minor ADJUSTMENTS

A NOVEL

Minor Adjustments is a charming romance with endearing characters and a story line that makes you ask yourself some hard questions. It's a book you'll remember long after you've read the last page.

Rebecca Talley,
author of *The Upside of Down*

Talented author Rachael Renee Anderson has done it again. *Minor Adjustments* is a heartwarming romance, set in sunny Australia, that shows love can conquer all. Once you start reading, *Minor Adjustments* is sure to grab your heart and not let go.

Marlene Bateman,
author of *Light on Fire Island*

Rachael Renee
Anderson

minor Adjustments

A NOVEL

Bonneville Books
Springville, Utah

Also by Rachael Renee Anderson

Divinely Designed
Luck of the Draw

© 2011 Rachael Renee Anderson

All rights reserved.

No part of this book may be reproduced in any form whatsoever, whether by graphic, visual, electronic, film, microfilm, tape recording, or any other means, without prior written permission of the publisher, except in the case of brief passages embodied in critical reviews and articles.

This is a work of fiction. The characters, names, incidents, places, and dialogue are products of the author's imagination, and are not to be construed as real.

ISBN 13: 978-1-59955-913-1

Published by Bonneville Books, an imprint of Cedar Fort, Inc., 2373 W. 700 S., Springville, UT 84663
Distributed by Cedar Fort, Inc., www.cedarfort.com

LIBRARY OF CONGRESS CATALOGING-IN-PUBLICATION DATA

Anderson, Rachael Renee, author.
Minor adjustments / Rachael Renee Anderson.
pages cm
Summary: Bachelor Devon Pierce is appointed guardian of the four-year-old son of an Australian exchange student who lived with Devon's family ten years earlier. The boy's father surfaces, causing complications, and a custody battle ensues.
ISBN 978-1-59955-913-1
1. Domestic fiction. 2. Custody of children--Fiction. 3. Fathers--Fiction. 4. Mothers--Fiction. 5. Parenting--Fiction. I. Title.
PS3601.N5447M56 2011
813'.6--dc22

2011014522

Cover design by Brian Halley
Cover design © 2011 by Lyle Mortimer
Edited and typeset by Heidi Doxey

Printed in the United States of America

10 9 8 7 6 5 4 3 2 1

Printed on acid-free paper

For my clever and charming Devon. You give the best squishes in the world. I love you.

acknowledgments

A hundred million thanks to Caroline Sterling, my brilliant, beautiful Australian barrister friend, who not only showed me around Australia but answered question after question after question. I couldn't have written this book without her.

To the fabulous team at CFI. Jennifer, for putting up with me in her gracious way; Brian, for designing a gorgeous cover that I love; and Heidi, my talented friend and editor, for making the book shine.

To Marlene, Rebecca, Braden, and Don, my awesome critique group, for helping me polish this manuscript and see problems I couldn't on my own.

And of course to my family. My mom, Linda, for being so willing and enthusiastic to read anything I write; my sisters, Lucy, Sarah, and Letha, for helping me with the plot and reading the choppy, earlier versions of this book; and Jeff, for his love, support, encouragement, and being so willing to help out when I need it most.

chapter one

A baby.

Well, more like a toddler. Maybe. The boy appeared steady on his feet as he stood on a chair, doodling on a whiteboard, so Devon wasn't sure how to classify him. At what age did kids outgrow the toddler stage?

"Can I help you?" asked an Australian-accented voice. An attractive blonde, businesslike in her dark tailored suit and high heels, stood on the other side of a gleaming, expensive-looking desk, a question in her blue eyes.

"Um, yeah. I'm looking for Stella Walker."

"You found her."

Devon had expected her to be older for some reason, with crow's feet and frown lines. Ornery. The type of person who liked to mess with people's lives. But Stella Walker looked young, maybe midtwenties, with a complexion devoid of any wrinkles. She neither smiled nor frowned—only scrutinized.

Well, scrutinize away. In twenty-four hours he'd be back on a plane and gone for good. "My name is Devon Pierce. We talked over the phone about a week ago."

Stella studied him a moment longer before punching a button on her phone. "Tess, would you mind if Ryan colored on your whiteboard for a bit?"

"Of course not." The accented reply was about an octave above Stella's. "Send him on down. Tell him I have a lolly lying about waiting to be found."

The boy grinned, dropped the marker, and hopped from the chair, barely glancing at Devon as he darted out the door. Stella watched him fondly, but when her eyes returned to Devon's, the poker face was back. "Thanks for coming all the way to Sydney."

"According to you, I didn't have much of a choice."

"You're from the land of the free, aren't you? You always have a choice."

Devon wanted to shine a flashlight in her face—anything to make those blue eyes blink and look elsewhere. "You said it was imperative I meet Lindsay's son and discuss this with you in person. You do know that imperative means—"

"I know what it means, but you still could've said no," Stella said. "But I'm glad you didn't."

"I'm glad that you're glad, but that doesn't change my decision. I'm not in a position to be anyone's guardian, so I'm clueless as to why I needed to fly out here." Where was aspirin when Devon needed it? "Do you mind if I sit down? I'm still dealing with jetlag."

Stella gestured to a green upholstered armchair. "Make yourself comfortable."

"Right," Devon muttered as he took a seat. He leaned forward and rested his elbows on his knees, willing his eyes to remain open. Having spent twenty-five-plus hours waiting in an airport and confined on a plane with not one, but two crying babies, Devon wanted nothing more than to sign whatever he needed to sign, get a decent night's sleep in his hotel room, and fly back to America.

Devon massaged his temples, attempting to relieve the mounting pressure. "Okay, so now that we've established I'm here by my own free will, can we please get on with it?"

Stella sat down and opened a file on her desk. "I want you to take Ryan for two weeks."

Headache forgotten, Devon practically shouted, "Two weeks?

Are you out of your mind? I've already told you, more than once, that I can't take the kid—not for two weeks, not for a month, and definitely not permanently. Nor can I stay in Australia for that long. I'm needed back in the States. It's called a job—maybe you're familiar with that definition as well?"

Stella continued to thumb through the file. "If, after two weeks, you still refuse to become Ryan Caldwell's legal guardian, you can return to America as free and alone as you left it."

The girl was insane. Did she really think he'd believe that? "You're telling me I'm required to take the boy for two weeks? By law?"

"Yes . . . you are." The hesitation in her voice belied her words.

"I'd like to see that in writing."

A pencil twirled between her fingers as she avoided eye contact. "Australia has thousands of laws. It would take me days to track down that specific one. But I'll be happy to let you see it as soon as I find it."

"Or I could simply call another lawyer."

"You mean solicitor," Stella said, as if he were a student and she his teacher. "In Australia, we're called either solicitors or barristers. Solicitors are mostly lawyers outside of court and barristers present cases in court."

Devon blinked. Why would he possibly care about that? "Uh, thanks for the tutorial."

"Well, I would've wanted to know."

"Why don't you push that button on your phone and get your friend on the line again. I'll double check with her about that so-called law."

Stella sighed. "Listen. For some reason Lindsay was adamant that you become Ryan's guardian. She wouldn't hear of anyone else. Not even—" Her knuckles turned white and Devon half-expected the pencil to snap from the pressure.

Or maybe it was Devon who was about to snap. "Why me? It doesn't make any sense. Are you sure Lindsay was in her right mind when she had the will drawn up?"

The pencil finally broke, although Stella didn't appear to notice. "Of course she was. She didn't even hesitate when she signed the will either. She wanted you, and only you. Why can't you even consider it?"

"Because I'm a single guy who knows nothing about kids and works hard for a living. I have absolutely no room in my life for anyone's kid—least of all a stranger's."

Elbows came to rest on the top of the desk, and Stella clasped her fingers together. "Lindsay lived with your family for a year. How can you not remember her?"

"It was only nine months, and thanks to my sister, I do remember her now—vaguely. She was five years younger than me, staying with us as a foreign exchange student, and she hung out with my younger sister. I was in high school and hardly ever home, so forgive me for not keeping her memory alive."

Stella glared at him.

Devon knew he could have been more tactful, but he didn't care. Stella wouldn't even look at the situation from his perspective. Instead, little Miss Chastiser sat on her throne and accused him of being selfish. It made him want to shake some sense into her, but he could only imagine the legal ramifications if he did that. Besides, they were getting nowhere, and Devon's hotel bed was calling his name. Loudly.

So he decided to give reason one last chance. "Please try to understand. I'm the owner of a company and work eighty hours a week. I live alone in a studio apartment in a busy city—not the best atmosphere for a child. If Lindsay had only taken the time to contact me or look into my situation, she would've realized that I'm the last person in the world capable of caring for a small boy."

Worry lines creased Stella's brow as she played with the broken pencil pieces. "You're right. Lindsay messed up. She should have called you, and I have no idea why she didn't. One conversation and she would've known there's no way you could ever make a decent—"

Again, Stella cut herself off, only this time Devon knew what she hadn't said. It was obvious. And it hurt. Mostly because it wasn't the first time he'd been accused of that fault.

"Father," he said, his voice cold and hard. "There's no way I could ever make a decent father. Right?"

"I was actually going to say guardian," Stella admitted. "And sorry. I didn't mean for it to sound that way, especially when I don't even know you. I was referring more to the circumstances than your parenting skills."

"Apology accepted."

Stella searched his face with pleading eyes. "But the fact still remains that Lindsay chose you. All I'm asking is that you give it a try. Two weeks. Fourteen days." She paused. "Please."

Her confident, rigid demeanor was gone, and she sounded . . . what? Depleted? Worried? Troubled? He wasn't sure, but suddenly he found it hard to say no. "There's got to be someone else in a better situation who actually wants to take him."

Stella winced at his words. "Even if there were, Lindsay insisted on you. She promised me that you were the right choice."

The office phone beeped, and a deep male voice erupted through the small speaker. "Stella, could you come to my office?"

"I'm in the middle of a meeting, Gerald."

"It's important and will only take a moment."

With raised eyebrows, Stella glanced at Devon. He nodded.

"I'll be right there." Then to Devon, she said, "Please excuse me," before striding out the door. Her long, blonde ponytail swayed along with her hips as she walked down the hall and disappeared into another office.

Devon frowned as he absently clasped and unclasped his fingers. Her earnest "please" had been like a blast of warm water when he'd expected cold, and it bothered him that she could nudge his conscience so easily. Why couldn't she have stayed brusque and demanding? The girl who made up fake laws and broke pencils? Instead she'd changed the rules halfway through the game. Cheated.

It wasn't fair.

The truth was, Devon could take a couple of weeks off—even longer, if he wanted. But why? Was Stella hoping he'd change his mind? That two short weeks was enough time to convince him to keep Ryan permanently? Devon almost laughed at the thought. Maybe if he was married or in a better position to be a parent. But he wasn't. And besides, he'd been told more than once that his world revolved too much around work and not enough around people and relationships.

Which was true. Devon lived, breathed, and practically ate work. It was his life, his motivation, his salvation. Without it, he'd have nothing but empty time. And time, without distractions, was an enemy to him. There was nothing worse than boredom.

But for some reason, Lindsay Caldwell had wanted him to be her son's guardian. Why? When her hazy thirteen-year-old face had finally registered, Devon remembered that Lindsay had hardly spoken to him during those nine months. She'd never really known him, much less the thirty-year-old version of him. Why would she choose a near stranger to look after someone who was so important to her? And why did Devon now feel like he'd be letting down her, himself, and maybe even God if he didn't try?

If only he could do away with his conscience. It had plagued Devon his entire life, grilling him to take back the Snickers bar he'd stolen when he was nine, making him feel bad for the chewed-up wad of gum he'd placed on a despised teacher's chair in seventh grade, and forcing him to rat out a friend for doing drugs in high school.

And now that same conscience goaded him to take Ryan for two weeks, telling him it was the right thing to do, that he could leave with a better feeling in his gut if he only gave it a try.

Two weeks. Just two weeks. Fourteen days. Devon could handle the boy for that long, couldn't he? At least then the stubborn and manipulative Stella would know from experience it wouldn't work out.

"You're still here," Stella said as she walked back into the office. "I assumed you'd be long gone by now."

"You didn't dismiss me," Devon said. "I was worried I'd be breaking another one of your many Australian laws if I left without your permission. With you being a solicitor and all, I figured I'd be rotting in some jail by nightfall."

"I'm not a cop."

"I'm sure you have connections."

"True."

"And I'm also pretty sure you'd be the prosecutor."

Her lips twitched. "Actually, it would have to be a police prosecutor, but . . . never mind."

The desire to argue seeped out of Devon. He knew he was going to cave, but not until he gave it one last pathetic attempt. "I'm not what you'd call father-figure material."

"Obviously."

She probably meant it as a joke, but it still hit a sore spot. Devon was tired of being told he'd make a lousy father when he'd never had the chance to prove otherwise.

Here's your chance, a voice whispered in his head.

Dang that conscience. "Okay, you win. I'll take him for two weeks, but that's it."

"Really?" She let out a breath. "Thank you."

"I mean it. Just two weeks. After that, no more guilt trips, okay?"

"Deal." Stella's smile spread across her face and enlarged her eyes. It was a good thing she hadn't looked at him like that from the beginning or Devon wouldn't have stayed strong as long as he had. At least now he could take some pride in the fact that he hadn't given in without a fight.

"So . . . what now?" Devon said.

"I need to get some information from you and then I'll introduce you to Ryan."

As she shuffled through the papers on her desk, Devon said, "The boy who was coloring on your whiteboard earlier—he's Lindsay's son?"

"Yeah, that was Ryan."

"How old is he?"

"Four."

"So, uh, not a toddler anymore?"

The smile was back. "No, not a toddler. A darling little boy."

Stella passed him a stack of papers that looked like an extensive job application. What was his name, address, phone number? Did he have a local address? And then a few more personal questions: Was he married? Did he have any children? What was his annual salary? Devon scribbled on the pages, answering all the questions briefly while he blinked and tried to relieve the sleep-deprived dryness in his eyes.

Signing his name, Devon handed the pages back to Stella. "Is that all?"

"For now. I'll go and get Ryan."

A few moments later she returned holding the boy's hand in her own. Crouching beside him, she said, "Ryan, I want you to meet Devon Pierce."

Dark eyes peeked at Devon under a mop of curly light-brown hair. "Hey, you have my same name."

"Yes," Stella said. "He does, doesn't he? And that means that you two are going to be really good friends." Turning to Devon, she explained, "His name is Ryan Devon Caldwell."

"Really? Was he named after . . ." No, he couldn't be.

"Yes," Stella confirmed. "Lindsay may not have made much of an impression on you, but you definitely made one on her."

Not knowing what to say, Devon opted for silence. Ryan, his namesake, shifted his weight from one foot to the other, as though the boy didn't like standing still. Maybe he was like Devon in that respect, needing to move and stay busy.

Offering Ryan a gentle smile, Stella said, "This is the man I've been telling you about. He was one of your mum's friends, and you get to stay with him for a few weeks. Will that be okay with you?"

"I want to stay with you," Ryan said, gripping Stella's hand.

She took a breath and let it out slowly. "I know. But I'm going to be very busy and you'd be bored. If you stay with Devon, he'll take you to lots of fun places, and he might even buy you custard."

Big brown eyes peered up at Devon. "You'll buy me custard? With mangos and strawberries?"

Devon had to laugh. As the oldest of three kids, all close in age, he'd never spent much time around children—especially small ones. By the time he became an uncle, Devon had already moved away and rarely saw them, which was fine with him. He never knew what to say to someone who was too shy or too little to carry on a conversation. But this boy seemed different.

"Do you mean frozen custard? Sort of like soft ice cream?" Devon asked.

Stella shook her head. "No. Custard is more like a thick pudding. It's Ryan's favorite dessert."

"Thick pudding, huh? Well, I'm still not sure what it is, but it sounds good to me. How about after we get some dinner we can try and track down some custard?"

"You talk funny."

Stella laughed. "That's because he's from America, and I'm sure he can teach you some neat new words."

Ryan looked skeptical. "What words?"

Good question. Didn't both countries speak the same language? Maybe Ryan had a fetish about learning new words. Hmm . . . what's a cool word a child wouldn't know? Devon said the first thing that came to mind. "Onomatopoeia."

"Ono-what?" Ryan giggled and Stella laughed.

"I meant some American slang words, not middle-grade vocabulary words," she said.

"Oh."

"You're weird!" Ryan said.

"It's nice to meet you too, kid." Devon turned to Stella. "So we're free to go now?"

She nodded, her expression resigned and almost sad. Devon didn't know what else to say, so he picked up Ryan's two faded blue duffle bags while Stella reached for the boy and easily lifted him into her arms, hugging him to her.

"I'll follow you out," she said.

When Devon pressed the button in the elevator for the parking garage, Stella said, "You have a car?"

"Of course. Why wouldn't I?"

"You found this building on your own?"

Was she really questioning his navigation skills? "Not exactly. It's called a GPS. You know, one of those modern-day wonders."

"Oh. Well, just so you know, it's usually easier to take the train around Sydney. There are a couple of stops near the hotel where you're staying, and you can go pretty much anywhere you want, so long as you don't mind a little walking."

"I'm not much of a train or subway person. I like my privacy and freedom, and I don't like to wait."

Stella shrugged. "Your decision."

Devon waited while she settled Ryan into the backseat. When Stella faced him again, tears glistened in her eyes, which made no sense. Devon was going out of his way to do exactly what she wanted him to do, and yet she was crying. Women.

"I guess we'll see you later?"

"Definitely." Stella blew Ryan a kiss and strode away, the clack of her heeled shoes echoing off the concrete walls of the parking garage.

Taking a deep breath, Devon slid into the driver's seat, put the hotel's address into the GPS, and turned up the radio. It took most of his concentration to remember to drive on the wrong side of the road, or at least it was wrong to him. Steering from the passenger seat was at odds with his universe. Why did the difference even exist? Were countries not able to communicate when roads were designed?

Through the rearview mirror, Devon saw Ryan staring out the window. Was he hungry, tired, bored? All of the above? Devon shifted in his seat and raised his voice above the sound of the radio. "You hungry?"

Ryan's eyes met Devon's in the mirror, and he nodded once before returning his attention to the passing buildings.

Devon tried again. "Pizza? Hamburgers? What do you like?" The boy's lips moved, but Devon heard nothing, so he sighed and turned off the radio. "Sorry. What did you say?"

"I like pizza, but not with pepperonis on it—just with cheese," Ryan said.

"Cheese pizza, huh? You sure you don't want pepperoni, sausage, ham, peppers, olives, onions, and tomatoes?"

"No. I just like cheese."

"How about a compromise? We'll get half with what you like and half with what I like. Will that work?"

"Okay."

"Now we just need to find a pizza place," Devon said.

"You can call someone and they will bring it to your house and ring the doorbell."

"Good idea," Devon said as he came to an intersection. The

computer voice said nothing, so he continued straight, which was strange because the road curved to the left, and downtown Sydney was in the opposite direction. Or was it? Devon didn't know anymore. A roundabout came into view, and Devon glanced at the GPS screen for direction. It was blank.

"What?" He tapped the screen. Nothing. A horn blared from behind, so Devon veered to the right and searched for a place to make a U-turn. Maybe he should stop and call Stella for directions. No, bad idea. His pride could take a beating only so many times in a day. Instead, Devon merged onto Liverpool Road and then veered east on The Great Highway, reasoning that he couldn't go wrong with a highway.

A few miles later, a sign for Pizza Hut winked at him from the side of the road. Devon grinned. Who needed a train? Not him. He didn't even need a map.

"Ryan, I've changed my mind. What do you say we go out for pizza?"

"Okay."

They ordered a half-supreme, half cheese pizza and ate while a nice waitress drew a map for Devon on a napkin. Then they returned to the car, and Devon whistled as he followed the directions, or at least tried to. The makeshift map depicted only straight streets, but after he turned off the highway all the roads wound this way and that, with cross streets coming at him like ties on a railroad track.

When the road dead-ended at a park, Devon tossed the napkin aside and pulled out his phone.

"Well, Ryan, we are officially lost. Any suggestions?" Devon said as he searched Google for a map.

"Mum says if you're lost to find a policeman."

"And what if there are no policemen around?"

"Mmm," Ryan said. "You should go to where they live and ask them."

Devon smiled as he typed in the nearest cross streets. The map was loading when an incoming call erased it from the screen. *Oh, for crying out loud.*

"Hello?"

"Hey, it's Stella. I just wanted to make sure you found your hotel okay and see how Ryan is settling in."

"We're almost there now. Ryan was hungry so we stopped for dinner."

"Oh. Is he doing okay?"

"He downed two slices of pizza and two glasses of soda. Now he's wondering when he'll get his custard."

Stella chuckled. "Well, at least I know he's not starving. Call me if you need anything."

"I will." Devon ended the call and loaded the maps application again, calculating the quickest way to the hotel. He threw the car into gear and made a U-turn, heading south. But navigating all the winding roads and one-way streets turned out to be a bigger problem than he'd anticipated, and before long, he was traveling through a long underground tunnel.

When the car resurfaced on the north side of Sydney, Devon felt like cursing—at least until the light turned red and a taxi pulled to a stop beside him.

Devon was quick to roll down his window. "Hey!" Thank goodness the taxi's windows were open.

The driver looked over and raised an eyebrow.

"Can you lead the way to the downtown Hylton Hotel on the south side?"

The guy smirked. "Lost?"

"You could say that," Devon admitted. "I'll pay you double."

The light changed and the guy nodded. "Sure, follow me."

Twenty minutes later, Devon followed the taxi into the underground parking and gladly paid the driver.

chapter two

Stella,

I know you're angry with me, and you have every right to be, but you stormed out without letting me explain, and I need you to understand my reasons.

Ryan needs a father. A good, solid, honest, and hardworking man. It's pathetic that I only know one man like that, and his name is Devon Pierce. I know it's been a long time, but if you only knew him, you'd understand. Not only will he give Ryan grandparents, aunts, uncles, and cousins, but he's kind, caring, humble, and will make a wonderful father. He will teach Ryan how to swim, shoot a basket, throw a ball, and surf (at least I think he knows how to surf). He will teach him how to open doors for the girls and treat them with kindness and respect. He will teach a son how a father is supposed to care for his child.

And he will teach him about God.

Are you shocked I just wrote that? I'm as surprised as you, believe me.

Please don't think I've made this decision lightly, that I'm giving my son to an old crush I had over a decade ago. I know I've never been much for religion, but when death is glaring at you, taunting you to defy it when you know you can't, it makes you wonder. Even hope. So I finally took your advice and started praying, hard and long, hoping that there was a God and that maybe, just maybe, He might point me in the right direction. One night, I was going through an old scrapbook and found some pictures of me with the Pierce family. It's hard to explain, but Devon's face seemed to rise out of the picture, like a 3-D image, and I knew he was the one I should choose.

I know that you love Ryan like he's your own, but you and I both know that you're not in a position to care for him. Nor do you have any family to rely on like Devon does. I also know that you're stubborn and willful enough to remain a part of his life. Please do! Although he'll be living in America, I want you to keep in touch. I need you to keep in touch. Teach my son about his roots, his history, his homeland.

And teach him about me. You're the only one who can tell him what his mother was truly like. Just don't make me out to be perfect, because we both know that's not true. Tell him it's okay to make mistakes, tell him he doesn't have to be perfect, and tell him that I love him so much and hope to be watching over him throughout his life. Tell him I want him to talk to me as if I'm still there. That when he's scared, lonely, sad, hurt, or happy, I want to know about it. I want to know everything.

Stella, you are the best friend I could have ever hoped to find, and I want you to know that I now thank God every day for your presence in my life. Please trust me in this.

Love,

Linds

Stella clutched the letter against her chest as tears seeped down her face. She had no idea why she'd reread the letter when she already had the words memorized. Maybe she liked to torture herself—or maybe, after her encounter with Devon, she needed to see Lindsay's words again, assuring her that she was doing the right thing by practically forcing Devon to take Ryan.

Forcing Devon to take him away.

Stella missed Ryan already. How would she be able to stand it? There was an emptiness in her apartment that hadn't existed until Ryan had come and gone. Even the couch seemed to miss him—it felt lumpier than usual, no doubt punishing her for letting him go.

And Stella deserved every lump.

Devon found the number and waited for his call to go through. Ryan had fallen asleep in the middle of the king-sized bed, looking so small curled up into a ball. Tiny, innocent, helpless—and completely unrepentant about stealing the only bed. Now where would Devon sleep? His gaze rested on the black contemporary sofa with metal armrests. Great.

First thing in the morning, he'd call the hotel about a room change. But right now, he had a different call to make.

A sleepy, grumpy voice groaned in Devon's ear. "Dev, I'm going to kill you."

"You never were much of a morning person, were you, Brady?" Devon kept his voice hushed as he made a beeline for the bathroom. He wasn't about to wake Ryan.

"The fact that you already know that and still called at six in the morning makes you the world's most pathetic friend. You know that, right?"

"Sorry. I guess I miscalculated the time change."

"Liar. Admit it—you didn't even think about the time change." Brady yawned. "I should be lucky it's six and not three in the morning."

"Come on, I'm not that inconsiderate."

"You've got three seconds to tell me what you want before I hang up on you."

Devon sat down on the closed toilet seat and rested his elbows on his knees. "I need you to hold down the fort at the office for a couple of weeks."

"A couple of weeks?" Brady suddenly sounded more alert. "Am

I talking to Devon Pierce? The Devon Pierce who hasn't taken a day off work since I've known him? Don't tell me you've actually decided to take a vacation."

Devon stifled a yawn. "Think you can handle it?"

"I know I can handle it," Brady said. "The question is, can you? I give you two days before you die of boredom and come back."

"Unfortunately, that's not going to happen. Things have gotten complicated here, and I've agreed to stay for two more weeks."

"Why?"

Devon rubbed his forehead. How much should he tell his friend, the VP of his company? Answering a slew of questions wasn't what he wanted to do right now, but Brady deserved to know something. "I've somehow agreed to look after the boy for a couple of weeks."

"You're joking."

"Afraid not."

Brady's laugh pounded through Devon's aching head. "How is it you can start a company from scratch, make it successful, and still be such a pushover? I can't figure it out."

"I'm hanging up now," Devon said. "Just keep me updated and call if you need me."

"Pushover," Brady repeated before Devon hit the button to end the call.

Devon picked up his toothbrush and vented on his teeth and gums. Brady was right. He was a pushover. Not only had Stella managed to get him on a plane to Australia, but she'd also manipulated him into babysitting for two weeks. He was an idiot for falling prey to such tactics. Devon should be on a flight back to the States, not stuck on the other side of the world with a four-year-old child.

He put down the toothbrush and another thought entered his mind. What in the world was he supposed to do with Ryan for two weeks in a country he knew nothing about?

No inspiration. No answers. No ideas. Nada.

He really was a pushover.

chapter three

"May I help you?"

The voice sounded loud through the hotel telephone, and Devon winced. Even after a decent night's sleep, his head still throbbed. "Yeah, I'm wondering if I can switch rooms. Do you have any suites available with two bedrooms?"

"I'm afraid not. We have a room with two queens or we have a master king suite, which has a king sized bed in an en-suite bedroom. Would you like to upgrade to that?"

Devon weighed his options. Deciding it was better to have a separate bedroom for Ryan, he asked, "Does the couch have a fold-out bed?"

"No. Sorry."

"Is it comfortable?"

"Uh . . ."

"Never mind." At least he wouldn't have to shut himself in the bathroom to make any nighttime phone calls. "I'll take it. When can you have it ready?"

"Probably an hour or two. I can ring your room as soon as it is."

"Thank you."

Propped up by several pillows, Ryan sat on the bed and stared at a cartoon on the TV screen. "Feel like some breakfast?" Devon asked.

Ryan's eyes sparkled and his head bobbed. "My stomach is making noises. That means I'm starving. Can we have custard?" Evidently he had a one-track mind when it came to his favorite dessert.

"How about we get dressed and go down and see?"

"Okay."

Custard wasn't on the hotel's breakfast menu, but after a quiet word in the waiter's ear, the congenial man brought out a bowl of fruit with a side of the thick pudding.

"I love custard!" Ryan said when he saw his breakfast. "Ta!"

The waiter grinned and patted Ryan's head. "Anytime, little bloke. Anytime."

An older woman with short, graying hair sat at a nearby table and waved an arm at the waiter. "May I have some too? It looks delicious, and my husband isn't here to tell me I shouldn't."

"Of course. I'll bring it right out."

"Thank you."

The waiter left and Devon asked the woman, "Are you from America?"

She nodded. "Texas. My husband is here for business and I came along just for fun. Unfortunately, he's going to be busier than he thought, so I'll be on my own much of the time." She gestured toward Ryan, who was devouring his custard. "Is he your son?"

"No. I'm just watching him for a few weeks. Speaking of which, have you been here long enough to know of any kid-friendly places to visit?" Devon would gladly take any suggestions.

She shook her head. "Sorry. We got here two days ago and I haven't ventured out much on my own because it makes me nervous. You might try the concierge though."

"Good idea." The few times Devon had traveled during the past decade had been for business—and business only. He couldn't remember the last time he'd asked a concierge for more than a decent place to eat. "If we figure out something to do, you're welcome to come with us."

She smiled. "I'd love to, if you're sure you don't mind. I hate sightseeing alone."

"Well, you're more than welcome, so long as you don't mind a tag-along."

"Heavens, no. I had four of my own and now have three grandchildren."

Devon gestured to an empty seat next to Ryan. "Want to join us? I'm Devon and this is Ryan, by the way."

She slid in next to Ryan. "I'm Colleen. It's wonderful to meet you both."

By the time they'd finished their meal, Colleen felt like an old friend. Her ready smile and quiet sense of humor entertained Devon and put Ryan at ease. They exchanged cell numbers and agreed to meet up later.

The suite was ready for them, so Devon picked up their bags, grabbed Ryan's hand, and rode the elevator up two floors. The new room was equipped with a separate master bedroom and a decent-sized living area. Even the couch looked more comfortable and slightly larger than the previous one.

Dropping the bags to the floor, Devon flipped on a cartoon for Ryan before calling the concierge. He spoke to a woman and jotted down some of her more interesting suggestions.

"Hey, Ryan, would you rather go up in a tall tower or walk across a really big bridge?"

No answer. The couch was empty, and the door was wide open.

"Ryan?" Devon rushed to the hallway. No sign of Ryan anywhere. Only a few hours into the two weeks and already Devon had lost the child. "Ryan!"

Ryan's chattering voice floated into the hallway from an adjacent room, and Devon let out a breath. *Thank goodness.* He jogged over to the cracked door and knocked.

"I'm so sorry," Devon said as he poked his head through the door. "Oh, it's you again."

Colleen's smiling eyes met his. "It's a small world, I guess. Turns out we're neighbors."

"I'm just happy to know Ryan didn't barge into a stranger's

room." Devon shot Ryan a meaningful look. "You need to tell me before you leave our room, okay?"

"But someone knocked on our door and left towels on the floor, and they weren't ours!" Ryan said.

Huh?

Colleen pointed to a stack of towels on a small table. "I think a maid must have brought you some extra towels. When Ryan answered the door and saw me going into my room, he thought they were mine and brought them to me. Such a darling and thoughtful child."

"Oh." Devon reached for Ryan's hand. "Come on, let's go. We need to go get ready. Then we'll come back to pick up Colleen, assuming she still wants to come."

"Count me in," she said.

"What do you think about going to see the Sydney Opera House?"

"It sounds wonderful."

"We'll be back in about twenty minutes."

"I'll be ready."

An hour later, they boarded a train at a nearby CityRail station and exited a few stops later at Circular Quay. The Sydney Opera House was nothing like Devon had ever seen. Comprised of massive fin-shaped arches, tiered on top of each other, the building looked like the sails on an old tall ship. Incredible.

If only Ryan had been equally impressed. Ten minutes into their guided tour, the boy's steps lagged and his grip on Devon's hand turned limp. Swinging Ryan up to his shoulders, Devon continued to follow the guide.

"Can we go to the park?" Ryan pleaded.

"As soon as we're done here," Devon said. "Assuming we can find one."

Colleen chuckled and fished a pack of Life Savers from her bag. "Tell you what, Ryan. If you can point out ten things shaped like a circle, I'll give you a circle treat."

Ryan wriggled down from Devon's shoulders, and Devon wanted to hug Colleen. Bribery. Brilliant. Why hadn't he thought of that? Devon needed to stock up on candy. Maybe even custard.

When the guide led them into the Utzon room, Devon's phone vibrated with a text from Stella.

How's Ryan?

Devon frowned. How often would Stella feel the need to check up on them? Hopefully not every few hours or she'd drive him crazy. He typed a quick reply.

Fine.

A few seconds later his phone buzzed again.

And you?

Fine.

Fine!

Devon smirked and shoved the phone back into his pocket. Serves her right for getting him into this situation. Moments later he got another text.

Next time I won't let you off the hook so easily.

Devon punched out a response.

What are you going to do? Put me on a courtroom stand and question me?

Not a bad idea.

Devon grinned as Colleen eyed him with curious eyes. "Work?"

"Not exactly."

"If you need to step outside to make a call, I can handle Ryan for a few minutes."

"No, it's fine." How could Devon even begin to explain? "It's a long story."

Glancing from the guide to Ryan and back to Devon, Colleen whispered, "Well, Ryan's got a mouthful of candy, and this guide is rather boring. I think I'd find your story much more interesting."

chapter four

"Rise and shine, sleepyhead." Devon tapped Ryan on the nose.

Scrunching his face, Ryan slowly opened his eyes before shutting them again.

"Come on, little man. I ordered pancakes with fruit and custard on the side."

Ryan yawned. "Custard?"

"Yep—your favorite."

Rubbing his sleepy eyes awake, Ryan sat up, and his gaze rested on the room service table. "You ordered it?" He swung his feet over the side of the bed. "How did you order it?"

"I picked up the phone and asked them to make it and bring it to our room."

"You mean somebody took it all the way up the elevator?"

"Just for you." Devon smoothed Ryan's hair, or at least tried to. The longish curls had a mind of their own in the mornings, jutting out this way and that. "Now, let's eat before it gets cold. It's almost nine, and the aquarium opens in an hour." After two days of sightseeing, Devon decided to see if Google could offer any better ideas than the concierge. Sydney Aquarium had been first on the list.

"What's a queryam?" Ryan asked, plopping down in front of his breakfast.

"It's a place with fishes and turtles and sharks. You'll love it."

"A shark? A real one that's alive?"

"Yep."

"But what if he tries to bite me?"

"I'll punch him," Devon said, taking the other seat.

Ryan's giggle sounded like animated popping bubbles, and a dimple appeared to the left of his mouth. "You can't punch a shark! He'll eat you up all gone."

The kid was cute. "Not if I make his nose bleed first. Then he'll need to find a tissue instead."

"But the tissue would get all wet!" Ryan laughed so hard he nearly scooted off his seat.

A knock echoed through the hotel room. Colleen had said she'd be spending the day with her husband, so maybe it was the maid service. Devon pushed his chair back and pointed at their breakfast trays. "Hey, you better stop laughing and start eating so we can go." He walked over to the door and pulled it open.

"G'day." Stella smiled as she swept past Devon.

"No, please, come on in," Devon said.

She ignored him and smiled at Ryan. "Sounds like someone's having a good time."

"Devon's going to punch a shark and make his nose all bloody if he tries to eat me!" Ryan said, still giggling.

It didn't sound quite so funny when Stella gave Devon an arched eyebrow look, as though blood and breakfast didn't go together. "Uh, he was only joking. We're planning a trip to the aquarium today."

"Oh, I love the aquarium. Mind if I tag along?"

Already Stella had managed to douse some fun in the room, and Devon wasn't sure he wanted her looking over his shoulder the entire day. But how to discourage her from coming? "It's Thursday," he finally said. "Don't you have to work?"

"Not today."

"You get to come to the queryam with us?" Ryan bounced up and down.

Devon sighed. So much for convincing Stella not to come. "Have you eaten yet, Stella?"

"Yeah." Her gaze drifted to their breakfast trays. "Custard for breakfast?" The way she looked at him made Devon feel like he was back in the first grade, getting a check mark next to his name.

"Custard makes us big and strong and we should have it every time we eat! Devon says so!" Ryan was all smiles.

"Does he now?" Another check.

Devon shrugged. "What can I say? The stuff is good. And it comes with fruit—which is a breakfast food." So there.

"Well, don't let me interrupt your, um . . . breakfast." Picking up a magazine, Stella dropped to the couch and settled in to wait. Devon could handle a few hours with her, couldn't he? Besides, Ryan seemed to love her, so she had to have some redeeming qualities.

They finished their breakfast and rushed to get ready. After a fifteen-minute search for Ryan's missing shoe, Stella finally found it in the drawer of a nightstand. Good thing too, because Devon would never have thought to look there. Who puts a shoe in a nightstand drawer?

Ryan. Or maybe the boogeyman, since Ryan didn't know how it got there either.

Ten minutes later, they finally stepped into the elevator. When Devon pressed the button for the ground floor, Stella once again arched that eyebrow. "Aren't we going to the parking garage?"

The question sounded so innocent—too innocent. If Devon hadn't already returned the rental car two days before, he would have pressed "P" and taken the car purely for pride's sake. "Ryan loves to ride on the train, so I humor him."

"Really?" Stella looked down at the boy. "You like trains now, Ryan?"

"Trains are noisy."

"I know," Stella said. "They are very noisy."

"But they don't get us lost."

If the boy didn't look so cute, with his large, guileless eyes, Devon might have throttled him.

"Lost?" Stella asked, still looking at Ryan. "Did the car get you lost?"

Ryan nodded, his eyes growing bigger. "Yeah, but then another car came and got us un-lost."

"Tattletale," Devon muttered.

"Another car?"

Devon rolled his eyes. "It was a taxi, okay? Now go ahead and say I told you so."

But Stella only smiled—a pompous sort of smile—and stepped out into the lobby when the elevator doors opened.

By the time they arrived at the aquarium, Devon wondered how long Stella planned to stick around. It was like he was constantly being watched and found wanting. Maybe he could rush Ryan through the exhibit and bring him back another day—without Nanny McPhee. But that small ray of hope died when Ryan ran to the first display window and pressed his hands and nose to the glass, twisting his head as he tried to follow the movements of the fish.

Devon groaned inwardly. Where was the Sydney Opera House when he needed it?

"What have you guys been up to the past two days?" Stella asked.

A neutral topic. Good. "We visited the Sydney Opera House, walked across the harbor bridge, and yesterday we went to the top of the Sydney Tower. Ryan wasn't too impressed with any of it, but I was. This city is awesome."

"You've never been here before?"

"Nope. Never had a reason to come."

Ryan shouted, "Look! It's a turtle!" His eyes radiated excitement, and Devon found himself wondering if the aquarium would sell him the turtle.

Stella smiled at Ryan before returning her attention to Devon. "Are you two getting along okay?"

"Sure." Devon shrugged. "He's been easy, you know?"

"What do you mean?"

How to explain? That Ryan wasn't annoying? That he said the most interesting things sometimes, making Devon want to laugh out loud? That Ryan was sweet and innocent and fun to hang out with? "I don't know. I've never been around kids much, and at first I had no idea how to act or what to say, but . . . well, he's been easy."

"Oh," Stella said. "When you put it that way, yeah, he is easy."

Ryan pointed to an animal that looked like a cross between a duck and a seal. "What's that?"

Resting his hand on Ryan's shoulder, Devon said, "That, my friend, is called a platypus."

"Platypus?"

"Yep, and the name fits, don't you think? I bet he even likes custard."

Ryan's eyes widened. "Really? Just like me and you?"

"You better ask Stella to be sure."

So Ryan did, as well as everyone else in the room, since his question rang out above the other murmuring voices. "Stella, do platypuses like custard?"

Stella's laugh sounded nice. Genuine. Happy. "No, silly. Platypuses would rather eat things like yabbies and prawn—other little animals that live in the water."

"Hey, I like prawns too!" Ryan's eyes brightened as he continued to study the mammal.

"Me too." Devon leaned over and whispered to Stella, "Does that make me part platypus?"

"Now that you mention it, you do have some similarities."

"Hey now."

She smiled and nodded toward the animal. "Did you know that when the first platypus specimen was sent to England, the British scientists thought it was a hoax?"

"How could they with the animal sitting right in front of them?"

"No idea. But it is rather odd-looking, isn't it?"

"I hope you're not still comparing us."

Stella laughed but said nothing more. Devon wondered if she'd added "strange" and "odd-looking" to his growing list of character traits.

As they toured the rest of the exhibits, Stella raised her eyebrows less and laughed more. It was as though her role of judgmental observer had been tossed aside and replaced with that of a casual acquaintance. Although Devon was grateful for the change, he knew it had nothing to do with him and everything to do with Ryan. The kid had a natural ability to draw people out and make them feel . . . Loved? Happy? Special? Devon still wasn't sure what made Ryan so likeable, but whatever it was, Stella obviously felt it too.

By the time they finally shooed Ryan from the underwater shark exhibit, Devon was ready to buy the boy an annual pass. Not that he actually would. Devon would be leaving in just over a week, and who knew if the people Ryan ended up with would ever bring him back. Their loss if they didn't.

They followed Stella to a nearby eatery for lunch. As Devon munched on the tasty fish and chips, he had a brilliant idea. "Hey Ryan, do you want to go to a pet store and pick out your very own fish?"

The dimple instantly appeared, and Ryan's eyes crinkled. "You mean one I can keep forever and ever?"

"And ever. Assuming you take good care of it and feed it every day."

"Can I have a shark too?"

"Do you think a shark would fit into our hotel room?"

Ryan grinned and shook his head.

"Maybe we can go back to the aquarium another day so you can see the sharks again."

"I know of a pet store in Surry Hills. It's only a short train ride from here," Stella said.

"Are you offering to come?" Now that the tension between them had ebbed, it would be nice having someone along who knew the area.

"Sure. I'd love to see what fish catches Ryan's fancy. And besides, I'd hate for you to have to call another taxi to get you un-lost."

Devon wanted to stick his tongue out but refrained. Obviously he'd been spending too much time with a four-year-old. "Just so you know, I almost got us to the hotel. We followed the taxi driver for maybe five minutes."

"And now you use public transportation."

"Let's just say that CityRail has grown on me."

Stella smiled. "It has that effect on people."

At the pet store, Ryan didn't take long to select his fish. It had been an easy choice, really. When the salesclerk held up a mirror to the blue Betta, and its gills puffed and fins flared, Ryan was entranced. The fact that it was also called a fighting fish finalized the decision.

Stella's cell phone rang, and she excused herself to take the call outside while Devon waited at the checkout counter as the clerk rang up their supplies. Meanwhile, Ryan wandered off, no doubt entertaining himself by looking at all the other tanks.

When Stella came back inside, she asked, "Where's Ryan?"

"He's still looking at the fish. I'm thinking he's destined to become a marine biologist."

Stella waited for Devon to finish signing the receipt, and together they headed toward the back of the store. They found Ryan standing on a short stool in front of an aquarium filled with goldfish, holding a bottle of fish food in his hand. An empty bottle of fish food.

"I feed the fish," Ryan said, all smiles. "See? They're hungry."

Sure enough, approximately forty fish were feeding off the entire contents of the emptied food container. Devon closed his eyes and groaned inwardly. He knew enough about goldfish to know they weren't supposed to eat that much. Fabulous.

When the sales clerk approached, Devon gestured to the tank. "I guess we'll be taking home those goldfish as well."

Stella's eyes widened. "Uh, maybe—"

"Yay! We get goldfish, too!" Ryan clapped his hands.

"Never mind," said Stella, lips twitching.

"Never mind what?" Devon asked while the clerk worked quickly to remove the food from the aquarium.

In a quiet voice, she said, "I was going to say that if you're worried the fish ate too much, it would be easier to pay for them, rather than take them home. But best of luck telling Ryan that now."

Devon blamed his idiocy on stress and lack of sleep.

"And you do know that goldfish don't play well with male Bettas, don't you?" Stella added.

Although it wasn't her fault, Devon still glared at her. "No, I didn't. I'd rather eat fish, not play with them. What's that supposed to mean, anyway?"

"It means you'll need a separate fish bowl for the goldfish, or the ones that survive, at least. And speaking of survivors, what do you plan to do if Ryan wakes up tomorrow and finds some of his fish floating on top?"

"I'll tell him we're eating them for breakfast."

"Yeah, that won't traumatize him."

Armed with a Betta, thirty-two engorged goldfish, food, two fishbowls, and Ryan's handpicked decor, Devon herded Ryan from the shop, more than ready to return to the hotel. What a day. He'd never been so grateful to board a train and sit on a hard plastic seat.

Three o'clock. Really? That was it? Maybe Ryan would take a nap when they got back. And maybe Devon would join him.

But Ryan didn't look tired at all. Instead, he poked at his new pets through their bags, giggling when he got the Betta to puff his fins. What would happen to the fish after Devon left? What would happen to Ryan? Would Stella find some nice adoptive parents who would let Ryan keep the fish? Would Ryan like his new parents?

The unwelcome worry attached itself to Devon's mind and burrowed in, making Devon shift in his seat. He didn't want to care about Ryan's future. He didn't want to care about Ryan. And yet the child's innocence reached out to him, begging for rescue.

A rescue you can't offer.

"Do they allow fish at the hotel?" Stella asked.

"No idea," Devon said. "If not, you don't mind taking them home, do you? For Ryan's sake?"

Stella's eyes widened. "How about we try sneaking them up to your room? If the maid has a problem with it, we'll talk about it then."

"Not a fish person?"

"They have really short life spans with me," Stella said. "I've never understood why."

"Did you feed them too much?"

"No."

"Are you sure? Because maybe that's where Ryan learned it."

"I didn't feed them too much, and it was before Ryan stayed with me."

"Maybe you should have sung to them."

"That would have only made them die sooner."

Devon chuckled. So Stella had a few faults after all. Good. It made her seem more human somehow, more relatable. "Well, we have something in common then. I can't carry a note either."

They shared a smile as the train pulled to a stop. When they got to the hotel, Stella walked in first to distract the front desk clerk so Devon and Ryan could get the fish to the elevator undetected.

They spent the remainder of the afternoon "decorating" the two fish bowls. Ryan was particular when it came to where the rocks and plastic coral belonged. In the end, the rocks were piled high on one side, so the fish would have a "mountain" to climb, and the coral was bunched together on the other side, so the fish would be able to hide in a forest.

"It looks awesome." Devon ruffled Ryan's hair. "The aquarium should hire you to design all their fish tanks."

Holding up the bags with the fish, Ryan said, "Can we dump them in now?"

"Dump away." When the fish were released in their new habitats, Devon breathed a sigh of relief. Maybe they could actually relax for a little while.

"The fish are hungry. Where's the food? I need to feed them," Ryan said.

"No!" Devon and Stella shouted in unison. The two voices together sounded loud, even to Devon's ears. Louder than he'd intended.

Ryan's expression fell. "But they're hungry!" He burst into tears. "I need to feed my fish or they'll die!"

Devon crouched beside him. "Ryan, if they eat too much—"

"They're hungry. They need to eat!"

"Ryan—"

"They're going to die!"

Devon stared as the boy's cries escalated. It was like watching Dr. Jekyll morph into Mr. Hyde. Only with Ryan, there had been no warning or strange concoction to blame. It had just happened.

Devon closed his eyes and prayed for patience. He was too tired for this. He wanted to give Ryan a good shake and say, "Get a grip!" But instead he turned to Stella for help. Maybe she had a miracle cure—a magic stick to slap on the ground and bring everything back to its rightful order.

But Stella was no help. She sat in an armchair with her arms folded while a tentative smile played on her lips. She might as well have asked for a bowl of popcorn and said, "You're on your own. I'm enjoying the show."

Devon turned back to the sobbing, hysterical child. "My fish need food!" Ryan said the words over and over.

"Ryan, calm down. Just let me explain why you can't feed them right now."

"I need to feed my fish!"

"Listen to me."

"They're hungry!"

"Ryan—"

"My fish are dying!" His little hands started beating on Devon's stomach.

Raising his voice to override the child's screams, Devon gripped Ryan's hands and gave it one last try, "If your fish eat too much, they will die."

"I don't want them to die!" Ryan screamed.

"I know. That's why you can't—"

But Ryan wouldn't listen. He broke free and frantically rummaged through the discarded bags from the pet store, searching for the food. Thank goodness Devon had already thought to hide it on top of the TV cabinet.

"Where's the food!" Ryan ran at Devon in a crazed way.

Not knowing what else to do, Devon picked up the boy and carried him kicking and screaming to the bathroom. Setting Ryan inside, he quickly closed the door and held it shut. Maybe a few minutes locked in a room would do the trick.

Not daring to look at Stella, Devon hunkered down outside the bathroom door and waited. He could only imagine what she thought of him now. Well, she could think what she wanted; it wasn't like she'd offered to help. In fact, if she'd listened to him from the get-go, they wouldn't be in this situation now.

Ryan started beating on the door. He must have dropped to the floor, because the poundings were coming rapid-fire, too hard for little fists but not for little feet. Well, better the door than Devon.

"Ryan, when you calm down, I'll let you out," Devon called.

That was a bad idea, because although the kicking stopped, objects started to hit the door. "Let me out!"

Devon cringed, wondering how long the tantrum would last. He wasn't about to open the door—not now. He had no desire to be clubbed in the head with his deodorant.

"So um, what time did Ryan go to bed last night?" A look of sympathy had replaced Stella's smile.

"I don't know. Probably around midnight."

"And what time did he wake up this morning?"

"I woke him up a little before nine. Why?"

Her eyes widened. "You woke him up?"

"The aquarium opened at ten, and he needed to eat breakfast first." Surely she understood that.

But Stella only chuckled. "He's tired, Devon. Too tired to think straight. That's why he's acting this way. Children need sleep. A lot of sleep."

Devon leaned his head back against the door and closed his eyes. Swell. First the car, the custard, the fish, and now this. So much for proving himself an adequate father. He didn't even know how much sleep a child needed.

Eventually the pounding and crying stopped, but Devon was still afraid to open the door. Afraid of the mess he'd find and afraid of reviving Mr. Hyde. Finally, he mustered the courage and cracked the door. Ryan was huddled in the corner, shaking. His eyes were red, his nose runny, and his breaths haggard.

"I wa-nt to fe-ed my fi-sh," Ryan stuttered.

In that instant, Devon wanted to rewind the last thirty minutes and happily hand over the bottle of fish food. He wanted to erase the red eyes and runny nose. He wanted to give back the happiness he had somehow taken away. But he couldn't. And if Ryan was going to be a fish owner, he needed to learn how to take care of those fish.

So Devon sat on the closed toilet seat and picked up Ryan, holding him close. "Ryan, fish can only eat once a day. If you feed them too much, their tummies will get very sick and they could die. You already fed them at the pet store, so you need to wait until tomorrow to feed them again, okay? You don't want to hurt them, do you?"

Ryan looked up with swollen eyes. "I get to feed them when I wake up?"

"How about after lunch?"

"And they won't die?"

Devon hoped the already engorged goldfish would still be alive come morning. "If any of those fish die, it's not because they're hungry, believe me. It's because they are old and ready to go to fish heaven."

"Did my mum go to fish heaven too?"

Oh great. How did they get on that subject? "Was your mum a fish?"

Ryan actually smiled. "No. She was a mum."

"Then your mum went to mummy heaven."

"Because she got old?" Ryan's trusting, brown eyes stared up at Devon.

It wasn't fair or right that this small boy should be without a mother or a father. Four years old and already alone. How could Devon explain? "No. Your mum just got very sick."

"Because she ate too much food?"

Devon smiled even as his heart hurt. He prayed for the right words to say. "No, kiddo. A different kind of sick. But she's happy now. Did you know that? She's in a nice place where she gets to watch you every day. It probably makes her sad when you're sad, so how about we try to be happy for her. Okay?"

"Okay."

Devon hugged Ryan closer and rested his chin on the boy's head. Stella stood in the doorway, watching. The light glistened off the tears in her eyes before she quickly turned away. What was she thinking? Had he somehow messed up again?

Lowering Ryan to the floor, Devon reached for his hand. "Since we have bigger tummies than fish, we can eat a lot more. What do you say we order some dinner?"

"The kind they bring to our room?"

"Yep."

"And custard too?"

"Of course. We can't have a meal without custard."

Ryan's dimple returned.

chapter five

After dinner, Stella snuggled with Ryan until he fell asleep. Tucking the blanket around him, she kissed him softly on the forehead. Her arms ached to pick him up and take him home with her, but it was impossible. Lindsay had made sure of that. Stella needed to accept the fact that Ryan would never be hers and move forward with her life. If only it didn't feel like she was losing her own child.

Have a care, Stella. She sucked in her breath and squared her shoulders.

Now, where were her shoes? Finding them by the couch, she picked them up and sat down to put them on.

"I hope you get paid overtime," Devon said. "You put in some extra hours today."

"This one's pro bono." Stella was grateful for Devon's dry humor. It helped to lighten the hollow, desolate feeling that had tunneled into her chest. In fact, she was grateful for a lot of things about him. His kindness, his patience, how great he was with Ryan.

"Where's Ryan's father?"

Stella stiffened. She'd known he'd ask sooner or later, and he had a right to know, but that didn't mean she wanted to talk about it. Not yet anyway. "I don't know. He's listed as 'unknown' in her file."

"Lindsay didn't know who the father was?"

"That's usually what 'unknown' means."

"She had to have some idea. Did you even try to find him?"

Stella met his gaze. Was he serious? "Lindsay didn't give me any names or descriptions, so how was I supposed to find him? Stop every guy I came across on the street and ask for a DNA sample? Run an ad in the paper? Even if she'd given me a name, Lindsay didn't exactly go out with winners. Do you really want to connect Ryan to some drunk stranger?"

Devon raked his fingers through his hair. "Sorry, I didn't know. I figured there was a reason Lindsay left Ryan to me and not the father. I just wanted to know why."

Stella sighed. "It's okay. I'm as frustrated as you are, believe me." How many times had she wished she wasn't so close to this case? So close to Ryan? It would be infinitely easier to approach it all from an impersonal point of view—to answer Devon's questions factually rather than emotionally.

Devon stood and walked over to the window. He studied the street below before turning back. "Thanks for being our tour guide today, even if you only came to check up on me."

He was right. She had been checking up on him, but it was also more than that. Stella had wanted to get to know the person Lindsay had chosen over her. "I'll admit I was curious to see how you two were getting on, but I also came to spend time with Ryan. I'm rather fond of him."

"So I've noticed. I take it you and Lindsay were good friends?"

Stella nodded.

"What happened to her? You mentioned she'd been sick, but that's it." Devon took a seat next to her, his brown eyes intense, questioning.

"Pancreatic cancer. It hit hard and fast. She was gone within six months. That's why I'm so attached to Ryan. They lived with me for a while at the end when Lindsay needed help. She had no one else."

"I'm sorry," Devon said, sounding sincere.

Stella fiddled with the fabric of her shorts, trying to think of a way to change the subject. Her emotions were too flimsy, and if Devon kept asking about Ryan and Lindsay, he'd soon have a weeping woman on his hands. She cleared her throat. "It was good of you to get Ryan some fish."

Devon cringed as he glanced at the goldfish. "I'm not sure what I was thinking. He was so excited at the aquarium; I guess I wanted it to last. I never expected it to instigate a meltdown."

"Don't blame yourself. Ryan spit the dummy because he was exhausted, not because of the fish."

Devon laughed and gave her a strange look. "Did you just say 'spit the dummy'?"

"Oh, uh . . ." Stella never realized how strange the saying could sound to someone who'd never heard it before. "A dummy is another word for pacifier. So when a child starts to scream or tantrum, out comes the pacifier. Make sense?"

"Sort of." Devon appeared drained all of a sudden—a look Stella understood well. How many times had she felt that way during the past months?

"If it makes you feel any better, I thought you handled Ryan well tonight."

"Yeah, locking a child in a bathroom definitely puts me in the running for a parent-of-the-year award."

"You didn't hurt him."

"Did you see his expression? Of course I hurt him."

Stella rested her hand on his knee. "Not physically. You could have done a lot worse, believe me. I work for a family law practice, so I know. And to be honest, I would have done the same thing. Ryan was out of control and needed to calm down. You did well."

"Thanks," Devon said, watching her again. "So is this the kind of case you usually handle?"

Stella settled back against the couch. "Sometimes. I've dealt with child protection, early intervention, and occasionally adoption. We've also represented families who have been affected by disasters."

"Do you like what you do?"

Stella nodded her head slowly. She'd been doing it three years now—enough to know. "Like any job, there are good and bad days, but overall the good balances out the bad. And it's definitely never boring."

"Lindsay was lucky to have you. Not everyone has a friend who can draw up their will and look after their child."

Her fingers fiddled in her lap. "I was the lucky one." Factually, what he'd said was true, but there were so many things she needed to tell him, so much he didn't understand. But now was not the time. Like Ryan, Stella wasn't her best self when exhausted. "I'd better get going. Let me know if you could use a tour guide again. I'm free on Saturday." She stood and walked to the door.

"Actually," Devon said, "if you know of any places I could take Ryan, I'd love to hear them. The concierge is fresh out—not that she had any great ideas to begin with. She was the one who suggested the opera house and bridge tour."

"She obviously doesn't have much experience with kids."

"No kidding. I was thinking of asking her to watch Ryan for a day, and then afterwards see if she has any better ideas."

Stella laughed. "You should. Maybe it would be the start of a new family-friendly training program at the hotel."

"As long as they'd create suites with two beds in them, I'd be all over that."

"Have you been sleeping on the sofa?"

"It's actually more comfortable than it looks."

Wow. Stella had assumed he'd let Ryan fall asleep in the quiet of the bedroom and then move him to the sofa later. Devon was either the kindest guy she'd ever met or completely ignorant. Probably a combination of the two. "You know, it's really good of you to let Ryan have his own bed, but he would have been just fine on the couch."

"Really?"

The hopeful expression on Devon's face looked adorable, and Stella hated to crush it. "Yeah, but good luck telling him that now."

"I should have known you'd say that," Devon said.

"I'm that predictable?"

"Afraid so."

Stella laughed. "Have a good night, Devon."

"Wait. You never told me if you knew of any good places to take Ryan. Really, I'm getting desperate."

Stella smiled. Of course she knew places—and not just for Ryan. Australia was a beautiful country and she loved showing off her native land to foreigners. "Have you been to the beach?"

"The beach? Is it safe for Ryan? I've seen Shark Week on the Discovery channel, and it seems like you guys have way too many shark attacks over here."

Stella laughed again—something she'd done a lot that day. It felt good. "I'm not sure why you're worried. If one comes near Ryan, won't you just punch it?"

"Good point."

"Then it's settled. I'll be by on Saturday morning to pick you up." Stella left with a wave. A smile played on her lips as she pushed the elevator button.

A moment later, Devon strode into the hallway. "I just realized how late it is."

"Which is why I'm leaving. Sorry. I hope I didn't overstay my welcome."

"No, of course not. But you shouldn't be riding the train alone at night."

"I actually do it all the time. It's really not a big deal."

"Sorry, but I have this annoying conscience that doesn't agree."

"So what are you suggesting? That I sleep here?"

"No way. There's only one couch and I'm not that chivalrous."

Devon knocked on the door of a neighboring hotel room, and a woman, probably in her fifties, with short, curly gray hair and bifocals opened the door. "Well hello, Devon. Can I do something for you?"

"Yeah, actually. Ryan's asleep and I wondered if you'd mind hanging out in our room for a little while so I can make sure Stella gets home okay."

The woman nodded. "Your timing is perfect. Dave is busy working on a presentation for tomorrow's meeting and won't stop typing on that ridiculous laptop of his. Since I'm in the middle of a good book, I'd love to read it in a quiet room. Just a moment." She went back in her hotel room, spoke a few words to her husband, and returned with a book in hand.

"I owe you one, Colleen."

"Just let me tend that little charmer one of these afternoons and we'll call it even," she said. "It would help me not to miss my own grandchildren quite so much."

"Deal. I'll be back as soon as I can."

Colleen looked back and forth between Devon and Stella. "Take your time. Dave's going to be working for hours yet. Sometimes I wonder why I even came on this trip with him."

"We're headed to the beach on Saturday if want to come."

Colleen squeezed Devon's hand. "You're such a dear, but Dave's actually free on Saturday, so we've already made plans."

"Next week, then."

Pausing outside Devon's door, Colleen glanced back at Stella. "I haven't known this young man long, but I can tell he's a good one." With a wink, she walked into the room and closed the door.

"I—uh . . ." *Really have no idea what to say.*

Devon re-pressed the elevator button. "It's okay. You can admit that you know I'm a good one. I won't let it go to my head."

"I think it's already gone to your head," said Stella. "Are you really going to leave Ryan with a stranger?" The elevator opened and Devon grabbed her elbow to pull her inside, but she resisted.

He sighed and leaned against the elevator door, keeping it open. "Colleen's not a stranger. Her husband's here on business and she gets lonely, so she's spent the past two days with us. In some ways she reminds me of my mom."

With her feet rooted, Stella said, "I'm still not sure that's a good idea. You really don't know her that well."

Devon smirked. "What, you think that sweet woman is going to kidnap Ryan and take him away?"

When he put it that way, Stella did sound a bit overprotective. "Stranger things have happened."

"You're just going to have to trust me then. You couldn't find a kinder, more patient person than Colleen. She's wonderful, and we're lucky to have her for a neighbor."

His hand tugged on hers again, and this time Stella allowed him to pull her inside the elevator.

As they descended, Devon leaned his shoulder against the wall and shoved his hands into his pockets. "Do you make a habit of going out on your own at night?"

"All the time. I'm telling you, I'll be fine."

Devon raised an eyebrow. "I'm sure you would, but my mother would tan my hide if she knew I'd let you ride across town on public transportation alone at night."

"Sydney is actually a really safe city."

"That's good to know, but I'm still taking you home. So stop arguing and just say thank you."

"Okay. I give up," said Stella. "And thank you." She'd been on her own for so many years that she'd forgotten what it felt like to be worried about. It was nice. Really nice.

"So how far away is your apartment, anyway?"

"Not that close," she said. "Listen, if I'd have known you'd do this, I would have left before it got dark. It's just that I wanted to—" When would Stella learn to think before she talked? She didn't want to talk about Ryan again.

"I know. You wanted to spend time with Ryan. What I don't understand is why you have trouble admitting it. It's not like you hide it well."

Stella bristled. What did he know, anyway? Nothing. Admittedly, Devon would know more if she'd tell him, but she wasn't ready. Nor was he ready to hear it. "I haven't been trying to hide it. I just don't want to talk about it right now."

"Fine by me."

The elevator door opened and Stella followed Devon out to the street and toward the train station. Sounds of rumbling engines, laughter, and faraway trains filled the humid night sky. The bright lights of the city masked the stars, but Stella searched for them anyway.

Are you looking down on us like you promised, Linds? Are you watching out for your son? If so, I could really use your help right about now.

But no answers came. No inspiration. And soon the starless

sky disappeared, replaced by the florescent lights on the concrete ceiling of the underground train station.

"Were you raised in the city?" Devon asked when the train started moving.

Stella shook her head. "No. I actually grew up in a small seaside town about ten hours north of here."

"Your parents still live there?"

Her parents. She hadn't been asked about them in years. Five long and lonely years. "No. They actually died in a car accident several years ago."

"I'm so sorry." His brown eyes looked sincere.

"It's okay," Stella said. "And before you ask, I was an only child, so besides an estranged aunt and uncle who live in England, I have no family."

"I'm sorry," he repeated. "And obviously, I have no idea what else to say."

She almost laughed at his blunt honesty. It was refreshing. "There's really nothing else you can say—unless you want to annoy me."

Leaning back, Devon rested his arm on the chair behind her. "What could I have said that would've annoyed you?"

Stella shrugged. How many people had Stella wanted to ignore, how many mouths had she wanted to tape shut? Even the people who'd gone through similar situations hadn't been able to comfort her. No one could. Only time. "Oh, you know. That things happen for a reason. They're in a better place. Not to worry because God is looking out for me, and somehow this experience will make me a stronger and better person. You know, words meant to bring peace but that really don't."

Devon's lips formed half a smile. "Well, not to be redundant, but things *do* happen for a reason and they *are* in a better place. And although I don't know you that well, I'm pretty sure you're a strong and good person."

Stella laughed. She couldn't help it. Devon had restated some of the comments that had once grated, and yet he had somehow managed to turn them into something different, and—well, charming. It was becoming apparent why Lindsay had been so captivated by him. "Thank you. And I know it's all true; it just wasn't what I wanted to hear at the time."

"You don't seem too annoyed now," he said. "Should I try again?"

"Do you *want* to annoy me?"

"I don't know. You're kind of cute when you're angry."

"And when I'm not angry?" Stella didn't mean to flirt or wheedle compliments, but the words tumbled out without asking permission.

"You're beautiful."

Her heart thumped a staccato rhythm. "What?"

"I said when you're not angry, you're beautiful." And then Devon turned and stared out the window.

Just like that.

Subject closed.

Which was good because Stella didn't know how to respond. She'd expected teasing, joking, maybe even a sarcastic remark. Not sincerity—which was exactly how he'd sounded. Honest. The kind of straightforward, no-nonsense, plain-speaking honesty that seemed so rare these days.

A fluttery sensation spread through her body, filling her. She'd felt it before, when Devon had sat a red-eyed boy on his lap and told him about his angel mother. The memory alone brought tears to Stella's eyes again. Without realizing it, Devon had reached inside her heart and touched it. Probably exactly what he'd done to Lindsay's all those years ago.

Since the day she'd watched Lindsay sign the will, Stella had tried to convince herself that her friend had made the right choice, that listing Devon as the guardian hadn't been a monumental mistake. But it wasn't until now that Stella finally started to believe it. Devon was a good man, a good person, and—whether or not he realized it—a good father.

The train slowed and a computerized voice announced the name of Stella's stop. Did Devon plan to walk her all the way to her door?

He stood and started following her off the train.

Should Stella say something? Tell him her flat wasn't far and that she'd be fine? Warn him that it might be a long wait for the next train?

"Which way?" Devon asked.

Stella pointed north. It was okay to be selfish once in a while, wasn't it?

"Hey, I wanted to say thanks for coming with us today," Devon said as he fell into step next to her. "It was really nice having someone along who knows their way around."

"I had fun." More fun than she'd had in a long time.

"What can I say? Ryan and I are fun guys."

"And humble," Stella teased.

"Just remember that you said it, not me. You're only humble until you admit it."

"Are you admitting it?"

"Nope."

Stella's laughter floated across the dim, lamp-lit street. A dog barked, a car drove past, and the few other people from the train dispersed and went their own way. It had been a long time since someone had walked Stella to her door. In the past, guys and friends had always met her downtown and said good-bye at the train station.

"Have you lived here long?" Devon asked.

"Three years and counting."

"It looks like a nice neighborhood—not that I can really tell in the dark."

"It is nice. The best part is that it's a short walk to the train station, which makes it close to work, shops, and the beach. I really like living in Sydney. At least for right now."

"Right now?"

"Having Ryan made me realize a bigger yard and some open space would be nice some day, especially if I ever have kids. But for right now it's great." They came around a corner, and Stella pointed at her white, boxy, contemporary flat. "That's my place."

Devon followed her up the walk and stopped outside her door. "There. Delivered all safe and sound. My mom would be so proud."

"If I ever meet her, I'll let her know she has a chivalrous son."

He grinned. "Please do. I'm sure she wonders at times."

"The times when you're arrogant?"

"I'm never arrogant. Only and always modest."

Stella smiled. "So you're admitting you're humble."

"No. I'm admitting I'm modest. Humility and modesty are two very different things."

"Not really."

"Yes really."

Stella shook her head.

"I can't believe you're giving me a hard time after I went out of my way to walk you home. That's pretty low, you know."

"You're right, and I'm sorry." Rising to her tiptoes, Stella kissed his cheek. "There. All better."

Devon grinned. "I actually do feel better. Now I know where to come if I ever get a real injury. Do you kiss those better too?"

"Sure, but one kiss a day is my limit." Stella smiled as she unlocked her door and let herself inside. "Good night, Devon. And thanks again for walking me home."

"No problem. See you Saturday."

Through the crack in her door, Stella admired his even stride and broad shoulders as he walked away. It was no wonder Lindsay had never really gotten over him.

chapter six

The last Saturday in February marked the end of Australia's summer. The wind whipped at Devon's face as the ferry carried them across Sydney Harbor toward Manly Beach. Hilly and lush tropical landscapes, sandy beaches, and high rises dotted the haphazard shoreline. With the bridge, the opera house, and the aqua blue water, every view could have been an image straight from a postcard.

The air was warm and humid, making Devon glad he was in the southern hemisphere. Back in Chicago, sleet and ice covered the ground, cars needed to be defrosted, and the surrounding bodies of water were frozen solid. As much as Devon looked forward to returning to work and his apartment, he didn't miss the cold.

They arrived at the beach early and claimed a spot near the water. The sun brightened the clear blue sky and highlighted the waves and rivulets in the ocean.

"Nice place," Devon said, surveying all of the people already there. "I can tell it's a popular beach."

"Yeah," Stella said. "But it wasn't until the early 1900s that people were allowed to legally swim in the ocean here."

"Why?"

She dropped the towels and beach bag to the ground. "It's an interesting story, actually. During the early settlement years, the men got so hot, they used to strip down and swim in the buff, so swimming was banned. Then people disobeyed, and after several arrests, a man named William Gocher told everyone he was going to bathe during the day, despite the law. He started a campaign to have the regulations changed—and it worked."

"Just like that?"

"It was more of a compromise. People were allowed to swim, so long as they wore clothing from their neck to their ankles. But the clothes became heavy and several people drowned, so they protested again, and before long, Manly Beach became a favorite place to sunbathe and swim."

"I can see why." Resorts, hotels, and high-rises surrounded them. Sort of a Honolulu meets Miami. Touristy and busy, but beautiful.

Ryan darted past, heading toward the ocean and carrying an empty bucket.

"Ryan, hold up!" Devon ran after him, grabbing the boy's hand as a small wave rolled over his feet. "You need an adult to be with you when you play in the water."

Trying to pull his hand free, Ryan said, "But I need water to build my castle."

Stella walked up next to them. "Yeah, you definitely need water, Ryan. Go on and fetch some." Devon started to follow until Stella's hand on his arm stopped him. "Ryan has spent his entire four and a half years coming to the beach on a regular basis. He knows he's not allowed to go in past his knees without an adult. Now stop hovering and enjoy the day."

"How was I supposed to know that?" Devon said, still not trusting Ryan.

"You weren't, which is why I just told you."

With water up to his ankles, Ryan stopped and waited for a wave. When it crashed over his legs, he scooped up a bucket of sandy water and trotted past them. The water toppled over the side as he walked, spilling half of its contents before he finally plopped down. He didn't seem to mind that his bucket was half empty—or was that half filled? Devon smiled, knowing Ryan would probably think the latter.

"See?" Stella said. "Told you so."

"Know-it-all."

Devon helped Stella spread out towels and set up the umbrella. The he dropped to his knees next to Ryan. "Can I help?"

Ryan's eyebrows drew together. "Do you even know how to build a castle?"

"Not as well as you, I'm sure. Why don't you teach me?"

Ryan nodded. "It needs to have four towers with a wall all the way around. Then we need to make a tall, tall tower in the middle."

"Is that where the princess lives?"

"No, that's where the ninjas live," Ryan said, like Devon should have known that already.

"Oh, right. Ninjas. Sure, why didn't I think of that?"

"Loads of ninjas."

"And what do they do?"

Ryan sighed, as though he had to explain something that shouldn't need to be explained. "They fight the fire dragons and push them into the river that's full of hot lava."

Devon bit back a laugh. The kid had an imagination, that's for sure. "Okay, then. Let's get this castle built before those dragons show up to fight. I'm thinking we need some more water."

While Ryan ran for more water, Devon looked over his shoulder to see Stella lying on her stomach, reading a book. Dressed in a white cover up with her hair pulled back in a ponytail, she looked relaxed and beautiful. "Hey, aren't you going to help?"

Her head swung around and her eyes flickered to his. "My degree is in law, not architecture. I'll leave the building to the boys."

Devon pointed to the pile of sand. "But the fire dragons are on their way and if we don't get this castle built, all the ninjas will be burnt to a crisp. How do you think that will make Ryan feel?"

"I'm sure he'll survive."

"Okay, but if things go south, you get to be the one to shut a hysterical four-year-old in the bathroom."

"Yeah, yeah." She smiled and returned her attention to the book.

Ryan stumbled back, lugging a bucket of water. He dumped it on the pile of sand, splashing wet sand all over Devon's board shorts. Looking down at the mess and then at the oblivious Stella, reading calmly in the shade, Devon frowned. Her morning of relaxation was about to change. After all, bringing Ryan to the beach and giving him a bucket had been her idea.

Devon whispered to Ryan, "It's really hot out here. I think it would be nice of you to pour water on Stella so she won't be hot."

Ryan grinned. "Okay." He raced to the water and refilled his bucket. Then he trotted to Stella and turned it upside down over her head.

Devon laughed. The kid had no fear.

Squealing, Stella rolled over, clutching a soggy book in her hand. "Ryan! Why did you do that?"

"Devon said you were hot."

The little tattle-tale. Ryan may not fear Stella, but Devon sure did. "I didn't tell him to pour it on your head. That was all him."

"Well, I think Devon is hot too," Stella said.

Devon grinned. "Thanks."

Stella's eyes narrowed. "I thought you were never arrogant. Ryan—"

But Ryan was already headed back to the water.

"Oh, no you don't." Devon lunged and grabbed Ryan around the legs, tackling him to the sand. After tickling more giggles from him, Devon said, "You can't get me wet, we're on the same team. Boys always stick together."

"Don't listen to him, Ryan!" Stella called. "You're on my team."

"No," Devon argued. "It's always boys against girls. Ask anyone."

Ryan looked uncertain, so Devon decided distraction tactics were in order. "Oh no! I hear the fire-breathing dragons coming. We need to hurry and get the castle built."

It worked. Ryan ran to his castle and started filling a bucket with sand. "I hear them coming! We have to hurry!"

Devon grinned, loving how easy it had been.

"Here, I'll help too," Stella said.

A blob of wet sand landed on Devon's head. A big blob.

"Oops, I missed. So sorry. I really was trying to help."

Devon wiped what he could from his hair. "Well, it was nice of you to try and help with something."

"I'm nice like that." Stella tried to brush the worst of the sand from the back of her cover-up. When she couldn't reach all of it, she pulled the knee-length dress to shake it free.

"Oh brother," Devon said. He stood and swiped his hand down her back, removing the worst of the sand. "In case you couldn't tell, you're on a beach, surrounded by sand. Did you really expect to stay clean the entire day?"

She glared at him and moved away from his touch. "You're making me sound like a wowser, which I'm not."

"Prove it."

"Fine." She plopped down on the sand next to them. "What do you want me to do, Ryan?"

Devon bit back a smile. Mission accomplished.

Stella's eyes drifted to Devon as he stooped to gather another bucket of water. His short, light brown hair had a disheveled, almost spiky look that she loved. With his brown eyes and broad muscular shoulders, she couldn't help but stare. Was there a girl waiting for him back in the States?

Focus, Stella, focus. The last thing she should be worried about was some hopeless attraction. In another week Devon would be gone, hopefully with Ryan in tow. And in order for that to happen, the boys needed to bond. And not just any bond—a strong and lasting one, like epoxy. Stella needed Devon to feel the same way about Ryan that she did.

"I think the dragons are getting closer," Stella said as she worked on the moat.

"I know. We have to hurry." Ryan's digging became frantic.

"Would it help if I put a powerful force field around the castle?"

The shovel stilled in Ryan's hand. "What's a force field?"

Stella moved her fingers like she was playing the piano and circled her hands over the castle. "A force field is like an invisible wall or shield, one that can block out dragons and fire, and keep the ninjas safe. In fact, I'll bet it will hold while we go take a dip in the ocean. What do you think?"

Ryan looked unconvinced. "Will the ninjas really be safe?"

"I promise. Come on, I'll race you to the water."

Devon was walking toward them, so Stella and Ryan grabbed his hands and tugged him back to the ocean. They played, splashed, threw a ball around, ate lunch, and finally finished the castle. Ryan wanted to add seashells to make the walls stronger, in case the force field stopped working, so Devon and Stella gratefully dropped to their towels, ready to soak up the warmth and sunshine.

Stretching his arms behind his head, Devon closed his eyes. "I could definitely get used to this."

Stella wanted to ask what "this" included, but she didn't dare. She could only hope Ryan was part of it. "Working eighty hours a week doesn't leave you much time for play, does it?"

"Nope."

A handful of warm sand streamed through her fingers. "When was the last time you took a real vacation?"

"A real vacation?" he asked. "Hmm . . . that would be in high school. Our family spent two weeks in Florida after I graduated. Ten years ago."

"Wow. I don't even know what to say to that."

"Pathetic, I know," he said. "But I've been busy and haven't had the time."

"Haven't *made* the time, you mean."

Devon's eyes opened and he rolled to his side, facing her. "No. I mean I haven't had time. Do you have any idea how much work it takes to start a company?"

"No. But I know you've managed to put your life on hold for two weeks to stay in Australia."

Brown eyes stared at her before he finally said, "You're right.

The company's more established now, so I could probably take some time off. And Brady's more than capable of handling things while I'm gone. It's just that I like what I do. My company means everything to me and it's hard for me to let other people take control, even for a little while."

Stella picked up another handful of sand. "What do you mean, it means everything to you? Don't you have a life outside of work?"

"Sure. I have friends and a small social life, but my job always comes first. I started the company from scratch and built it to what it is today. You can't do that and not have it consume your life."

"What about your family? Lindsay mentioned you came from a close family."

"I am close to my family. But they're still in Oregon, where I grew up. I live in Chicago and only go home for Christmas. We text and call each other a lot, though."

Stella felt a heavy, disturbing weight settle in her stomach. For some reason, she'd assumed he lived near his family. It was one of the reasons Lindsay had chosen him—a big reason.

Stella's fingers clenched around the sand. Why hadn't Lindsay called Devon before her death? Why hadn't she gathered more information? Why? Flipping onto her back, she squinted against the afternoon sun. *Did you really know what you were doing, Linds? Did you? Or is this some horrible punch line of an old teenage crush?*

Stella honestly didn't know what to think anymore.

No wonder Devon was hesitant to take Ryan. Who would look after him while Devon worked? Some day care center? The idea made her ill.

Unfortunately, it was still better than the alternative.

Lindsay, why couldn't you have picked me? I could have made it work. Somehow, I would have made it work. But Stella could no longer plead her case. Lindsay was gone, placing Ryan and his future on an unknown, undefined course—one that Stella could only hope and pray would end up like the sky that day, sunny and bright.

Shoving her worries aside, Stella forced her mind to other things. "So what does this company of yours sell?"

"It's an internet security site. Basically we help to protect people against viruses, hackers, or scams. We also offer filters that people can download for free to keep most of the crap on the internet off their screens. So when I say that the company is established, I mean that we no longer have to worry about paying our employees. But we still have to worry about keeping our products updated and recent. It's a constant battle, and we have a lot of competition. For right now, we're on top, but it's going to take a lot of work to stay there."

"Impressive."

"Thanks."

Stella's arm shaded her eyes from the sun as she studied Devon. He seemed like a take-charge sort of person, not one to bury himself behind a computer, writing code. "I would have never pegged you for a computer nerd."

He chuckled. "Guilty—although not so much anymore. I started off as a programmer with the dream of owning my own company. I wanted the flexibility to pick my hours and be my own boss, but I've had some rude awakenings since then. Ironically, I've put in twice the number of hours as most of my employees, and I don't remember the last time I took a day off just because I wanted to. And as for being my own boss—yeah right. The board of directors and stakeholders are really the boss."

Ryan continued to plaster the sides of his castles with broken bits of seashells. What would he be like as an adult? Still happy and laid-back? Or would life change him as it did so many people? "Wouldn't it be great if life turned out the way we dreamed it would as kids?"

"Maybe."

"Maybe?"

Devon shrugged. "If it had all been as easy and smooth as I'd imagined it, I wouldn't be who I am today."

"And who are you today, exactly?"

He chuckled. "I really have no idea."

Stella smiled, brushed some sand off her legs, and stood up. "Well, I'll let you figure it out while I go pay a visit to the loo."

chapter seven

Stella's slim figure made its way across the beach, somehow looking graceful as her feet wrestled with mounds of soft sand. She really was beautiful—and a complete mystery, but maybe that was part of her attraction. One minute she seemed anxious and worried, and the next, calm and collected. Devon didn't understand her.

Or why he even cared.

He was lounging on a beautiful beach in Sydney, Australia. A dream vacation for most people. And yet all Devon could think about was a mysterious girl and a four-year-old boy.

Who was no longer adding seashells to his castle.

Where did he go?

"Ryan?" Devon sat up and scanned the surrounding area. No Ryan. He wasn't in the ocean either. Leaping to his feet, Devon called, "Ryan!"

No answer. No boy.

The crowded beach now looked like a page out of *Where's Waldo*.

"Ryan!" Devon yelled. He'd been there only seconds ago. He couldn't have gone far.

A girl lying on a towel ten yards away set her book aside. "Lost someone?"

"Yeah, a boy. Four years old."

She scrambled to her feet. "Which way did he go?"

"I don't know."

"What's he wearing?"

"Uh . . . navy blue shorts. Red hat."

"Okay. I'll head this way, you go that way."

Devon nodded and jogged to the left, shouting Ryan's name along the long stretch of beach. By the time he neared the end, several others had joined in the search, and cries of "Ryan" drifted up and down Manly beach.

Ryan, where are you?

Had he gone out in the ocean? Had a large wave carried him out to sea? Had he drowned? Been attacked by a shark? Been kidnapped? Was someone driving off with him right now? The nightmares came at him like an onslaught of killer bees.

Deep breaths.

Calm down.

Ryan knew not to go in past his knees. He couldn't have drowned. No. He must have gone for a walk and gotten lost. *But does he know to stay away from strangers? Not to take candy from them and get in their cars?*

Stop it already!

Devon ran, calling out Ryan's name and searching the beach as he went. Maybe the girl with the book had found him. Please let her have found him.

Stella stood by their towels, holding the hand of a small boy with a red baseball cap. Stopping, Devon doubled over and tried to catch his breath. Ryan. He'd been found. He was fine. He hadn't drowned or been kidnapped. Everything was okay. Ryan was okay.

Devon suddenly wanted to throttle him. "You scared me to death, Ryan. Where have you been? I've been looking everywhere for you."

"As well as half of the people on the beach," Stella said. "You sure know how to get a search party moving."

Devon glared at her before returning his attention to Ryan. "Well?"

"I went with Stella," said Ryan.

"No you didn't. I watched her walk away."

Stella had the nerve to grin. "I guess I didn't hold your interest long enough because Ryan caught up to me just outside the loo."

The girl was unbelievable. How could Stella make fun of him at a time like this? Could she at least try for some sympathy? Her cheeky grin widened.

Apparently not.

Knowing he was about to wring both their necks, Devon spun around and went for a walk.

A long walk.

The hike from Manly Beach to North Head was breathtaking. A lush plateau of green looked like its edges had been crudely chopped off, exposing jagged cliffs that were splattered with creams, oranges, and browns. The ocean waves splashed across the rocky coastline below while a light breeze danced over Devon's skin, cooling him.

He was officially in awe of New South Wales.

Stella gripped Ryan's hand as they stood overlooking the ocean. "Did you know that most of *Mission Impossible II* was filmed here? In fact, somewhere along these cliffs they shot that scene where Nyah nearly jumped to her death."

Devon took a step back and pulled Ryan with him. "I'm beginning to think you're the queen of random facts, Stella. First the platypus, then Manly beach, and now North Head."

"Those aren't random facts," said Stella. "They're interesting tourist facts. But if you want random, I can give you random."

Always full of surprises. "Okay, sure. Let's hear it."

"Did you know that if you chew gum while peeling onions, it will keep your eyes from stinging?"

"Seriously?"

"It's true. I've tried it."

Devon grinned. "Ski goggles work too. What else you got?"

"Hmm . . . Intelligent people have more zinc and copper in their hair."

Devon laughed. "Where are you getting these so-called facts from? The *National Enquirer*?"

"You mock, but I'm telling you, they're true. Go look them up for yourself."

"Maybe I will."

"And maybe you'll learn a random fact of your own."

"Like how all blue-eyed blondes are eccentric?"

"You obviously don't have extra zinc and copper in your hair."

"I'm tired," said Ryan. "Can we go home now?"

Devon lifted the boy into his arms, and Ryan's head dropped to his shoulder. Little hands wound around Devon's neck as Ryan snuggled against him. Trusting him.

Devon tightened his hold. There was something about Ryan . . . something different, something unique. It was like an added responsibility, but one Devon didn't mind so much.

A large boulder rested a few steps away, and Devon sank down in front of it, leaning back. Ryan relaxed against him as his breathing deepened.

Stella collapsed beside him. "Feel like carrying me back as well?"

"Sure, why not?" Devon said. "Hey, I want to apologize about earlier. One minute Ryan was there and the next he was gone. It sort of freaked me out."

"So I noticed."

"Funny."

Stella smiled. "It was partly my fault. I should've made sure you'd seen him follow me."

"I should've been watching him better."

"You mean instead of watching me?" Her eyes laughed at him.

"Are you flirting with me?"

Her smile vanished and she looked away. "Why would I flirt with you? It would be pointless." She cringed. "Uh, what I meant to say was—"

"I'm leaving in a week and you'll never see me again."

Blue eyes reconnected with his. "I'd better see you again."

What? Wow. She really was flirting with him.

"Now don't go selling tickets on yourself. I only meant that if I don't see you, I won't see Ryan, and that's not okay with me."

Whoa. Slow down a second. Did she just imply . . . ?

"What are you talking about?"

Red-cheeked, Stella stammered, "I mean—if you plan to take Ryan home with you, that is."

The girl had some nerve. Devon couldn't take Ryan. Sure, he cared about the boy, but there was no way Devon could raise him. Maybe if he had a wife or fiancée or lived closer to his family—but he didn't.

"Stella, when are you going to realize that I'm not in a position to take Ryan? I can't. I have no idea how you convinced me to stay for two weeks or why I'm even here, but you did—which is the only reason I haven't left. If you keep pressuring me about Ryan, though, I'll be on the next plane out of here. Understand?"

Stella nodded and then turned away, but not before Devon saw the pain on her face. Was she going to cry? If so, tears wouldn't work on him. Devon refused to be coerced into taking Ryan home permanently.

Almost unconsciously his arms tightened around Ryan, and Devon found himself wishing things were different. If the truth be known, he wanted Ryan to come with him. He'd love nothing more than to offer the child a home filled with love and security. But he couldn't.

And now Devon would have to leave knowing there was nothing he could do.

Sometimes he wished he'd never met Stella Walker.

But then traitorous and betraying images slapped him in the face. Stella, with her gorgeous blue eyes and cheeky grin. Stella, comparing him to a platypus or snuggled on the couch with Ryan. Stella, splashing Ryan in the ocean and spouting random facts. Stella, Stella, Stella. For a girl he'd known less than a week, Devon sure had a lot of memories of her.

In her own frustrating, beseeching way, Stella had touched

him. Which would make saying good-bye to her and Ryan that much more difficult.

Devon took a breath and slowly let it out. "I'm sorry."

There were no tears, only a sad resignation. "I'm sorry too."

"I'm not sure why you want me to take Ryan, anyway. It's only been a week, and I've already lost count how many times I've messed up."

"Don't kid yourself. You're wonderful with him."

"Really? Because I remember you once said that I'd never make a good father."

"I've been known to say things I don't mean when I'm frustrated." Her fingers reached out and gently brushed Ryan's curls before falling to Devon's shoulder. "You're generous, patient, and caring—the type of person every boy should have in his life. You would make an amazing father, if you only had the desire to try."

Not again. Devon closed his eyes. "Stella, please . . ."

"I know," she said. "I promise not to push you anymore. Just promise me you won't leave until you have to."

"I won't."

But somehow, Devon knew he'd come to regret the promise.

Ryan finished his prayer and crawled into bed. "Will you read me a story?"

A story? This was a new request. Devon searched the room, hoping a children's book would suddenly appear. "Sorry, bud, but I don't have a book. Maybe we can get one at a bookstore tomorrow. Would that be okay?"

"I have one." Ryan jumped from the bed and ran to his bag. Unzipping a side pocket, he pulled out a beat-up hardback book. It pictured a wooden doll on the cover with the words, "You Are Special."

A flood of good memories rippled through Devon. He'd been eight when his family moved to Oregon, where he'd struggled to fit in and make friends. He started pretending to be sick so he wouldn't have to go to school. One day, Devon arrived home to find *You Are Special* lying on his bed, tied up with a bright green bow. His mother had read it to him nearly every night that entire school year, even after he'd made friends. And every night she'd kiss him good night and say, "You're special too. Don't ever forget that."

Devon's fingers glided over the cover. "I know this book," he told Ryan. "My mom used to read it to me."

"My mum always read it and said I'm special."

Devon blinked at the moisture in his eyes. "She's right. You are special."

"Can we read it?"

"Sure."

Devon picked up the boy, swung him around a few times and threw him onto the bed, loving the sound of his giggles. He scooted next to Ryan and smiled when the child snuggled up to him.

Together, in the dimly lit hotel room, they read the book. Devon would read a page and then Ryan would explain it with his own enthusiastic words. It was almost déjà vu for Devon, bringing back memories when his own mother had done the same thing.

The story ended, and Devon turned the last page, recalling the message his mother had written in his book years before. His breath caught. The words were faded, but they were still there. "Devon, I hope you never forget how special you are to me, to your dad, and to God. I love you! Mom."

Why had Lindsay taken it? The thought settled inside Devon as Ryan's little arm came to rest on Devon's chest. His finger grazed Ryan's cheek. Whatever her reason, Devon was glad she had. Somehow the knowledge that his book was now Ryan's favorite made it all the more special.

chapter eight

Stella stared at the open file on her desk. It was Monday, the beginning of a new week, and the skies were clear and blue. It should have been a great day, but the words from the file seemed to pop off the pages and smack her in the face.

Ryan Devon Caldwell

Mother: Lindsay Ellen Caldwell, deceased.

Father: unknown

Mother's parents: George and Betty Caldwell

Stella shut the file, hoping it would lessen the hatred and fear that came with those last two names. Her eyes drifted closed. *Please, God, please bring Devon around.*

"Looks like you could use something stronger than a lolly, but it's the only thing I have on me," Tess said, throwing a wrapped piece of candy at her.

Stella caught it and set it on her desk. "Ta, love. I haven't talked to you in a few days. How's Jeremy?"

A diamond glistened from Tess' left ring finger. "He wants to move up the wedding date to September."

"A beach wedding will be a bit chilly in September."

"I know, which is why I still want to wait until January," Tess said. "But he has a brother living in England, and they haven't seen each other in three years. Turns out, his brother is coming to Sydney for a business trip in September and Jeremy wants him to be the best man."

"His brother won't come back in January for the wedding?"

"Can't. His pregnant wife is due about then."

"How about November? It should be warm by then."

Tess shook her head. "Jeremy's parents have a three-week vacation booked. And October is close enough to September, so we might as well have it then."

"Well there you have it," Stella said. "If I had a gavel, I could pronounce the case closed."

"But I've already found the loveliest dress with short, capped sleeves."

"You could always wear a sweater."

Frowning, Tess said, "Some friend you are. I want my lolly back."

Stella's hand clamped over the candy. "No way. Besides, you'll be radiant no matter what you wear or where you get married. And just think how much Jeremy will owe you for this one. You could probably ask for anything."

A slow smile crossed Tess's face. "You're right. I never thought about it that way. He told me the other day that he wants to wait awhile before we have a baby. Maybe I can use this as leverage to make it sooner."

Stella laughed. "It's a good thing you're a solicitor. If he does agree to that, you'll know to get it in writing."

"True. Now, what about you? How are things going with the American?"

If only Stella knew. "He's a good guy. I just wish he'd stop thinking about why he can't take Ryan and focus on how he can."

"What are you going to do if he doesn't?"

"What can I do? I'll have to turn the matter over to the Department of Human Services." Stella hated saying the words out loud. Speaking them seemed to make it more of a possibility. A possibility she wasn't willing to consider yet—not when there was still a speck of hope. "I've been thinking about taking a few days off work. Do you think Gerald will mind?"

"Of course not. He thinks you work too hard anyway."

"I want to spend some time with Ryan before I can't anymore."

"I know. I need to talk to Gerald anyway, so I'll let him know." Tess offered her a look of sympathy and stood. "Eat the lolly. It's the red kind that brings good luck." She blew a kiss and left the room.

Pulling the wrapper from the candy, Stella popped it into her mouth. She needed all the luck she could get.

As Stella rode home on the train that evening, she sent a text to Devon, asking if it would be okay if she tagged along to the zoo the following day.

His reply came seconds later.

Tag away.

Tag away? What did that mean? That he'd tolerate her presence? That he didn't care either way? Stella shoved her phone into her purse. Why did she care what he thought, anyway? Ryan was the one she wanted to spend time with, right?

Right.

And Devon.

Stella couldn't think about Ryan without Devon's name forcing its way though, like a child seeking attention. Unfortunately, Devon didn't seem to have the same problem. What was Stella hoping for, anyway? That he'd be overjoyed to see her again? That he'd decide to stay in Australia permanently? She almost laughed at her absurd daydreams. Well, overjoyed or not, he'd have to put up with her "tagging" for a few more days.

Her phone buzzed again.

In the mood for some ice cream?

A smile spread across Stella's face as she typed her reply.

Only if it's New Zealand Natural.

You'd know best. Where? When?

Stella was waiting on a bench at a train stop when they appeared. Ryan grinned and ran to her while Devon followed at a leisurely pace.

"How was work?" he asked.

Who wanted to talk about work? "What are we, some old married couple?" Stella teased, hugging Ryan.

Devon shrugged. "Fine, if that's the way you want it. I guess we won't tell you about our day either."

Pulling free, Ryan gushed, "We saw tigers and monkeys and rhinos and zebras and elephants and a wombat!"

They'd already gone to the zoo. Without her. Stella forced the smile to remain on her face. Why did Devon tell her to "tag away" if they'd already been? "You went to the zoo today?"

Devon shuffled his feet, looking sheepish. "Sorry. When I got your text, we were in the middle of the bird show. I skimmed through the message and didn't realize you'd mentioned the zoo until I reread it when we were on our way to meet you."

If only Stella didn't feel as though she'd missed out on something special. "Sounds like you guys had a fun day," she said to Ryan.

"Yeah, and now we get ice cream!" Ryan's enthusiasm, as usual, was infectious.

As they made their way out of the train station, Stella couldn't resist saying to Devon, "So you reread my text?"

"Are you fishing for compliments?"

"Maybe. I had a long day. I could use a nice compliment about now."

Devon chuckled. "In that case, I reread your text over a hundred times and savored every last word. In fact, I plan to read it again and again when we get back to the hotel tonight. I'm sure it'll keep me awake half the night."

"Only half the night? That's it?"

"Blame Ryan. He wears me out."

A laugh escaped her mouth. "In that case, all's forgiven."

When they arrived at New Zealand's Natural, Devon held the door for her and Ryan. They ordered their ice cream and found a small table tucked away in the corner.

"Ice cream is good!" Ryan said, digging in.

"Better than custard?" Devon asked.

"No."

Stella cleared her throat. Now or never. "So, what are your plans tomorrow? Since I invited myself to the zoo and you've already been there, mind if I come along to wherever you're going?"

"I was actually surprised to get your text. I figured you'd be working most of the week." Devon took a bite of his ice cream and then examined it. "This stuff is amazing. Why don't we have this in the States?"

Hello, I'm over here. "Believe it or not, I took a few days off work."

"You did?"

"I'm not a workaholic like you." Maybe Devon didn't want her along. Was he trying to think of a way to tell her to bug off? *Enough, Stella. You're acting like a teenager.* What Devon thought didn't matter—it was Ryan who mattered. That's why she'd taken the time off.

"So, would it ruin your plans if I hung out with you guys?" Stella asked again.

"Since when did you need an invitation?" There was a teasing glint in his eyes.

"Since now."

"Then consider yourself invited, if that's what you want," he said. "Although we haven't planned anything for tomorrow yet."

"But you do want me to come?" Stella nearly groaned. Did she really just say that? Why hadn't she said a simple, "Thanks," and left it at that? *Honestly, Stella, you need help.*

"I see you're fishing again."

Stella played with her ice cream. Why did he have to be so unreadable? She wouldn't have to fish if he would give her some idea of what was going through his mind—at least where *she* was concerned. It was a simple question, really. Did he want her to come or not?

As if reading her mind, Devon leaned over the table and picked up her hand. "Yes, I do want you to come—but only if it's pressure-free."

A wonderful, tickling sensation coursed through her fingers and up her arm. "I already told you I won't pressure you anymore."

Devon returned to his ice cream. "Perfect. Then what should we do tomorrow?"

"How about a bushwalk?"

Ryan's eyes lit up and Stella wanted to hug the darling boy. "You mean a real one? In the mountains?" Not waiting for an answer, he turned his dimple on Devon. "We get to go on a bushwalk and see real live kangaroos!"

"Hey, I didn't say anything about kangaroos," Stella said.

"A bushwalk sounds great." Devon winked at her. "And seeing real live kangaroos sounds even better."

So much for a pressure-free outing.

The following morning, Stella chauffeured Ryan and Devon to the Blue Mountains near Katoomba. As they wound their way up the road, Ryan wouldn't stop talking about kangaroos. Stella hoped the clearing at the top would contain the usual mob. She wanted a front row seat to Ryan's excitement when he saw them.

Stella parked the car and led them past an old and decrepit knee-high wooden railing. Peering through the trees, she smiled. A mob of kangaroos was clustered in a clearing not far from them.

"I see them!" Ryan shouted, his little legs bouncing along in anticipation.

Devon and Stella shared a smile and quickened their steps to keep up.

"Don't get too close," Stella called as they neared. Several kangaroos looked their way but soon lost interest.

Ryan burst into giggles and pointed. "Look! They're hitting each other!"

"It's their way of playing, I think. Like when we wrestle." Devon studied the kangaroos. "They're interesting animals, aren't they?"

Maybe to him. To Stella, and most Australians, kangaroos were more like vermin. "When early European explorers described what they looked like, the English thought they were crazy. They called them travelers' tales until a man shot one and brought the hide back to England. It was stuffed and put on display."

"First the platypus and then the kangaroo," Devon said. "The English aren't very trusting, are they?"

"I guess not."

When Ryan had seen enough of hopping marsupials, Stella drove them to the trailhead of one of her favorite hikes in the Blue Mountains. In the middle of a rain forest, eucalyptus trees, ferns, and moss-covered boulders framed a well-worn dirt path. Every now and then a tropical flower would appear, stark and lovely against the green backdrop.

The sweet scent of vegetation, chirping birds, and fresh air—Stella never tired of bushwalks, especially ones that snaked through the dense and humid areas of these mountains. There was something calming about nature. Peaceful—a feeling that had been missing from her life recently. It had been too long since Stella luxuriated in sliding her worries aside. Way too long. She sent up a silent prayer of thanks for the gentle reminder.

Thank you, Father. I needed this.

Ryan stopped to point out a bug, and Devon crouched down beside him. Next it was a plant or something else Ryan found interesting. Each time, Devon was there, making Ryan feel important. It showed in Ryan's dimple and his proud, dark brown eyes. A feeling of rightness stirred inside Stella, bringing with it a penetrating warmth. For all of Lindsey's skepticism about the existence of a God, her friend definitely had a spark of inspiration there at the end.

Devon was exactly what Ryan needed.

The knowledge filled her, buoyed her, lifted her. Stella wished she could capture the impression and somehow inject it into Devon. He needed to feel what she felt—to know what she knew. If only she could tell him; if only he'd listen.

Ryan's wails cut through her thoughts. Ahead, Devon peeled Ryan off the ground and hugged him, rubbing his back and murmuring into his ear.

Stella rushed forward. "What happened?"

"He tripped."

Brushing hair from Ryan's forehead, Stella said, "Hey, tough guy, you okay?"

"My knee hurts," cried Ryan.

Devon pried the tiny body away from him. Sure enough, a few drops of blood oozed from a skinned knee.

"Ow! Ow! Ow! I need a bandage!"

"It's okay—it's just a little scratch," Devon soothed.

Stella dropped to her knees and rifled through her backpack. She pulled out a small first aid kit. "Here we are. Let's get this on and you'll be good as new."

Ryan cries intensified until the bandage was intact. Before long, he was bounding along on his own again, his skinned knee forgotten. Stella loved that about children—how easy it was for them to forget.

"I'm thirsty," Ryan said. "Really, really thirsty."

Stella almost laughed at Devon's expression. He was probably reliving the fish incident and petrified of another meltdown. She fished out a water bottle from her bag, untwisted the cap, and held it out to Ryan. "Here you go."

"Thank you," Devon mouthed in obvious relief.

Ten minutes later, the drink was gone, as well as Ryan's enthusiasm for the hike. "I'm hungry," he whined.

Devon turned to Stella, looking drained. "Please tell me you have a snack in that Mary Poppins bag of yours."

"Of course." Stella pulled out some black licorice. "But not until you say, 'Stella Walker is practically perfect in every way.'"

"You read my thoughts." Devon accepted the licorice and offered some to Ryan. Then he took a few for himself. "Do you mind? I could use a little energy boost."

"Have as much as you want."

The licorice seemed to keep Ryan happy while the path led them under a timid, drizzling waterfall. It was Stella's favorite part of the hike. She wanted to carve it out of the mountain and relocate it to her back patio.

Ryan's little fingers reached out to touch the tumbling drops. Then he leaned forward, trying to catch the water in his mouth.

Devon pulled him back. "Yeah, that's probably not the best water to drink."

Five minutes later came the plea, "I need to pee."

Devon turned back to Stella and winked. "Finally, something I can handle."

She laughed.

When Ryan complained of being tired ten minutes after that, Devon hefted him to his shoulders. Stella followed behind, admiring his strength and patience. They trudged along for a few more minutes until Devon stopped abruptly. He pointed. "What are those?"

"They're called stairs."

"Very funny," Devon said. "There's over a hundred of them."

"I know. It's the last part of the hike. They'll take us up to the Katoomba scenic railway."

"You're serious."

"Unless you can fly, up we go," Stella said, noticing his sweat-soaked t-shirt. "I can carry Ryan for a while if you'd like."

He shook his head and started forward, mumbling something about her questioning his manhood.

Stella pretended not to hear. "You have to admit this bushwalk is beautiful."

More grumbling came as he trudged up the stairs.

She tried again. "You'll thank me for this someday."

"Hear that, Ryan? Someday we're going to thank her for getting us tired, thirsty, hungry, and hot, and then making us climb the longest staircase I've ever seen."

Ryan giggled. "Giddy-up, horsey."

Quickening her steps to get around them, Stella lifted her camera to her face. "Look like you're having fun."

Ryan grinned and Devon made a face. A few pictures and over a hundred stairs later, they finally arrived at the top and entered the visitors' center. Stella held back a chuckle when Devon lowered Ryan to the floor and stood directly under one of the air-conditioning vents, raising his face to the cool air.

"Just so you know, Stella, that was not a short, little hike. Ask Ryan. He'll agree with me."

"Did you have fun, Ryan?" Stella asked.

Nodding, Ryan said, "Can we go down the stairs now?"

Stella directed a triumphant look at Devon. "See? Ryan's fine. He's not complaining."

"That's because he had a horse."

Stella laughed.

When Devon had finally cooled down, they took a ride on the Katoomba scenic railway. It was short, but with a 50-degree slope, it was also the world's steepest railway incline, originally used to bring coal and kerosene shale from the mines. Anything involving history always fascinated Stella.

"That wasn't very long," said Ryan. "Can we go again?"

Stella clasped his hand and swung it back and forth. "Maybe another day."

"Okay," said Devon. "Maybe that was worth the hike. Maybe."

"Oh, come on, admit it. You loved it all—even the hike."

Brown eyes met hers, and Devon smiled. "Maybe. But not the stairs. I definitely did not love those."

During the drive back to Sydney, Stella stopped at an overlook of a rock formation called The Three Sisters. With the Blue Mountains for a backdrop, it was picturesque, and Stella couldn't resist showing it to Devon.

"Why does he have paint all over him?" Ryan's voice sounded loud above the prattle of other tourists.

A painted, almost naked Aborigine was sitting on the ground, playing a didgeridoo. Stella hoped the man hadn't heard Ryan. "That's the way they dress where he's from," she said quietly.

"They don't brush their hair either?" Ryan studied the man's tightly curled, black, bushy hair, then took a step forward to get a closer look. "What's he doing?"

Stella tugged on his hand, hoping to draw him away from the man, but Ryan pulled free and walked over to him. "What's that?" He pointed to the long, cylindrical, almost cone-shaped instrument the man held.

Stella turned to Devon. "Are you going to just stand there or do something?"

"What do you want me to do? I don't think Ryan's offending the guy. In fact, I'm pretty sure he's made a friend."

Sure enough, Ryan plopped down on the ground next to the man. The Aborigine demonstrated how to blow into the didgeridoo before letting Ryan have a try. Stella cringed and started forward, but Devon's hand on her harm halted her progress.

"Really? You're going to let him blow into some stranger's instrument?" she asked.

"Yep." Devon smiled, watching as Ryan tried, but failed, to make a sound come out. The man demonstrated again and Ryan gave it another try, blowing harder. A whisper of a sound echoed through the canister and Ryan's dimple appeared.

Stella rolled her eyes, pulled her camera from her bag and snapped a picture. If Devon was going to let Ryan blow on a filthy wooden instrument, the least she could do was capture the memory. The man smiled at Ryan and offered his hand. Ryan pumped it up and down before bouncing back to Stella. "Did you see? I played it all by myself!"

"You're brilliant," Stella said as she led him to the other side of the overlook. Over her shoulder, Stella saw Devon walk up to the Aborigine, nod, and drop a wad of cash in a cup near the man's side.

It was a simple act but one that left an imprint on Stella's heart. A scared imprint. She didn't want to care about Devon any more than she already did. Becoming too attached would be pure stupidity. Things were already complicated enough.

When Devon rejoined them, Stella pushed her concerns aside and pointed out three burnt orange and yellow rock formations situated side by side on the edge of a cliff. They looked like the tops of three melting ice cream cones.

"They're called The Three Sisters," Stella explained. "And that bluish haze hovering above the trees in the background is caused by oil from the eucalyptus trees. That's how the Blue Mountains got their name."

"It's beautiful." Devon scooped up Ryan so he could get a better look.

Stella asked someone to take their picture before they headed back to the car. During the drive back, Ryan fell asleep almost immediately, and Stella wished she could do the same. It had been a long but wonderful day.

As they neared the hotel, reality descended. Another day gone. Now Stella only had a few days left to convince Devon to sign the guardian papers. Could she do it? Would he listen? Would he care?

Devon had been so quiet since they left the overlook. What was he thinking?

"I had fun today," Stella said.

He glanced in her direction. "Yeah, me too."

"Thanks for being such a good sport and letting me show you a little more of our country."

"Thanks for being our tour guide again. You really do have a beautiful and unique home."

"So do you."

"You've been to America?"

"Once. Lindsay used to go on and on about it. And after hearing all her stories about the time she spent with your family, she convinced me to take a short holiday there a few years ago, right after I'd graduated."

"You went to Oregon?"

Stella nodded. "And Washington and California. We flew into Seattle and made our way down the coast. My favorite place was Yosemite. I loved all the redwoods."

"Lindsay went with you?"

"No. Another girlfriend of mine went with me. We called it our final holiday before we started working. Lindsay wanted me to look up your family while I was there and stop by."

"Did you?"

Stella shook her head. "But we did take a detour through your hometown—so I could tell Lindsay I went there. And she was right. It's a beautiful place. Do you miss it?"

"I do, but mostly I miss my family. Chicago's my home now."

"You like it there?"

"It's not Oregon, but it's nice enough. I could do without the frigid winters, though."

"Why Chicago if it's so far from your family?"

"I got a job there after college. When I decided to start up my own company, the people I knew and trusted lived there, so it was easier to stay rather than move back home and start over."

The sun hesitated over the horizon, and Stella wished she could call it back. Time was slipping by too quickly. "Thank you for putting your life on hold for a couple of weeks. I'm sure it hasn't been easy."

"Actually, it's been surprisingly easy. I'm beginning to think I'm dispensable now."

"That's good. Maybe we'll see you back here at some point then."

"Yeah. I'd like that." Stella could feel his eyes on her. One look and she got all warm and tingly. Weak and pathetic.

Well, it was time for that to end. Time to be strong. For Ryan. With only a few days left until Devon's flight, it was now or never. "I need to talk to you."

"About what?"

"Ryan."

Silence. The air turned stuffy, even the supposedly fresh air blowing in through the vents. Rubber hitting asphalt and a purring motor suddenly sounded deafening.

Talk, Devon. Say something. Anything. Get mad at me for breaking my promise if you want. Don't just sit there. That's worse than anything.

"Stella, we've already had that conversation. You promised not to bring it up again."

"I know, but there are some things you need to know."

"What things?"

The rearview mirror showed Ryan stirring in his sleep. "Not now. It's been a long day and we're almost to your hotel. Do you think your friend Colleen might be able to watch Ryan tomorrow afternoon so we can talk? I'll even make you a meat pie."

Devon sighed and returned his attention to the passing scenery. "If she doesn't have plans, I'm sure she'd love to. I'll ask."

chapter nine

It was an odd experience to leave Ryan with Colleen and board the train alone. It felt wrong, in a way. Like a part of Devon was missing. He tried to shrug the feeling away and focus on the buildings darting by, but the feeling held tight. In three days Devon would leave Ryan behind, and as much as he hated to admit it, the thought brought an increasing amount of gloom.

He'd miss the kid.

He'd even miss Stella. In an almost infuriating way, she'd wriggled into his thoughts and maybe even his heart. At times she could be so maddening that he wanted to shake her. But then there were those other times, Stella's charming and endearing times, when she spouted off interesting and random facts, played and talked with Ryan, or made Devon feel . . . what? Encouraged? Inspired? Whatever it was, Devon liked it. He liked her.

Why?

Was it because she lived on the other side of the world? Out of his reach? Was this a case of liking what he couldn't have?

Maybe.

Or maybe not. Stella was different—the kind of different that made him excited to see her, even though he knew she'd pressure him to become Ryan's guardian again. He was like a mouse lured to the cheese in a mousetrap. Only worse, because he knew it was a trap. Pitiful.

But Devon would stand his ground. As difficult as it would be to say no and walk away, he knew his life back in Chicago could not incorporate a child—nor a long-distance relationship. For whatever reason, Lindsay had wanted Devon to be part of her son's life, so he would. He would offer financial support, even promise to visit and call as often as he could. He'd make Ryan a priority in his life.

Just not the chief priority.

Great. Devon hadn't even talked to Stella and already he felt guilty.

He stepped from the train and slowly walked to her apartment, stopping on her front porch. The door stared at him ominously, but he knocked anyway.

Stella opened the door and her bright blue eyes looked at him beneath the rim of a baseball cap. In her jeans and T-shirt, she looked informal and athletic. Gorgeous.

Devon stifled the urge to turn and run.

"G'day," she greeted him. "Thanks for coming."

Yeah. Like a lamb to the slaughter. "Thanks for feeding me."

"Don't thank me yet—you may not like what I made."

"I'm not really picky when I'm starving."

Stella laughed. "And on that flattering note . . ." She opened the door wider and waved him inside.

Curious to see the place she called home, Devon followed. The apartment was small and simple: tan walls, a blue couch, white kitchen cabinets. It was the patio off the kitchen that drew his attention. With stone pavers and a variety of potted plants and flowers, it felt like a mini oasis. A small table and two cushy chairs made it the perfect place to relax.

"This is nice," Devon said, walking outside.

"Ta," she said. "Someday I'll move somewhere with an actual garden, but for now, this works for me. Do you want to experience my favorite part?"

"Experience?"

"Hold on." Stella disappeared inside and returned with a small container. "Hold out your hand."

He obeyed, and she dumped what looked like Kosher salt into his palm. "What's that?"

"Sugar. Now hold up your hand and don't move or say anything." She whistled up to a tree that towered over the patio.

"You're making me nervous," Devon said. "Did you just turn me into some sort of bait?"

"Shhhh," she said.

A small, parrot-type bird flew from the tree and landed on his wrist, pecking at the white crystals. Another bird soon followed. Talk about awesome. "You have trained parrots?"

Stella laughed. "No. They're wild. And they're larakeets, not parrots."

"You're telling me that wild birds fly from the trees and eat out of your hand?"

"Welcome to Australia."

"This place keeps getting better and better."

While they ate, Stella kept the conversation light. She didn't eat much, but Devon devoured the food. The meat pies were incredible—nothing like the potpies back in the States. He wondered if licking his plate would be too uncouth. "I wish I could take all Australian food back with me."

"You obviously haven't tasted Vegemite yet."

"What's Vegemite?"

"It's a spread we put on sandwiches and toast. Something most Americans hate. I have some inside if you want to try it."

"Bring it on. I haven't tasted anything here that isn't great."

Stella shrugged and went back inside. A few minutes later she handed him a slice of bread with black paste spread across the top. "Bon appétit."

Devon took a big bite and immediately wished he hadn't. It reminded him of the time he'd stolen a beef bouillon cube from his mom's pantry, thinking it was a treat. He'd bit right into it, even chewed it once or twice before realizing it wasn't candy—at least not a candy he'd eat on purpose. Vegemite had a similar taste, only worse. There were no words for the bitter, salty paste. Disgusting didn't do it justice.

Not caring if Stella thought him rude, Devon spit it into a

napkin. "Okay, I obviously spoke too soon. That stuff is horrible." He gulped down the rest of his water.

Stella laughed. "You're definitely American."

"You really like that stuff?" She couldn't possibly. It was revolting.

"Yeah." She started collecting their plates and glasses.

"Here, let me take those," Devon said, pushing his chair back.

"It's all right, I got it." Stella stumbled over Devon's chair leg and deposited her unfinished meat pie on the front of her shirt.

Devon bit back a laugh. "You should have eaten all your lunch like a good girl."

Looking like she wanted to throw the plate at him, Stella said, "How nice of you to pin the blame on me. It was your chair I tripped over, after all."

"Maybe you should have watched where you were going."

With a glare, Stella said, "I'll be right back."

Devon followed her inside, and while he waited, he rinsed the dishes and loaded them into the dishwasher. Under the sink, there was a bottle of soap, so he added some before turning it on. There. What girl could stay mad at a guy who did the dishes? Helping himself to another handful of sugar, he walked back out to the patio and whistled for the birds.

"Thanks for doing the dishes," Stella said, sinking down onto a chair.

"It's the least I could do after such a terrific meal."

"I couldn't let you leave Australia without tasting meat pies."

"Or Vegemite," Devon reminded her, pulling out the other chair. "Although I'm not about to thank you for that one."

"Hey, Ryan loves it too. In fact, you should take some back with you—" She winced. "I'm sorry. I keep doing that, don't I?"

"Yeah, you do." And Devon was tired of it—more than tired. He'd made it more than clear that he wouldn't become Ryan's guardian. Couldn't. It was time for her to stop assuming. Time to accept the situation for what it was. Lindsay had chosen wrong, and Stella needed to deal with that and focus on finding Ryan a good home with two great parents. He deserved nothing less.

Devon settled back in his seat and crossed his arms. "Why

don't you just tell me whatever it is you want to say. Then I can tell you once and for all that I can't become Ryan's guardian."

Her expression solemn, Stella nodded. "If you don't take Ryan, our state government will become his guardian and will be responsible to find him carers." She paused. "And they'll start with Ryan's nearest relatives."

At least she was finally being open with him. "And his nearest relatives are . . . ?"

"Lindsay's parents. George and Betty Caldwell."

"And that's bad because . . . ?"

"Because they aren't nice people, Devon," she said. "They're religious and devout Catholics, but they're also cold, strict, and unfeeling. Sounds contradictory, I know, but I really don't think there's a speck of love in either one of them. That's why Lindsay hated religion so much."

"Have you met them?"

"A few times. Lindsay used to tell me stories about her life with them. Although they never physically hurt her, they yelled a lot and berated her—even in front of me. Lindsay was raised to think of herself as ugly, brainless, clumsy, and annoying.

"In middle grade, she heard about a foreign-exchange program offered through her school. She jumped at the chance and somehow managed to convince her parents to let her go. Lindsay described those nine months with your family as the best ones of her life. Your mother treated her with love and kindness, and your sister was a great friend who taught her about hair, makeup, and clothes.

"And you—well, Lindsay said you'd smile and say hi. That you told her she was smart when she came to you with a math question, and that she was talented when she drew you a picture to say thanks. She said you opened doors for her and told her that ladies were always first. She called you her prince, you know.

"Although we grew up in the same town, we didn't really become friends until the tenth grade. I found her crying in the bathroom one day after some guy she went out with had slapped her around. She didn't think much of herself, which was why she picked losers. She said they were all she was good enough for.

"After graduation, she ran away from home and got a waitressing job in Sydney. We kept in touch, and a few years later I found out she was pregnant. At the time, I thought it was the worst thing that could have happened to her—another setback. But I was wrong. Ryan transformed her. Lindsay stopped dating, found a decent job, and became . . . almost confident. She used to say that her baby would have the best mother in the world." Stella choked on the last words and fell silent.

Which was good because Devon wasn't sure he wanted to hear any more. He hadn't known what Lindsay's life had been like, what struggles she'd had to face. Nor had he known that a few kind words spoken so long ago would have meant so much. A one-time comment of, "you're smart," shouldn't be a highlight of someone's life. Devon should've made more of an effort to befriend her back then.

If only he'd known.

"And Lindsay *was* the best mother," Stella continued. "When Ryan was born, she started working part-time from home, and with a little help from the government, she got by okay. She doted on Ryan and showered him with love, affection, and compliments. The first time Lindsay held him in her arms, she called him her handsome and brilliant little man. I know, because I was there.

"She was over one time and Ryan spilled his milk. Lindsay immediately tipped her own glass over and said something like, 'How fun! You are the best game-inventor!' He giggled, and for the next couple of months, until the 'game' got old, Lindsay constantly cleaned up spilled drinks. I told her she was crazy, but she said that her son would never hear a negative word from her. Ever. And I'm sure he never did."

No more, please no more. Devon wished he'd never come. He wanted to forget everything or somehow make Stella take it all back. Erase. Delete. Strikethrough. Whatever it took, he wanted it gone.

There had to be another alternative. Some other way. "If you know all this about the Caldwells, why can't you get Ryan placed somewhere else, with parents who can give him the kind of home he deserves? You've got to have some connections."

Stella shook her head. "You don't understand. If the Caldwells want to take and raise Ryan, there's not much I can do to stop them. Sure, I can take them to court and challenge the placement, but I can't prove anything. On paper they're the perfect choice. All I have are a bunch of secondhand stories from a deceased friend. It would be their word against mine, and you have to know how those types of cases play out."

"So what you're saying is that if I don't become Ryan's guardian, he'll end up with the Caldwells?"

"Unless they, like you, don't want him."

"What are the chances of that happening?"

"To be honest, they don't even know they have a grandson. Lindsay would die all over again if she thought they'd ever meet."

"You didn't answer my question."

"It's because I don't have an answer. Your guess is as good as mine."

Devon let out a breath. This was too much to take in. Too much pressure. "So why me? Why not you? I get that Lindsay thought I was a nice person, but that was ten years ago. You were her best friend and already knew and loved Ryan. Why did you let her list my name?"

"Ironically, Lindsay didn't choose me for the same reasons you say you can't take Ryan. I work full-time and I'm single. She couldn't see me making the situation work, and she didn't want Ryan being raised by a nanny or a care center. She also wanted Ryan to be part of an extended family, which I don't have."

Devon clamped his mouth shut. He wasn't prepared for this.

"Listen." Stella leaned across the table and covered his hand with hers. "Lindsay promised me she would contact you before she passed away. I'm not sure why she didn't, but I do know she felt right about choosing you. She knew you came from a wonderful family, and I'm sure she assumed you still lived near them. Maybe she even thought you were married."

Unseen walls closed in around Devon. The humid air felt hot and sticky. Thick. "Why didn't she pick my sister then? Emily's married, she's a stay-at-home-mom, and she has a couple of kids. She would have been a way better choice."

"She wanted you."

"But she hardly knew me! I don't get it." Devon stood and paced the small patio, wishing now it was bigger. The arguments he'd come prepared with were no longer valid. He'd been broadsided. Stella had known all of this from the get-go and kept it from him, choosing to dump it on him three days before his scheduled flight home. Why?

The answer came in an instant. She'd wanted Devon to get to know Ryan and care about him. She wanted him to feel responsible. Because if he cared, he couldn't possibly let Ryan go to the Caldwells.

Which left only one choice.

Him.

Devon was thrust back to the ninth grade when Nancy, the prettiest girl in school, had flirted with him. He'd felt flattered, even a little arrogant. But then he found out she'd only acted that way to make his best friend jealous. It had been his first real and painful experience with manipulation—but it was nothing to what Stella had done.

"Exactly why did you want me to take Ryan for two weeks?" Devon's eyes dared her to be honest.

With a pleading look, she said, "I needed you to come to love Ryan the way I do—to care about the outcome of his life."

"And you think his life will be that much better with me?" Devon almost shouted the words.

"Yes," Stella said, her voice shaking. "I do."

"You know, you've got some nerve—"

"I've got nerve?" Shoving her chair back, Stella stood. "I don't know why you're blaming me for this. I wasn't the one who lived with your family for nine months. I wasn't the one who had a baby on my own. I wasn't the one who listed you in her will. And I wasn't the one who died!" With her palms planted on the table, she dropped her head, shoulders shaking. When her eyes finally met his again, tears coursed down her cheeks. "I was the one who tried to convince Lindsay to choose me."

Devon felt an almost physical impact, as if her words had literally struck him. He took a step back. He needed to get away.

He needed time to think and less suffocating air to breathe. He needed Stella's tear-filled eyes to look at someone else.

So he turned and walked away.

Through the patio door and into the kitchen—Devon stopped short when he saw bubbles. Lots of bubbles. They oozed from the dishwasher, covered the floor, and seeped into the great room.

"What the heck?" This couldn't be happening. Not now.

"Oh look, you mopped the floor too," Stella said from behind.

Devon struggled to push the claustrophobia aside, at least long enough to deal with the mess. "There was only one kind of soap under your sink. I figured it was dishwashing detergent."

"I'm out of dishwashing soap."

Devon turned on her. "Why didn't you say anything? You knew I loaded the dishes."

Pushing past him, Stella said, "I didn't know you turned the dishwasher on."

"For crying out loud! Who washes dishes and doesn't turn it on?"

"It wasn't even full!"

"So?"

Stella glared before she stepped through the bubbles to stop the machine. "Just go. Please. Just go."

Gladly. Devon didn't need to be told twice and practically bolted for the front door.

"Wait," her voice called out as he grabbed the handle. *What now?*

"Please." Stella shoved a wrinkled envelope into his hand. "Read this before you make any decisions."

Stuffing it into his pocket, Devon flung open the door and left.

chapter ten

Devon didn't know how long he'd been on the train or where it was headed. It didn't matter. What mattered was that he was getting away from Stella. And Ryan too. As if distance would alleviate the pressure and allow him to think.

If only Lindsay Caldwell had never come to America.

Devon knew it was harsh, but he didn't care. He wanted to confront Lindsay and tell her she'd made a mistake—a horrible mistake. That she needed to come back and set it straight. But Lindsay was gone. And like a squashed bug on a windshield, she'd left a big splat behind.

Devon's palm hit the back of the seat in front of him, and several passengers turned to stare. At the next stop, he left the train behind. Crossing a street, he looked up at the sky. *Why God? Why me?* It was as though he was being punished, but for what? Committing an act of kindness? If Devon had been rude to Lindsay or simply ignored her, he wouldn't be in this situation now. But he'd been nice, complimentary even.

And how had she thanked him?

By messing up his life from her grave.

"I'm sorry I'm so late." Devon left the door open, hoping Colleen would take the hint.

No such luck. Colleen smiled but remained seated in the armchair. "I don't mind. Ryan is a delight, and we've had a wonderful time together. He's now snug as a bug in bed."

"Thanks for watching him for me."

"Did you have a nice time with Stella?"

"Sure." *Until she shoved me under the bus.*

Eyebrows raised, Colleen said, "For someone who just spent the majority of the day with a pretty girl, you don't look happy."

"It's been a long day."

"So you don't like her then?"

Was this really happening to him after the day he'd been through? "I do like her. She just told me some things that made me angry. In fact, if you want to know the truth, we had lunch together and then I spent the rest of the day riding around on a train and walking." Devon collapsed on the couch. "On a positive note, I now feel as though I'm learning my way around downtown Sydney."

Colleen's expression fell. "Oh, I'm so sorry. Would you like to talk about it?"

"No, but thanks for asking. And thanks again for taking care of Ryan. I owe you."

Colleen stood and picked up something she'd been crocheting. It looked like a blanket. "You should call your mom."

Devon wanted to laugh at her random, unasked-for advice. He wanted to smile. But finding humor in anything now felt too foreign. Too impossible. "Yeah, I'll be sure to do that."

"Good." Colleen patted his cheek. "Mothers always know the right thing to say. They're a gift straight from heaven, you know. And I'm not just saying that because I'm a mom."

The door closed, and Devon tossed aside her advice. What could his mother possibly say, anyway? Nothing. She could only listen and worry, which was exactly why he wouldn't call. Why make someone else shoulder his problems?

They're a gift straight from heaven. The words echoed in Devon's mind.

It was true. His mom was a gift from heaven. How many times had she been there for Devon? Hugged him when he was sad. Helped him with school projects, read to him, listened to him. Given him advice. And right now, more than ever, Devon needed some advice. Some good advice.

So he pulled out his phone and called Lydia Pierce.

"Devon, is that you?" she whispered. "What's wrong?"

"Why does something have to be wrong for me to call you?"

"It's five in the morning, sweetie. Usually you call at a reasonable hour."

Could nothing go right today? "I'm sorry, Mom. I wasn't thinking. I'll call back in a few hours."

"Nonsense," she said. "I'm already awake and headed to the family room so I won't wake your father. Now what's going on? Is Ryan okay? I really wish you'd call more often."

"I talked to you three days ago."

"Exactly."

Devon sighed. "Sorry. I've been busy."

"I know and I understand. What can I do for you?"

"I need some advice, Mom."

"Well you came to the right place," Lydia teased. "I really should write a book one of these days."

Devon actually smiled. It felt good. Even managed to release some of the aching pressure from his head—enough to get him talking, at least. The words gushed out as Devon told his mother everything. From the Caldwell's nastiness to Stella's duplicity, Lydia heard it all.

When he finished, Devon waited for her words of wisdom. She'd know what to do. How to turn it all around so that Ryan would end up with a good family and Devon could return to America alone.

But no answers came. No words of wisdom. "Mom? Are you still there?"

"Yes," Lydia said. "I'm just wondering what it is you want me to say."

"How should I know? You're the one who could write a book. You tell me."

Her throaty chuckle spanned the globe and sounded loud in his ear. "Ah, sweetheart, I'm afraid this is one of those situations where I can't tell you what to do. It's your life. You need to decide what the right thing is for yourself."

"That's just it. No decision is a good one. Ryan gets screwed either way."

"I disagree," Lydia said. "I think you'd make a wonderful father."

Of course she would think that—she was his mother. "And what about my job? Am I supposed to take him with me to work?"

Silence.

"Mom?"

"Honey, in your mind, this is a lose-lose situation. You're not seeing the big picture. All you're seeing is the here and now, when what you really need to do is think about the future. Regardless of what you decide, everyone's life will continue to move forward. Whether Ryan comes home with you or not, he'll grow up and live his life, with you or with someone else. If you decide to bring him back with you, you'll find a way to make it work. In other words, stop worrying about the now and focus on making a decision you can live with."

Devon felt like cursing. Where was the door number three? The "everyone goes home a winner" solution? Nowhere. There wasn't one. Not even his gift of a mother could find one.

"Uh, thanks, Mom, but I should go."

"I know you'll make the right choice. I love you."

"Love you too."

Devon dropped his head to his hands. Why wish for a third door when there really wasn't even a second?

Why hadn't Lindsey added a contingency? Something to the effect of: "If Devon can't or won't take Ryan, I want my son to be raised by Stella Walker." It was like Lindsay had kept it out on purpose, knowing it would force Devon to take her son. The ultimate manipulation. The ultimate trap. And it had worked. A ball and chain was now clamped around Devon's ankle, and there was no way to break it free—not if he wanted to live with himself.

Slowly, Devon picked himself up off the couch and rummaged around in his suitcase for pajamas. He needed sleep and lots of it. Maybe things would look better in the morning. More clear. Wadding up his khaki shorts, he paused when a crackling sound came from the back pocket. The letter. He'd forgotten all about it.

Sinking down onto the couch, Devon removed a wrinkled and creased paper from the envelope, unfolded it, and read Lindsay's letter. Then he reread it.

Devon couldn't remember the last time he'd cried, but by the time he'd refolded the letter, his eyes were wet with tears. Lindsay's words had penetrated through the walls of stubbornness and found a way to his heart. A feeling of hope drowned out all other emotions, bringing with it the clarity he'd needed. Stella had tried to explain, but it had taken Lindsay's words—Ryan's *mother's* words—to finally make him understand.

In Lindsay's mind, she hadn't picked him. God had.

With care, Devon slid the letter back into the envelope. Someday Ryan would be old enough to understand, and Devon planned to keep it safe until that day. There were some words only a mother could say. Colleen had been right after all. Mothers really were a gift straight from heaven.

Devon knew what he needed to do. He'd known it all along but hadn't wanted to consider it or even think about it until now. Every part of him screamed, "No. There has to be another way." But deep inside, Devon knew there wasn't.

With shaking hands, he called Brady.

A raspy voice answered. "Man, you've got to get yourself some sort of nightlife in that city so you'll start calling me at a reasonable hour."

"Sorry, bro, I'm not thinking right. I'll make it quick. Have you heard from Walter Hawkins lately?"

Silence. For almost a full minute, Brady's even breathing echoed through the phone before his friend finally asked, "Why?"

Devon sat on the couch next to Ryan. "Hey, bud, I need to talk to you man to man."

"What does man to man mean?" Ryan grinned. "That sounds funny."

"Well, I'm a man, and you're a man, so when we only talk to each other, it's called man to man."

"I'm not a man. I'm a koala!" During the past week, Ryan had become a fan of *The Koala Brothers*.

Devon patted his knee. "Fine, can we talk man to koala then? Come here."

Ryan scooted away. "I'm not a koala. I'm a boy."

"Get over here before I tickle you senseless."

Ryan giggled and ran. After ten minutes of chasing, tickling, and wrestling, Devon finally managed to get Ryan to sit on his lap.

"Hey, how would you like to live with me?"

"Forever?"

"Uh huh."

Brown eyes widened. "Here? Where we eat custard every day?"

Devon shook his head. "No. We'd move to America, where I live. You'll come back with me and stay with me there. We can get a house with a big yard and a swing set and everything."

"But how will we get there?"

"On an airplane."

"I get to ride on an airplane? Yay!" Ryan nearly jumped down before Devon caught ahold of him again.

"Whoa, I'm not done yet. If you decide to live with me, that means that after the airplane ride, we won't come back to Australia for a long time. You will live in America and go to school in America, and you'll always be with me."

"Can Stella come with us?"

Devon paused. How to make Ryan understand? "No. She needs to stay here, but we will come back to visit her sometimes, okay? And you can call her anytime you want." Except during the day. The time difference wouldn't exactly be kid-friendly, but they'd find a way to make it work.

Ryan's excitement fled as quickly as it had come. "But I want Stella to live with us too."

"Maybe she can come to America sometime."

"To live with us?"

"No, to visit."

Ryan frowned at the floor.

It had never occurred to Devon how attached a four-year-old could become to an adult. How hard had it been for Ryan to lose his mother? How difficult would it be for him to leave Stella? Ryan deserved stability and love. He deserved to be a child. And from here on out, Devon would see that he got it. He'd be there for Ryan the rest of his life.

And Stella would too . . . from a distance.

Inspired, Devon said, "Hey, what do you say we buy a camera for Stella's computer? That way when we call her, you can see her on the computer and she'll be able to see you. Just like you see people on the TV. Would you like that?"

Ryan nodded, a partial smile returning to his face.

chapter eleven

Devon's flight was scheduled to leave the following morning, and Stella still hadn't heard a word from him. What was going on? What had he decided to do? Did he plan to show up and hand Ryan over, or would Devon become Ryan's legal guardian?

Stella had debated calling him several times, but what could she say that wouldn't make things worse? Nothing. Waiting was her only choice.

That and missing them both.

Sometime during the next twenty-four hours, Stella's entire life would change. And not for the better. Either way, Ryan and Devon would drift away from her. Either way, she lost.

It was Friday night, and Stella wanted to curl up in a ball and hope the melancholy would scatter away in her tears. But she was made of sterner stuff than that. So she cleaned. Stella washed her blinds and windows, reorganized her closet, wiped down all the walls, and dusted every square inch. But it didn't help. Every time she looked at anything in that wretched flat, it would remind her of a little boy or a man.

Maybe Stella should spend her time looking for a new place to live.

A knock interrupted her thoughts. Her pounding heart

deterred her for only a second before she rushed to the door and flung it open.

Devon. There. On her doorstep. Looking handsome and . . . nervous? With his hands shoved in his pockets, he rocked back and forth from his toes to his heels. Had he come to tell her no?

"Where's Ryan?" Stella said.

"With Colleen. I needed a chance to talk to you alone before we go back to get him."

Get him? What did that mean? Was he going to leave Ryan with her? Trying for a calm voice, Stella said, "Come on in."

Devon drifted toward the back patio but stopped when he got to the kitchen. "Your floor looks nice. Very shiny and clean."

"Yeah. Who knew my dishwasher could double as a floor cleaner?"

He half smiled before stepping out to the back patio. Taking a seat, Devon gazed up at the tree. "I'm going to miss this place. No one back home is going to believe me when I tell them wild parrots eat from your hands."

"Larakeets."

"Whatever."

Stella pulled out the other chair. She wanted to shriek, "Out with it!" but clasped and unclasped her fingers instead. What had Devon decided? What would become of Ryan? Why wouldn't he just tell her and get it over with?

"I've decided to become Ryan's legal guardian."

Stella's heart dropped to her toes as tears wet her eyes. After months of stewing and worrying, everything was finally looking up. Ryan would have a wonderful father. Ryan would have a great life. Ryan would be okay.

Ryan would leave Australia and perhaps never return.

Stella took a deep breath. *This is good, Stella. This is what you wanted.* But the words didn't compensate for the ache that filled her body. She didn't want them to go.

"Thank you," Stella said. "So, so much. You're an answer to my prayers. Lindsay's too. And I'm so sorry I didn't tell you everything to begin with. I just didn't think that . . ." Her words drifted off.

"No, you didn't think, or maybe you thought too much. Regardless, I understand why you did what you did."

"You do?"

"Yeah."

Stella wanted to throw her arms around him. Even after all she'd put him though, Devon had somehow forgiven her.

"Does Ryan have a passport?"

"Yes." Stella hoped Devon wouldn't be offended by yet another assumption on her part, but he didn't seem surprised.

"Good," he said. "I've changed my flight. I'm taking Ryan to Oregon. We'll spend a week or so with my family, and once he's comfortable, I'll return to Chicago alone."

"But—"

Devon held up his hand. "Just let me finish before you start questioning my decisions." Standing, he walked to the edge of the patio and leaned against a pillar. Minutes floated by before he finally said, "I've decided to sell my company."

Stella gaped at him. "But—"

His hand shot up again. "Please, Stella."

She forced her lips together. *No, no, no! This isn't right! It's not what I want you to do, and it's not what Lindsay would have wanted you to do either. You shouldn't have to give up something you love so much. Surely there's another way. There has to be another way.*

"Someone has wanted to buy it for years, but I've never considered selling—until now, that is. They've already made me an offer and I've already accepted, which is why you haven't heard from me in a few days. I needed to figure some things out before I signed any guardianship paperwork."

Devon took a breath and let it out. "So, as I was saying before, I'll leave Ryan with my parents while I fly back to Chicago and complete the sale. Then I'll pack up my stuff and return to Oregon, and Ryan and I will start over there, near my family. It makes sense. More sense than trying to work full-time and raise a child on my own. Besides, it's what Lindsay would have wanted."

Was it? Stella felt a sickening pit fill her stomach. She'd been too preoccupied worrying about Ryan and his future to really stop and consider what she was asking of Devon. Stella figured he'd simply cut back on his hours and maybe hire someone to care for Ryan. Wasn't that what most people would do?

Devon isn't most people, said a voice inside her head.

No. He wasn't. He was a good, honest man who would make the best father for Ryan. Stella only wished he didn't have to give up so much in the process. "I'm so sorry. I didn't set out to ruin your life."

"You didn't ruin my life. You may have upset it for a while, but as my mother so kindly pointed out, it's only temporary. Things will all work out in the end."

If only he looked more convinced. "What will you do?"

Devon actually smiled. Well, almost. "I don't know yet, but maybe Ryan can help me decide. He's already told me all the pets he wants to get, so maybe we can open our own zoo."

A zoo. Stella wanted to simultaneously laugh and cry. Here Devon was, about to give up something that meant so much to him, and he was joking about becoming a zookeeper. "Great idea. Ryan can be in charge of feeding all the animals."

"Hey, I think you just gave me our marketing pitch. We'll spread the word that we have the fattest animals on the planet and people will flock to it just to watch them try to move."

Stella laughed, and their eyes met. A wonderful, prickling sensation filled her body, and she couldn't resist walking over and throwing her arms around him. "Thank you," she whispered. "Thank you, thank you, thank you."

Devon's arms tightened around her as he pulled her closer. Closing her eyes, Stella rested her head against his chest, relishing the way his touch made her feel. Warm, happy, alive.

Maybe if she never let go, he wouldn't leave.

But he did, and took Ryan with him. They stayed a few extra days to finalize the paperwork and then late in the afternoon on Tuesday, Stella drove them to the airport. She parked the car and followed them inside, where they paused near a window just outside security.

Stella knelt and gathered Ryan to her. "I'm going to miss you, kiddo." She tried to blink away her tears as she held him tight. "I want to hear from you all of the time—at least once a week, you hear?"

Ryan frowned. "I want you to come too."

"I promise I'll come for a visit soon, okay?"

"Okay." A plane flew by overhead. Ryan turned around and pressed his nose to the window. His excitement was obvious, and Stella tried not to let it depress her.

Slowly, Stella faced Devon, not knowing what to say. How could she say good-bye to someone she shouldn't care about but did? "Did you know that the word "stewardesses" is the longest word typed only with your left hand on a keyboard?" Stella blamed her nerves for the ridiculous comment.

Eyebrows arched, Devon chuckled. "No. But I'll be sure to steer clear of that word since I have enough trouble using a keyboard."

He held out a gift bag he'd been carrying. "This is for you. From Ryan. It's a webcam so he can see you when he calls."

"How sweet. Thank you." The reality hit Stella like a blast of cold water from a hose. It was a thoughtful gift, really it was, even though there was already a webcam on her laptop, but it also reminded her that she couldn't touch, hug, kiss, or cuddle Ryan like she wanted. It meant distance.

Devon offered a half smile. "I don't know what else to say. And obviously you don't either, which is a first."

He was right. She didn't. Although there were several things Stella wanted to say: Please don't take Ryan away from me. Please stay a while longer. I think I'm falling for you, and I can't stand the thought of you leaving and taking Ryan.

"Keep in touch?" she finally said.

"We will."

Little fingers were still pressed to the glass. "Will you tell him every night that I love him?"

"I promise."

"Thanks." Well, this is it. Devon would pass through security and board the plane, and Stella's arms would ache to wrap themselves around him. Not touching him went against every natural instinct her body possessed.

But Devon surprised her. He picked up her hands and pulled her to him, tucking her into a warm embrace. Then he held her close as a few tears trickled from her eyes and soaked into the fabric of his shirt.

"When can we ride on a plane?" Ryan asked, bouncing toward them.

"You're one of a kind, Stella Walker," Devon whispered in her ear and kissed her forehead before releasing her. Then he held his hand out for Ryan and stepped into the security line. Ryan waved until they'd rounded a corner, but Devon looked back only once.

chapter twelve

It had been a long flight, which was ironic because no time had passed. At least not according to the clock affixed to the wall of the airport. Devon and Ryan had left Sydney Tuesday night at eight and landed in Portland the same Tuesday night at seven-thirty. Crazy. The International Date Line sure knew how to mess with people's minds.

Lydia Pierce found them in the baggage claim area. "Oh you darling boy, come and give your grandma a hug!"

Ryan smiled tentatively but hung back, looking unsure of the large woman towering over him. Devon's mom loved to bake and loved to eat. As a result, she had gained a few pounds over the years and was beloved by all who knew her. There was no happier person on earth. Even Mrs. Claus couldn't compete.

Ignoring the boy's shyness, Lydia scooped him up in her arms and squeezed him tight. "You're even more adorable than I'd imagined. We're so glad you're here."

Ryan didn't protest, but he didn't say anything either.

"Don't worry, champ." Devon rubbed the top of his head. "One taste of her cookies and you'll never want to leave."

"Cookies?" Ryan asked, the first shadow of a smile appearing on his face.

"Oh, you like cookies, do you?" Lydia asked. "That's good, because I have some waiting for you at home. Your grandpa is making them as we speak."

"Dad's making cookies?" Devon asked. "Since when did he become so domestic?"

"Since we didn't get them made in time to pick you up, and I told him I got to see Ryan first."

"Sounds like Dad's going soft."

Devon must have fallen asleep during the drive because it seemed like only a few minutes before Lydia pulled to a stop in the driveway.

"We're home," she said.

With its faded yellow siding and dark green shutters, the house still looked the same. It was good to be home.

"Do we get cookies now?" Ryan asked from the backseat.

"Of course," Lydia said. "Let's go find some and meet your grandpa."

Ryan allowed Lydia to hold his hand, and they found Jack Pierce in the kitchen, pulling a fresh batch of sugar cookies from the oven. He looked ridiculous wearing a red and white floral apron tied under his protruding belly, especially since flour covered his navy blue shirt.

"Welcome home, son, it's good to have you back," Jack said, clapping Devon on the back before bending down. "And you must be Ryan. I hope you like cookies because your grandmother insisted on doubling the batch."

Ryan's wide eyes rested on the frosting and candy sitting on the counter. Lydia plopped him onto a barstool and placed a cooled sugar cookie before him, handing him a butter knife.

"You're wearing ruffles, Dad. Ruffles," said Devon.

Jack looked down and grabbed at the strings, pulling it loose before tossing it on the counter. "Confound it, Lydia! I told you this thing would only make me look like a spineless pansy!" He glanced at Devon. "She's the one that insisted I wear this ridiculous getup."

"And you obviously agreed," Devon said.

"I did not."

"And yet you wore it."

Jack glared at his wife.

Lydia chuckled. "I tied it on while you were rolling out dough and talking to Emily on the phone. You were so distracted you didn't notice."

Devon grinned. "Well, it's a good look for you. Maybe next time you could put a matching bow in your hair. Oh wait, you'd need hair for that, wouldn't you?"

Jack snorted. "I might still have hair if I'd stayed single and never had children." He walked around the table and took a seat beside Ryan, who was dumping sprinkles on his cookie.

"You're really good at decorating," Jack said.

"I know. My mum said I'm the best in all of Australia."

"Well, now you're the best in America too," Jack said. "Hey, pass me those candies, will you?"

While grandfather and grandson frosted cookies, Lydia helped Devon bring in the bags and take them to his room. The bed looked soft and welcoming.

"Ryan's adorable," Lydia said. "He's going to fit right in—cute little accent and all. Your father is already smitten."

Devon fell back onto the bed and tucked his hands under his head. "What am I doing, Mom? I don't know the first thing about kids—or parenting."

Lydia sat beside him and patted his knee. "No one does when they first become parents. It's a learning and growing process. If something works, you go with it. If something doesn't, you learn the hard way never to try it again. You get to know your child and what works and won't work with him. The problem is that as they grow, they change." She chuckled. "It's definitely challenging, but you've always liked to be challenged."

"You're not helping." Devon's eyes drifted shut. He couldn't keep them open any longer.

"Tell me more about Stella. She sounds nice. Is she smart . . . pretty?"

Devon yawned. "All of the above, but don't go getting any matchmaking ideas. Australia is literally on the other side of the world."

"I know, but a mother can always hope." Lydia paused. "Have you heard from Beth yet? She called last week."

Devon's eyes flew open. The bright light fixture burned his eyes, but he didn't care. Devon cleared his throat and tried to make his voice sound normal. "What'd she want?"

"Your new cell number. I guess she ran into Brady a few days ago and heard about your trip to Australia."

"Does she know why I was there?"

"I assume so, but she didn't say much and we didn't talk long," Lydia said. "She hasn't called you yet?"

"Not that I know of."

Lydia leaned over and kissed his forehead. "I'm so happy you're back and that you've brought Ryan with you. Why don't you get some sleep, and I'll make sure Ryan goes to bed when he gets tired."

"He might not want to sleep alone in a new place."

"If he doesn't, I'll bring him in here. Now get some shut-eye, will you? Everyone's coming over tomorrow night."

Lydia turned off the light, leaving him alone in the dark, empty room. Devon hadn't slept much on the flight and needed rest, especially since his two loud, crazy sisters and their families were coming tomorrow. But he wasn't tired any longer.

Beth had called.

Beth, the girl he'd once been crazy about. The girl he'd almost married. What did she want? It had been over eight months since she'd spoken to him; eight months since she'd broken off their engagement. Had she changed her mind? After the way Beth had ended things, Devon couldn't think of any other reason she'd call.

Groaning, he rolled to his side. If Beth still loved him, if she wanted to try to make it work again . . .

Well, he honestly didn't know how he felt about that.

Stella snapped a file shut and glared at her cell phone, willing it to ring. The afternoon sunlight hid behind dark, graying clouds, a perfect complement to her mood. Devon and Ryan had landed ages ago, so why hadn't they called? For the past three hours, Stella hadn't been able to concentrate. Didn't Devon realize she'd be worried about Ryan? About him? One quick phone call. That's it. Only a few minutes, a brief sentence or two, and Stella could rest easy. But did Devon care? Obviously not.

Well, Stella wasn't one to sit around and wait for the phone to ring, at least not for more than three hours, so she took a breath and picked up her phone.

"Yeah?" Devon's groggy voice answered.

Oh great, she'd woken him up. "Hi, it's me."

"Beth?" He sounded half awake.

Who is Beth? "Um, no, it's me, Stella."

"Stella?" Devon flattered her with a yawn.

"Really? You've forgotten me already?" Stella said. "I'm the girl you promised to call when you arrived."

"What? Oh, yeah, I'm sorry. You woke me up, and I'm a little out of it. How's it going?"

"I was just about to ask you the same question. You never called or sent a text. I was worried . . . about Ryan."

"Sorry," Devon repeated. "I didn't sleep much on the flight, and I was so tired by the time we got here, I fell asleep before I thought to call. If it makes you feel any better, I'm still wearing my clothes."

Stella smiled. Oddly enough, it did make her feel better. "Sorry for waking you. I just wanted to make sure you arrived safely and that Ryan's doing okay."

"He's more than fine. My parents already love him."

Of course they did. It was Ryan, after all. Who wouldn't love him? Stella ached to snuggle with him, to be the recipient of one of his treasured kisses and hugs. America was too far away.

"Stella?"

"Sorry." Stella hoped he couldn't hear the sadness in her voice, the misery. "I'll let you go back to sleep now. Just promise to keep me updated."

"I will."

Proper etiquette dictated she say good-bye, but Stella couldn't make her mouth form the words. She didn't want to end the call. She wanted him to tell her about the flight. What had they eaten? What did they watch? When did he plan to fly back to Chicago?

And who was Beth?

"Stella?"

"Yeah?"

"Tell me something."

"What?"

"I don't know. One of your random facts. I'm feeling brain-dead and could use something to get me thinking."

"You're serious," Stella said.

"Deadly."

"All right, you asked for it." She thought for a moment. "Did you know there's no real word in the English dictionary that rhymes with 'month'?"

"There has to be," Devon said.

"Tell me one."

"I'm thinking."

Stella waited a few seconds. "You're wasting your time. There really isn't any, I promise."

"I'll get back to you on that one, but I'm sure I'll think of something."

"It has to be a real word, you know."

"Yeah, yeah," Devon said. "In the meantime, how was your day?"

Stella paused. Should she be honest or make something up? Honest. He'd probably see right through anything else. "Lonely. I think it's going to take some time to adjust to life here without you or Ryan."

"If it helps any, I wish you were here with us. My parents would probably want to adopt you too."

"They sound wonderful. I hope I can meet them one day."

"Well," Devon said. "You'll never guess what my dad was doing and wearing when we showed up."

"Tell me."

Devon launched into a description of just the sort of details Stella craved to hear. He told her about Ryan's reaction to his new grandparents and how quickly he'd made himself at home. Then he told her about the flight and their overly perky flight attendant. He told her how Ryan wanted to see the X-ray machine's monitor at the airport and about how he'd tried to ride on the carousel with the luggage.

Stella's laughter filled her small office, and a few rays of sunlight actually peeked through the clouds. It was enough. "Give Ryan an extra hug for me."

"Will do."

"Oh, and Devon?"

"Yeah?"

"Thanks. I needed that."

chapter thirteen

As promised, Emily and Cora, Devon's two perky sisters, arrived the next evening for dinner. They both lived about an hour away and usually only came for Sunday dinner, but that week they'd made an exception.

Devon and Ryan were out back grilling steaks when Emily's voice echoed through the house. "H-e-l-l-o! We're here!" she called. "Where's that big brother of mine and my new little nephew? Come on, show yourselves people! My kids have been dying to meet their new cuz!"

Ron, Emily's husband, mumbled something about hearing loss.

Pretending he hadn't heard, Devon ruffled Ryan's hair. "I think it's time to turn the steaks. Ready?"

Dressed in a child-sized Home Depot apron, Ryan looked like a miniature Bobby Flay. He held up a spatula that was almost as tall as him. Devon grinned and picked him up, helping to turn the steaks.

"There you are!" Emily had found them. "Guys, they're out back!"

Ryan gripped Devon's neck when Emily threw her arms around them. "So good to see you! We've been so excited to meet you, Ryan!"

"How've ya been, sis?" Devon said.

Three small children ran out, then stopped to stare at Devon and Ryan. They looked so much older to Devon than they had at Christmas.

"Hey guys, come and meet Ryan," Devon said.

They stood rooted to the stairs, saying nothing.

"Where's Grandma?" one of them finally said, taking a step back toward the house.

"She and Grandpa ran to the store for a few things. They should be back soon."

Emily shook her head at Devon. "They're still afraid of you, you know. If you would've at least tried to talk to them at Christmas, they would probably like you."

Devon frowned at the kids. "You guys don't like me?"

They shook their heads and ran back inside, tripping over the threshold in their rush.

"Why don't they like me?" he asked Emily. "I wasn't mean to them."

"You didn't play or talk to them either. To them, you are a big, scary man who stares."

What? Devon was not. Leave it to Emily to be so dramatic. He lowered Ryan to the ground. "What do you think, Ryan? Am I a big, scary man?"

"No." He giggled. "You're a big, scary meat pie!"

"Meat pie?" Devon said. "I'll show you who's a meat pie!"

Ryan squealed and ran, but Devon was quicker. He grabbed the little boy, hoisted him over his shoulders, and ran in circles around the backyard. Then he somersaulted Ryan down to the ground and chased him again.

One by one, Emily's children crept through the patio door and watched. When the oldest tentatively stepped into the yard, Devon chased him too. The other two soon followed, and Devon allowed them to tackle him to the ground.

"Emily, help!" Devon said.

But no help came. In fact, the opposite happened. Two more squealing girls ran into the yard and jumped on him. Cora's family had arrived. Devon wrestled, tickled, and chased all of the children until he couldn't anymore. Out of breath, he searched for some sort of help; at the very least, something to distract the kids. But Emily, Cora, Ron, and Jeff only stared from the sidelines, open-mouthed.

"Who are you, and what have you done with our brother?" Emily called.

Devon pointed toward the house and yelled, "Oh look, I think I hear Grandma and Grandpa inside. I bet they have treats." The kids all ran for the house. Even Ryan. Whew. It worked.

Ron slapped his shoulder. "Good to see you, man."

Devon nodded, trying to catch his breath. "I thought I'd show your kids I'm not so scary, after all. Please tell me Mom and Dad are back."

"You're in luck," Jeff said. "They came in with us."

"I hope they have treats."

"They always have treats." Cora gave Devon a hug. "I wish I would have caught that on camera. I'm still in shock."

Pointing to the smoking barbeque, Ron said, "Uh, you may want to check on those."

Crap. Devon darted toward the grill and lifted the lid, cringing at the charred meat.

"Yeah, that's how Dad cooks them too," Ron said, looking over his shoulder.

Jeff clapped Devon on the back. "Don't worry. I think I've pretty much decided to become a vegetarian anyway. At least on the days we eat here."

Ron laughed. "Yeah, me too."

Later, when they gathered around to eat, Devon tied the apron back on Ryan and lifted him to his shoulders. "I want all of you to know that chef Ryan here helped man the grill. And since he's new to the family, I'm sure you'd all love to show your appreciation by eating the steaks."

Ron and Jeff glared from across the table.

After dinner the kids ran off to play, leaving the adults to clean up. As Devon wiped down the table, he realized that for the first time in a long while, he felt as though he fit in—like he belonged again. It's not that his siblings had ever intentionally excluded him, but there were only so many conversations about potty-training, sleep-deprivation, or school assignments he could tolerate before excusing himself to find something more interesting to do.

But now things were different. Now Devon could relate to some of their tales of parenting and he even contributed once or twice. It was nice, and he had Ryan to thank for it. Somehow, the boy had helped Devon to span a gap that he couldn't on his own.

Well, almost span.

Ron hugged Emily from behind while she rinsed dishes, and Jeff playfully snapped a dishrag at Cora.

Suddenly Devon missed Stella.

Stella smiled when her Skype account rang. One o'clock—right on time.

Since that first night, Devon had called almost every night before Ryan's bedtime. The call coincided with her lunch break, so Stella was able to close her office door and enjoy a nice little chat with her two favorite guys.

Today, however, there was only one set of brown eyes watching her. "Where's Ryan?" she asked.

"In bed. He had a busy day and was . . . well, let's just say that cranky is putting it nicely."

"Were there any fish involved?" Stella teased.

"No, and please don't mention fish around him. I know I promised to buy him some more once we got here, but he hasn't asked about it yet, and I'm hoping he'll forget."

Stella laughed. A lone blue Betta swam in a fishbowl on her bookcase next to a few goldfish in another bowl—a good-bye gift from Ryan. Stella had promised to take good care of his pets, but so far, five goldfish had died. At least the Betta still seemed to be healthy. "Two goldfish were dead when I got to the office this morning," Stella admitted. "I don't know what I'm doing wrong."

"They miss Ryan."

"They must. Maybe I should frame a picture of him and put it on the table next to them. Do you think that would work?"

"Would you want it to?"

Stella shook her head. "Probably not. I don't mind the Betta, but the goldfish are boring and pretty disgusting when they're floating on top of the water. If they didn't remind me of Ryan, I'd have dumped them down the loo days ago."

"So the truth comes out. You're not all heart after all."

"Not where fish are concerned."

Devon chuckled and then cleared his throat. "Um, there's a reason I called without Ryan tonight. I need to talk to you."

"What about?" When he didn't answer right away, Stella's heart thumped a little faster. Was something going on with Ryan? Was he okay?

"I've decided to take Ryan with me to Chicago."

Stella blinked. "Why? Who will take care of him while you're at work?"

"Beth."

Beth. That name again. The way Devon looked away from her made it sound ominous. Like he was preparing her for something bad, something Stella wouldn't want to hear. *Then don't say it.*

"She's a girl I used to date . . . uh, used to be engaged to."

Engaged? Devon had been engaged? When? Stella stifled the urge to slam her laptop shut. Normally, the poor resolution of the webcam bothered her, but today she was grateful for it. Maybe he wouldn't see that her smile was fake.

"Used to be engaged to?" she asked. "How long ago?"

"Eight months," Devon said. "Beth broke off the engagement, and I haven't heard from her until a few days ago. She wants to give our relationship another try."

If there was a proper response to this, Stella didn't know what it was. Congratulations? Yippee? Golly-wolly? All of them sounded absurd, not to mention phony. So Stella did the only thing she could do. She nodded and tried to look interested. Glad even. Which was exactly what she should be. Happy. Happy for him and happy for Ryan. Maybe Beth was exactly what they needed.

If only it didn't hurt so much.

"She wants to date again and see where it goes from there."

"Oh." Why was he telling her all of this? Devon couldn't possibly know how much she cared or he wouldn't say such things—at least not until she had time to mend, to move on.

"Stella?"

"Yeah?" She fought for a calm, collected composure.

"I don't know. I guess there's not much more to say. Now that Ryan's a part of my life, Beth wants me to bring him to Chicago so she can meet and spend time with him. I just thought you should know."

Ryan. Beth wanted to meet Ryan. Get to know him. Why? Who was this girl who thought she could waltz back into Devon's life and expect to be part of Ryan's? And why was Devon okay with it?

"Are you sure it's a good idea to introduce Ryan to her now? Before you know if it will work out?"

"No," Devon admitted. "But I already know Beth and I know what we're like together. What I don't know is if Ryan will change that. I mean, how can I know if Beth's still a good fit for me if Ryan's not around? Does that make sense?"

In a depressing way, it did. "Why did she break up with you if she still had feelings for you?"

Devon sighed. "After we got engaged, Beth invited me to spend the weekend with her family. While we were there, I spent a lot of time on the phone trying to deal with some problems that had come up at work. And when I wasn't on the phone, I was distracted, thinking up solutions. Her family is big. With the noise and chaos, we both got a little testy and argued.

"After we got back to Chicago, we planned to go out to dinner and sort things out, but an emergency came up at work and I had to cancel. That night, she stopped by the office, gave me the ring back, and told me she was sorry but it wouldn't work out. She needed to marry someone who valued her more than a job. Someone who would be around, who liked kids, and who would one day make a good father. She said that wasn't me." Devon paused. "And she was right."

"No. She just didn't know any better. You've already proven her wrong."

"Thanks, but I've changed a little since then. And to be honest, I did think her nieces and nephews were really annoying."

Stella laughed. "Maybe they'll grow on you in time."

"Yeah."

"Doesn't she have a job? How can she watch Ryan for two weeks?"

"She works for her uncle and can pretty much get time off whenever she wants."

"Oh." Stella connected and disconnected two paperclips, wishing things were different. That she could be the one to watch Ryan. That she could be the one who Devon wanted to—*Stella, stop!* "Well, I hope things work out for the best. Have a safe trip and keep in touch, all right?"

"I promise."

And he would. Stella knew that much. What she didn't know was if she really wanted him to anymore. If only she didn't care so much about Ryan. If only she hadn't promised Lindsay she'd remain a part of his life.

Stella powered off the computer and walked to the window. People passed by on the sidewalk below, headed somewhere. Were they going out with friends? Home to a wife or a family? Or were they on their own, like her, walking toward a destination, but aimless just the same?

Stella needed to get away. Away from the office and away from her flat. She needed a distraction—somewhere that would remind her that being single and unattached had its perks.

But where?

"Hey, girl." Tess walked into her office and sat on the green upholstered chair. "You look about as cheerful as I feel."

"Bad day?" Stella asked.

"It started off well, until Jeremy called and said he can't make it to the U2 concert with me tonight," Tess said. "We've had the tickets for months, and I'm not about to stay home because my fiancé can't go. You interested?"

A slow smile replaced Stella's frown. "Definitely. Your timing couldn't be better."

chapter fourteen

Devon kept a firm grip on Ryan's hand as they walked through the Chicago airport. The gray, filthy snow piled high on the side of the road was an unwelcome reminder of the cold that would be waiting for them outside. He should have bought a warmer coat for Ryan.

A group of people passed by, revealing a tall, elegant girl with long, shiny black hair. Beth. With her clear blue eyes, she looked as beautiful and exotic as ever. Her high-heeled boots beat a staccato rhythm against the checkerboard marble floors. "Hello, Devon."

"Hey."

She threw her arms around him, and Devon resisted the urge to breathe in her perfume—a light scent she knew he loved. Eight months was a long time, especially after all that had happened between them. Devon half-heartedly returned her hug with his one free arm and then pulled away. "Beth, this is Ryan."

Beth smiled and crouched down to Ryan's level. "Hi Ryan. It's great to finally meet you. I'm so excited to spend time with you."

Ryan watched her in silence, neither smiling nor frowning. He looked more bored than anything. The poor kid was worn out and probably sick of meeting new people.

They followed Beth to her car, and she drove them to a nearby restaurant for dinner. An elegant and expensive French restaurant.

"Uh, Beth, I'm not sure Ryan will like this place," Devon said.

With a smile, she said, "Give me some credit, will you? They have a kids menu with American food like hamburgers and chicken nuggets. Besides," she said, reaching for Devon's hand, "you love French food."

"But Ryan doesn't, and he's not American."

Beth looked over her shoulder and flashed Ryan a brilliant smile. "Hey, you like chicken nuggets, don't you?"

Ryan shook his head.

She tried again. "Have you ever eaten a chicken nugget?"

Another shake.

"Well, how do you know you don't like them if you haven't tried them?"

"I don't like them." Ryan looked at Devon. "Can we have custard?"

Before Devon could answer, Beth said, "Sure—for dessert. We can get some frozen custard on our way back to Devon's, okay?"

Ryan frowned. "I don't want custard that's freezing. I'm cold."

Right then, Devon wanted to pick up Ryan and take him back to Australia. A place Ryan knew. A place he was familiar with. A place he called home. It wasn't fair that a small, four-year-old boy should have to go through so much change in such a short amount of time.

He threw Ryan an apologetic look. "Sorry, bud, but they don't have custard in America. They only have something called pudding, which is sort of like custard, but not as good."

Ryan's lips quivered, his eyes bright with unshed tears. "I don't want chicken. I want custard."

Devon thought fast. "What about noodles? Like the kind Grandma Lydia made you?"

"The long snake kind I can slurp?"

"The very same."

The dimple didn't appear, but at least Ryan offered a solemn nod. One potential disaster averted.

Beth didn't say anything until she had reversed the car and pulled from the parking lot. In a quiet but firm voice, she said,

"You shouldn't give in to Ryan when he acts that way. You basically just taught him that he'll get what he wants whenever he whines."

"Beth, we've been up since six o'clock this morning. Our connecting flight was delayed, and it's been a long day. Ryan's in yet another new place, meeting another new person, and he's tired. So am I."

Her expression softened and she smiled. "Does that mean you're going to throw a tantrum too?"

"I just might if there's a long wait."

Beth laughed. "That I'd love to see."

They stopped at the first Italian restaurant they found, and thankfully didn't have to wait long to be seated. When the waiter brought menus, Devon hoped Beth would make up her mind quickly. Before, she'd always taken forever to decide, and Ryan wasn't in a patient mood that night.

That hope died a tortuous death when the waiter came back the fourth time. By then, Ryan had shaken salt all over the table, spilled his water, and crawled under the table, nearly taking the tablecloth with him. Instead of concentrating on the menu, Beth had made comments such as, "Ryan, let's not play with the salt and pepper okay?" and "Ryan, don't climb under the table. It's not polite." and "Uh-oh! If you would sit still your water wouldn't have spilled."

Devon wanted to shout, "Will you just order already?" Didn't she realize that Ryan would behave better with a plate of food to eat? Where was the waiter with their bread, anyway?

"Beth, why don't you let me handle Ryan while you decide what you want?" Please, please just order something.

Beth gave him a frustrated look before returning to the menu. When the waiter came a fifth time, she asked him for a recommendation.

"I guess I'll try that, thanks," she said.

Finally.

"I'm hungry," Ryan said. "When can we eat?"

"Soon, honey," Beth said. "They're making it right now."

Where were the crayons and paper placemat when Devon

needed them? And where was that bread? Couldn't the waiter tell Ryan was bored and hungry?

"Here you go," the waiter said, setting a bowl of hot breadsticks on their table. "Sorry it took so long, but they're fresh from the oven."

Devon wanted to hug the guy. "Thanks."

Ryan reached across the table and grabbed two breadsticks, one in each hand.

"No, sweetie, just take one at a time." Beth's voice brought goose bumps to Devon's arms. But not the good kind. The kind that came from fingernails on a chalkboard. Why couldn't she try to get to know Ryan instead of continually pointing out his faults?

Ryan is acting more troublesome than usual, he tried to tell himself. But it didn't help. If Devon hadn't already asked Beth to go to a different restaurant, he would have had the waiter box up their order.

But the food finally came, and things went better after that. Thank goodness.

As they walked out of the restaurant, Beth said, "I thought it would be fun to see a movie."

Ryan wrapped his little arms around Devon's leg. "I want to go home."

"Beth, if it's okay with you, I think I'm going to take Ryan home and put him to bed. We're both pretty tired."

Beth nodded and drove them to Devon's apartment complex. Instead of dropping them off at the front entrance, Beth parked in the visitor parking.

"Are you coming up?" Devon asked.

"If it's okay. I know you're going to be working late during the next two weeks, so I should probably familiarize myself with Ryan's bedtime routine."

She had a point. Although now Devon was worried about how Beth and Ryan would get along. Would she be kind and fun? Patient? Or would Beth constantly tell Ryan not to do that, not to do this, not to have fun. No.

The word slammed into Devon, leaving a sick feeling in his gut. Lindsay had loathed that word and all it implied, and yet here

Devon was, handing Ryan over to someone who had no problem saying it. What had he been thinking?

Devon held Ryan's hand as the elevator glided upward. After Ryan went to bed, he would talk to Beth. Let her know that Ryan was special and wonderful. That Ryan had been through a lot and what he really needed right now was a healthy dose of love. Maybe then Beth would understand and not be so critical.

Maybe.

If only Stella were here. Devon missed her. He missed the girl who adored Ryan and who believed he could make a good parent. The girl he could leave Ryan with and not worry because she loved him like her own.

Beth didn't.

Not yet anyway.

Devon sighed as the elevator arrived at his apartment. He needed to give Beth a chance—for both Ryan and himself.

chapter fifteen

Devon arrived at the bowling alley twenty minutes late. When he'd phoned Beth to let her know he'd be getting off work earlier that night, she'd spontaneously planned a night out. And Devon was glad. For the first time in three days, he would get to see Ryan awake.

The large, open room reflected the glow of the black lights. Florescent pinks, yellows, and greens covered the walls like graffiti. Beth had called it "midnight bowling" even though it was only seven o'clock.

People milled about eating, drinking, bowling, and playing video games. Across the room, Ryan, wearing a glowing white shirt, pushed a neon green bowling ball down a ramp. It rolled slowly down the slick wooden floor, bounced off the bumpers a few times, and knocked over the two remaining pins. He jumped up and down as an excited squeal floated across the room. "I did it! I knocked all the pins down!"

Devon grinned and moved forward to greet them.

"Give me rocks," Beth said to Ryan, making a fist.

Ryan balled his fingers and punched Beth's fist with his own. "Oh yeah, oh yeah, I'm good!"

Beth winced and pulled her fingers away, then scooped Ryan

in for a hug. "You are totally going to beat Devon when he gets here."

"Who's going to beat me?" Devon asked.

Ryan charged straight into his arms. "Yay, you're here!"

"Sorry I'm late."

Beth shrugged. "I figured you would be, so they've been letting us practice. I'll go tell them we're ready now."

"Thanks." Despite Devon's initial concerns, Beth had been great during the past few days, playing the role of nanny. Even after a long day with Ryan, she still greeted Devon with a smile each night. She would rub his shoulders while they talked, then leave when Devon started yawning. She really was wonderful.

So why couldn't he get close to her again? Why, whenever he stopped to catch his breath, would his thoughts drift to a certain blue-eyed blonde in Australia, rather than to Beth—someone he was once engaged to marry?

Devon couldn't say, nor did he want to worry about it any longer that night. He'd rather enjoy the evening and hang out with his favorite little guy.

"Come on. You need to pick out your ball." Ryan tugged on his hand. "I'll show you where."

"Will you help me pick one out?"

Ryan nodded and dragged Devon over to the racks of balls. "I like that one." He pointed to a fifteen-pound neon orange ball.

"Great choice."

Ryan bowled first, so out came the ramp and up came the bumpers. The ramp went away for Beth's turn, but the bumpers remained. When Devon's turn came, the bumpers disappeared.

"You're that scared I'll win?" Devon asked Beth.

"I like to think of it as insurance," said Beth. "Now how about a bet for old times' sake?"

"Sure, why not?" A group of teenagers bowled a few lanes down. They looked nice enough. "Let's say the loser has to convince one of those kids to let them bowl their turn?"

Beth grinned. "Deal."

For the next hour, they bowled, laughed, and taunted. When Beth got a strike, Ryan jumped up and down and gave her five.

"I'm winning," Beth mouthed to Devon, her smile wide.

This is good. This is what I want. Right?

Right.

Then why did it feel like something was missing—someone was missing?

You're an idiot, Devon. Stella's an infatuation—nothing more.

Even if she were more, she couldn't get much farther away than Australia. Beth, on the other hand, was here—right in front of him. Available and ready for a commitment.

In the tenth frame, Beth landed another two strikes, making her the official winner. She glanced meaningfully at the scoreboard and then flashed Devon a "Well, what are you waiting for?" look. He followed her gaze to the group of teenagers.

Crap. The bet. Would Beth really make him do it? Yes. Beth had never been one to let him off the hook. Groaning, Devon picked up his ball and sauntered to a girl who was just about to bowl.

"Hey, do you mind if I have a go?" he asked.

The girl paused. "Are you talking to me?"

"Yeah. I've been eyeing your lane all night. The floor looks smoother and faster, and since I have a sort of fetish about which lanes I'll bowl on, I wanted to try it out." The look on the girl's face made Devon feel like he'd grown two heads. He struggled to keep a straight face. "Please? If I promise to get a strike for you?"

"Uh, sure . . ." She stepped aside. "You better get a strike though."

"No problem." Devon lined up, ignoring the muffled laughter of her friends. A few steps forward and he launched the ball down the lane. Pins went flying—all but two. A 7-10 split.

Woops.

The girl glared. "Thanks a lot."

"Uh, sorry about that. I guess this lane isn't so great after all. Thanks anyway, though, and good luck with that." Devon nodded toward the pins as he walked away.

Beth greeted him with giggles. "That was priceless."

"I'm glad you think so." He could still feel the girl's glare burning into his back. "Time to go, Ryan."

"But I want to play another game," he whined.

"Sorry, but other people are waiting to use the lane, so we need to go."

"I don't want to go!" Arms crossed, Ryan stomped his foot.

No. Not a tantrum. Not now. "How about we stop for dessert on the way home instead?"

Ryan appeared mollified until Beth said, "No, Devon. Ryan doesn't get rewarded if he whines or cries."

Ryan's face crumpled, and his words came out as a half-cry, half-whine, "But I want dessert!"

"We don't get what we want when we cry and whine," Beth repeated. "Now come on. It's time to go."

Ryan's cries escalated, and Devon felt the stirrings of a headache. Maybe Beth was right—maybe he shouldn't have bribed Ryan, but the boy was only four. Could he really be expected not to whine when he wanted to keep bowling? And why did Beth feel the need to take over? She might as well have said, "Devon, you obviously don't know what you're doing." Why couldn't she just stand back and let Devon handle things his own way?

Stella would have.

Ahhhh! He needed to stop comparing them.

Sighing, Devon picked up a screaming, wriggly boy. After fighting to get him buckled into the car, Ryan wailed during most of the ride home. By the time they pulled into the complex's parking lot though, he'd fallen asleep. Thank goodness.

"You don't need to come up with us," Devon said when Beth turned off the engine. "I'm sure you're tired and want to get home."

"Oh . . . yeah, thanks. I guess I'll see you in the morning then?" She looked disappointed.

"Thanks, Beth. Tonight was fun."

She leaned over and brushed her lips across Devon's. When she backed away, worry lines creased her brow before she masked it with a smile. "See you tomorrow."

chapter sixteen

Devon drove into his parking space in the underground lot of his apartment and stretched his neck from side to side. It was late, dark, and cold outside, but winter was nearly over and the brief moments of sunshine reminded him that spring was on its way. He left the engine running and picked up his phone.

The first night in Chicago, Devon had called Stella to keep her updated on Ryan. After that, there wasn't much to say about Ryan since Devon rarely saw him. Still, he called every night. He liked hearing Stella's voice; liked the way she could coax the tension from his shoulders and make him smile.

"G'day." The dimly lit parking garage seemed to brighten at the sound of her charming, Australian-accented voice.

"Hey," Devon said.

"You sound tired."

"I never want to look at another business or legal document ever again. Selling a company is a lot more complex than I ever realized."

Stella laughed, a lilting sound that infused him with energy. Devon pressed the phone closer to his ear.

"When will you officially sign?" she asked.

"Friday." Only two more days and his company was no longer

his. Two more days and he'd officially be unemployed. What then? How would Devon stay busy? Where would life take him? He didn't know.

"Did you get the package I sent?"

"Yeah. It came yesterday. And thanks. I've always wanted to sign a stack of papers with a platypus pen."

"You mock, but platypuses are good luck over here."

"Really?"

"Sure."

"Liar."

"Well they should be," Stella said. "Has Ryan eaten all of the TimTams yet? He loves those."

"All gone. But he did share a few with me and even taught me how to make a TimTam slam, which was brilliant of him. Those cookies are awesome. I'm trying to find where I can buy them here."

"He is brilliant," Stella agreed. "And TimTams are the best."

"Which leaves me to wonder why you never told me about them while I was in Sydney. I would have bought an extra suitcase and stuffed it full."

"Now you have a reason to come back."

"A very good reason," he said, thinking more about Stella than the cookies. "So what random fact are you going to entertain me with today?" It had started as a joke, something to tease her about, but the tradition stuck, and Devon looked forward to hearing the crazy, random things she spouted off every night.

"Did you know that dueling is legal in Paraguay as long as both duelers are registered blood donors?"

She never disappointed him. "Seriously?"

"It's the truth."

"Are they that desperate for blood over there or something?"

"Blood or brains, I'm not sure which."

Devon laughed, knowing he should end the call. Beth was waiting. But there was something magnetic about Stella that made him want to keep the connection alive, at least for a little longer. She had a way of hugging him with her voice.

"You doing okay?" Stella asked.

"I'm good."

"Okay. Tell Ryan I love him and miss him."

"I will. He misses you too. In fact, he told me this morning that I needed to take the platypus pen to work and sign all the papers today. That way I wouldn't have to be gone any more days and we could call you again from the computer."

"I'm looking forward to that too." There was a short pause before she said, "Until tomorrow?"

"Tomorrow it is."

The parking garage lost its brilliance as Devon ended the call and headed toward the elevator. Another twenty-four hours and he could call her again. Hear her voice. Picture her smile. Wish she didn't live in Australia.

Upstairs, Devon found Beth curled up in a recliner, reading a book. She closed it when she saw him. "How did everything go today?"

"Fine." Not wanting to talk about it again, Devon made his way to the kitchen and opened the microwave where he found a plate of spaghetti. Beth was thoughtful like that.

"Thanks for this," Devon said, holding up the plate. "How was your day?"

Beth came up behind him and massaged his shoulders while he ate. "It was good. We went to the indoor playland at the mall and rented a movie tonight. Ryan is such a sweetheart. I've really loved spending time with him."

"He seems to like you."

"I'm glad." Her hands stilled and she pulled up a seat next to him. "But what about you? Do you like me too?"

Devon chewed slowly on the noodles, turning them into mush. Once he swallowed, he'd have no excuse not to answer the question, so his jaw continued to move up and down. Why hadn't he prepared for this conversation? He'd known it would come sooner or later.

Finally Devon swallowed. "Of course I like you." It sounded lame, but he couldn't pretend something he didn't feel. Not any longer. He liked Beth, yes, but more as a friend than a potential wife.

Looking away, Beth said, "Ryan told me he gets to fly on another airplane on Saturday."

Devon should have known Ryan would say something. Why had he waited so long to tell her? "I'm sorry. I was going to talk to you tonight about that."

"It's just that I thought things were going pretty well with us and that you'd want to stick around for a while to see . . . We've hardly spent any time together. I feel like you're leaving before you've really given us a chance. Or are you planning to take Ryan home and come back?"

The hope in her eyes made Devon want to grimace. Beth was right. He hadn't given her a chance. Not really. But what chance was there when he couldn't get Stella off his mind?

"Listen." Devon reached for her hand. "When you first called, I hoped that things could work out between us—that we could find a way to pick up the pieces and start over."

"There's a 'but' coming, isn't there?"

"Beth, you're gorgeous, intelligent, kind, and you've been so great with Ryan . . . but things are different now—between us anyway. I really don't think we're a great fit anymore. Maybe I've changed, or maybe Ryan has changed me, but our differences seem bigger to me than they used to be."

Beth frowned. "I don't understand how you can say that when you've spent most of your time at the office. I mean, you're basing that assumption on what? The few hours we've spent together? What kind of basis is that?"

Devon hated conversations like this. There was never a win-win, not when two people felt differently. Taking a breath, he tried again. "I know it seems unfair and maybe you're right, but—"

Beth leaned over and pushed her lips against his. Her fingers circled his neck and pulled him closer, as if her passion alone could change his mind. At first Devon kissed her back, hoping to feel a spark of something—anything. But when thoughts of Stella intruded, he backed away, knowing he wasn't being fair.

Hurt filled Beth's eyes. "How can you not feel anything? We used to have such great chemistry."

"There's someone else." Devon immediately wished the words back. Idiot. So not the right thing to say right now.

Beth's eyes narrowed. "I don't understand. If there's someone else, why did you let me think that things could work out? Why did you bring Ryan and let me believe he could be mine one day?"

How to explain without making it worse? "Honestly, Beth, I thought there was a chance. I really did love you and I thought those feelings would come back. I wanted them to come back. Otherwise I would have left Ryan in Oregon."

"You're not making sense. Why would you want to feel something for me if there's someone else?"

"Because . . ." How could he explain?

Jaw clenched, Beth turned away from him. "Who is she?"

"Someone I met in Australia."

"You were only there two weeks!"

"I know, and I'm sorry." Devon hadn't been fair to her. He should be prosecuted and sentenced. But to what, exactly? Public humiliation and a good flogging? Two hundred hours of community service? What was the appropriate punishment for hurting someone you cared about?

Devon covered her hand with his. "Listen, Beth. I want to thank you. For everything. I really appreciate you watching Ryan for me. And don't worry about tomorrow. He can come with me."

Tears sparkled in her eyes as she shook her head. "No. I'll watch him until you've signed the contract, if you'll let me. It will give me a chance to say good-bye. He's really grown on me, you know."

"He has that effect on people."

Slowly, Beth stood and picked up her purse. "I'm sorry too. I should have had more faith in you, seen what you could become. If only I'd known . . . I'd never have broken off our engagement."

"There's someone better for you out there, Beth. I know it. You deserve someone great."

"Yeah, I do." Beth smiled through tear-filled eyes. "Good-bye, Devon."

"Good-bye, Beth."

Five o'clock. Time for Stella to head to the train station and home to her small, empty flat and wild larakeets. That is, unless she left the city and headed north to Byron Bay. So, so tempting.

If only it wasn't a ten-hour drive.

Stella sighed and shoved her cell phone into her bag. Devon had officially signed the paperwork today. His company was no longer his, and tomorrow they'd fly back to Oregon. When they'd talked, Stella hadn't dared ask who "they" included. She hadn't wanted to know.

But then she'd pictured Devon holding hands with Beth, kissing Beth, proposing to Beth. A small happy family flying back to Oregon together. Stella should have asked. At least then she would have known the truth and not been left to imagine the worst.

When Devon finally called the following afternoon, Stella lounged on her patio, enjoying the fresh air as she tried to concentrate on a book. "Hey," she said.

"I know I promised you could talk to Ryan on the webcam tonight, but he fell asleep on the drive home from the airport. I didn't want to wake him."

"That's all right. I'll talk with him tomorrow."

"Thanks for understanding."

"How did everything go?"

"Well, I'm now officially unemployed. But on the bright side, Ryan managed to charm our flight attendant into giving us extra packages of snacks, so if we ever find ourselves starving on the street somewhere, at least we'll have some peanuts."

Stella smiled. "So, how does it feel to be free?"

"Free. That's nice. It sounds so much better than unemployed. And it feels strange—not to mention a little scary. I'm not sure what I'm going to do with all my time now. Maybe I could take up meditating."

"I'm sure Ryan would sit quietly by and let you."

Devon chuckled. "Yeah, I guess you're right. But we plan to start house hunting on Monday, so that should give us something to do."

"Us?" Stella bent and unbent the corner of a page in her book.

"Uh . . . Ryan and me. Remember? Little boy? Curly hair? Any of this ringing a bell?"

So much for finding out the easy way. "What about Beth?"

"What about her?"

Honestly. Was he doing it on purpose? "Is she with you? Did you get back together? Are you engaged again?"

"Oh, didn't I tell you? It didn't work out." Said so simply and just like that. Over and done, like Beth was never a big part of his life.

"For you or for her?"

"For me or for her what?"

For a smart guy, Devon was certainly dense. Stella slowed her words down. "It didn't work out for you, or for her?"

"Oh." He paused. "For me, I guess."

And . . . ? And nothing. Of course there was no additional explanation. Did Stella really think there would be? *Let it go, Stella. Just let it go.*

"What happened?" she asked.

"I don't know. Things just weren't the same."

"Really? That's it?"

"What else do you want to know?"

"Is it *over* over, or are you still hoping things will work out eventually?"

"Why does it matter?"

Because I like you, you idiot, and it's driving me crazy not to know. "Your future affects Ryan, so I'm curious."

"It's *over* over, okay?"

"Oh. I'm sorry to hear that," Stella lied. "You doing okay?"

"I'm fine. It was actually a good thing I took Ryan with me. Without him, I might not have realized we weren't a good fit."

"Ryan didn't give her a hard time, did he?" Stella pictured Ryan somehow sabotaging the relationship. If so, he deserved some more TimTams.

"Of course not. Ryan charmed her like he does everyone."

Of course he did. Of course he charmed Beth. She'd probably fallen for him just like everyone did. Poor girl. Stella didn't have to imagine what Beth was probably going through right now. "Is she okay?"

"For crying out loud, Stella. I'm fine, Ryan's fine, and Beth is fine. Everyone's fine."

I'm not. "Okay, then."

"Great. Are we through with the twenty questions now? Because I don't want to talk about this anymore."

"Sure." Stella waited for him to change the subject. When he didn't, she said, "I guess I'll talk to you later?"

"I'll have Ryan call tomorrow night." Then he was gone.

Ryan. He would have Ryan call. Not Devon. As much as Stella looked forward to seeing Ryan's face light up her monitor, she also felt an achy emptiness inside—a feeling that was becoming all too familiar.

Leaving the patio behind, Stella walked inside her flat, grabbed her purse, and headed for the door. She needed to get out.

She needed to get a life.

Devon found his mother feeding Ryan a Vegemite sandwich in the kitchen. Yes, Vegemite. Another gift from Stella. Everywhere he went, something reminded him of her. Why did she have to live in Australia anyway? Why couldn't she live somewhere closer? He'd even take New York or Florida right now.

Devon dropped down on a barstool next to Ryan. Maybe if he kicked a door or threw something at a wall. It always seemed to make Ryan feel better.

"What's it going to take to get you to like peanut butter like normal American kids?" Devon asked.

"Peanut butter is yuck." Ryan munched away on his sandwich.

"No it's not."

"Yes it is."

"No. It's not."

"Yes it is."

"No—"

"Boys!" Lydia shook her head at Devon. "Honestly. I thought you were an adult."

"Ryan brings out the kid in me. So where's my sandwich?"

Devon got the look—the one that said, "I'm not your servant, fix it yourself." He hadn't seen it in years, not since high school. It actually made him smile.

"But you made Ryan one."

"Fine." Lydia pulled the Vegemite from the cupboard. "If that's what you want."

"Okay, okay, you've made your point." Devon went to the refrigerator and rummaged around, pulling out deli meat and cheese—the stuff normal sandwiches consist of.

Lydia wiped her hands on a dishtowel. "I need to run to the grocery store. Can I trust you two to behave while I'm gone?"

"I'll be good," Ryan said, and for that he got a kiss on the cheek.

"You're not the one I'm worried about." Lydia cast Devon a meaningful look, picked up her purse, and left.

"Thanks a lot," Devon said. "You've officially ousted me as the favorite child."

"What does ousta mean?"

"Never mind." Devon threw cold cuts onto a slice of bread and rejoined Ryan. "So tell me, what kind of house do you want to live in?"

"A teepee in the jungle."

Devon nodded, as though seriously considering it. "That's a great idea. I mean, who needs a big house with a cool bed, a play set out back, or a big yard for a dog—" Wait. Did he really just say "dog"? Crap.

"I want to live in a house with a dog!" Ryan bounced around on his chair. "Can we get more fish too?"

Yes, fish. Fish now sounded great. Way better than a dog. "I don't think it's a good idea to have both pets. The dog might hurt the fish. So would you rather have a lot of colorful and awesome fish or a dirty, smelly dog?"

Ryan grinned. "A dog, a dog!"

Swell, Devon. Totally brilliant. It's no wonder you're jobless. "We'll need to find a house with a yard and a fence first."

"Yay! Can we get a really big dog?"

"Sure, why not?" Devon bit into his sandwich and chewed slowly. At least he'd neutralized one problem. Ryan no longer wanted to live in a teepee in the jungle.

chapter seventeen

Devon lugged the last cardboard box inside and dropped it on the kitchen counter of his new home, next to the dozen other boxes he'd already brought in. There wasn't much. He'd been too busy working to buy more than the necessities, and his apartment in Chicago had been fully furnished.

Unlike this house. It was a four bedroom, colonial rambler, peeking out from behind massive maple and pine trees. The half acre lot with a fenced backyard had been the selling point for Ryan.

"A big dog will fit here," he had said.

But Devon liked it for another reason. The faded, crumbling paint on the front porch. The windows that struggled to open and close. The scratched and warped wooden floor. The squeaky, dysfunctional cupboard doors. Although the overall structure was solid, the surface needed a makeover—and Devon now had the time and inclination to give it one. He'd worked for a general contractor each summer during college and now looked forward to using those skills to stay busy—at least until he could figure out what he wanted to do next.

Since the house had been in foreclosure, it had taken several months of negotiations and waiting on the bank. In August, they'd finally agreed on a number, and Devon signed two weeks later. Hallelujah. Although he'd wanted to get some of the renovations done before they moved in, Ryan refused to wait any longer. He wanted his dog.

So Devon loaded up Jack's truck and moved them in, knowing they'd be "roughing it" for a few days. The newly purchased beds, sofa, refrigerator, and washer and dryer wouldn't arrive until the following day, so it was pizza for dinner and "camping" on the floor of the family room. Ryan was as excited as a puppy and Devon another day closer to owning one.

"Hello?" Lydia called from the front room. "We're back with the pizza."

Ryan burst into the kitchen, carrying a large pizza box. Lydia and Jack followed behind with another.

"Can we get my dog now?"

Devon chucked Ryan's chin. "Not until Friday. Just like I've told you ten times already."

"Is tomorrow Friday?"

Lydia took the pizza from Ryan and set it on the counter. "No. Friday is still three sleeps away."

"Can I go to bed now?"

Devon laughed. "Sure. But that won't make Friday come any sooner." A dog was actually starting to sound pretty good. At least then Ryan would stop his incessant begging.

After they'd eaten and Devon's parents had left, Ryan asked, "Can we go get my dog now? Please?"

Devon wasn't sure he could take three more days of this. "How about this? We'll go to the pound and look, but you won't be able to bring him home until Friday. Deal?"

"Yay!" Ryan ran for his shoes, putting them on in record time.

Unfortunately, the pound was closed. They were twenty minutes too late. "We'll come back tomorrow after your bed is delivered," Devon promised. "But only if you don't ask until it's all put together in your room, okay?"

"Okay." Ryan's expression fell, but he didn't whine, argue, or throw a fit. Such progress deserved positive reinforcement, so they went out for ice cream.

Later that night, Devon stared at the family room ceiling, waiting for Ryan to fall asleep. He wanted Stella all to himself that night, just like he had once or twice a week since Chicago.

At first Devon hoped that by getting to know her better, she'd become more of a friend than a romantic interest. But now he was worse off than before. Devon knew he needed to stop their frequent contact, but Stella was too addictive. There was no way he could go without their private conversations, at least not cold turkey. He needed to wean himself off her, taking away one phone call a month. When he could handle that, he'd up it to two.

And he would start tomorrow.

Ryan's breathing slowed, and Devon crept to the front porch steps. Most of the stars were hidden by the trees, but the cool, night air felt good. Refreshing. Combined with the sweet scent of pine, Devon already felt at home in his new house. Even more so when he heard Stella's voice.

"How does Ryan like the new house?" A few weeks ago, she'd dispensed with the greetings, which Devon liked. Sometimes it felt as though they'd never really ended the conversation from the day before.

"He loves it. In fact, he thinks we should camp on the floor of the family room every night."

"You should."

"No we shouldn't."

"Good luck convincing him of that tomorrow."

"No kidding. I'm probably going to have to bribe him with a real camping trip."

"Are you talking about a tent in the woods, with a campfire and a starry sky?"

"Something like that."

"Have you ever been camping?" she asked.

"Yeah. My dad and I used to go all the time. Fishing too."

"I thought you weren't a fish person."

"I'm not a pet fish person. But catch and release—that I can handle."

Stella laughed. "Your parents were okay with Ryan moving? I know they're pretty attached to him."

"It helps that we're only fifteen minutes away, so they'll still see him a lot. Then there's always Sunday dinner."

"It sounds wonderful."

It would be better if you were here. "It is."

Stella paused and then cleared her throat. "I wanted to ask you something. My friend, Tess, is getting married and she's asked me to be her bridesmaid. The wedding will be here in Australia, but her fiancé is from California so they're planning a big event there as well. She wants me to come along."

"Whoa, slow down." Devon straightened and pressed the phone closer to his ear. "Did you just say you're coming to America?"

"I haven't decided for sure yet, but it's a free ticket, and I could use a short holiday," Stella said. "Jeremy's family lives in a small city just north of Sacramento, and I figured if I'm that close, I'd really like to see Ryan . . . and you. If you're okay with it, that is."

Am I okay with it? Was she serious? "Of course I am. Ryan will be thrilled."

"I can't take too much time off work. The dinner is on a Thursday, so I'll rent a car and drive to Portland on Friday and stay for a few days. Tess can schedule my flight to leave from the Portland airport on Sunday night. Would that work?"

One lousy weekend? That's it? "Sure. I wish you could stay longer though."

"Me too, but I need to get back."

Three days. Only three measly days. Maybe Ryan could charm her into staying longer. "Well, we'll take what we can get. When are you coming?"

"Four weeks."

chapter eighteen

Stella shoved one last pair of shoes into her suitcase before kneeling down to zip it closed. Had she forgotten anything? In only four hours she'd board the plane. After that, there'd be no going back.

Five more days and Stella would get to see Ryan again. Get to hug, kiss, snuggle, and watch him kick a ball. She'd be there just in time for his last soccer game of the season. She couldn't wait.

But she'd also see Devon. Jittery knots rummaged around in her stomach, which was absurd. After all, a future with him was impossible, something Stella could only daydream about. But dream she did. Devon's smile, his laughter, his genuine kindness, his humor—him. He was wonderful.

And completely unavailable—at least for her.

So why go to America? Yes, Tess had asked her to come, but her friend didn't need her there. The reception in California would be a small one, with no official place for a bridesmaid. So why torture herself? Why go when her time with Ryan and Devon would be so short and end with yet another good-bye?

Because Stella missed them. Badly. The temptation had been too great to resist. She would spend one last weekend with them and then do whatever it took to move on with her life. It would be like savoring that one last bite of chocolate cake. Delicious and wonderful, and definitely worth the calories, but when it was gone, it was gone.

The few days in California went by fast. Stella was on her own most of the time, but the day before the dinner, she and Tess snuck off for some shopping and a little girl time. After that, Tess was busy, and then there were too many other people who wanted to wish the bride and groom well.

By the time Friday morning rolled around, Stella was eager to get on her way.

"Thanks for coming." Tess hugged her good-bye. "I'll see you in a few weeks."

"Enjoy the Caribbean. I'll expect you to have a beautiful tan when you come back."

"I'd better." Tess grinned. "And you be sure to kiss that American before you leave."

Stella laughed. "Yeah, sure. No problem."

Ten hours later, Stella pulled to a stop in Devon's driveway. She was here. Finally. Trees framed the cozy red brick house, and the freshly cut grass was a soft blanket of green. All Stella needed to do was get out of her car and walk to the door. Her fingers played in her lap, refusing to tug on the handle. *You can do it, Stella. You've come too far to be scared off now.*

The front door opened and there they were. Devon, with his perfect smile, and Ryan, grinning and holding tightly to a dozen multi-colored balloons.

Stella shoved open her door and rushed forward to engulf Ryan in a hug. It felt so good to hold him again. To see those precious brown eyes, adorable dimple, and glowing smile. How could she stand to leave in three days? Not even three. It was now closer to two.

Ryan wriggled from her grasp and thrust the balloons into her hand. "These are for you. Dad let me pick them out all by myself."

Dad. The word resonated in Stella's heart. How right. How fitting. "Ta, love." She kissed Ryan's cheek before he had a chance to escape. "I've missed you so much, and I love the balloons. They're perfect."

"I told Ryan we could get you flowers or balloons. He chose those," Devon said.

"Can I play with them?" Ryan asked. "I want to show them to Aussie."

"Of course." Stella smiled as she passed the balloons back to Ryan. He quickly scampered back inside, as though Stella's presence was no big deal.

"I guess we need to work on his gift-giving etiquette," Devon said. "And his welcoming etiquette."

"I'm not sure what I'd do with a dozen balloons anyway, but I couldn't have asked for a better welcome. Thank you."

"No problem."

Awkward silence.

Stella rocked back and forth on her heels. *Ryan, how could you leave me? Don't you know desertion's a crime?*

Stella was about to go hunt him down when Devon took a few steps forward and held out his arms. "Do I get a hug too?"

Stella's laugh sounded forced, even borderline frenzied. Clamping her mouth closed, she stepped into his embrace and rested her head against his chest. Thump, bump. Thump, bump. Thump, bump. The rhythm of his heartbeat had an almost hypnotic effect. Combined with his fresh scent, hard chest, and strong arms, Stella had never felt so welcomed. Like she was home.

"I'm glad you came," Devon said.

"Me too." Stella forced herself to pull back. "So when did Ryan start calling you Dad?"

He smiled. "A few weeks ago. I didn't ask him to or anything, he just said it one day. It was strange at first, but I really like it."

"It fits."

"Thanks." Devon reached for her hand. "Come on in. I'll give you the official tour. The place still needs some work, but Ryan and I have made a little progress."

He continued to hold her hand as he led her though the house. Although Stella could tell Devon had been working hard on the renovations, sheetrock mud, tape, and texture decorated the walls, the cabinets were without doors, and the floors felt uneven beneath her feet. "This house is a bit dodgy, isn't it?" she teased.

"Oh come on. Where's your vision and imagination?"

Stella laughed. "If it's any consolation, I'm sure it will look beautiful when you're finished."

Devon led her back to the family room, where a ghastly, white painted brick fireplace covered an entire wall. Or at least the brick did. The opening for the actual fireplace looked more like a mouse hole. How had Stella missed that the first time through? "Uh, did Ryan paint that?"

"Would it make you like it any better if he did?"

"Maybe." Even the mantle was horrid. Like someone had nailed a two-by-six to the brick and threw a bucket of white paint at it. Stella shook her head. "Sorry, I still don't like it. Probably because I know Ryan can paint better than that."

"Actually, the fireplace came with the house—but I got a great deal."

"I hope so." Stella's smile softened the words. "And I'm sure in a few months it will be lovely." It couldn't get much worse.

"You'll have to come back to see if you approve . . . that is, if you want to." His slight hesitation was adorable.

Stella met his eyes. Of course she wanted to come back. In fact, now that she was here, she didn't ever want to leave. If only she didn't have a job and responsibilities back in Australia. If only her life wasn't there. A life Stella needed to get on with.

"You're hesitating," Devon said. "That's not usually a good sign."

"I have to be honest with you. I want to be a part of Ryan's life more than anything, but it was really difficult for me when you left and took him with you. Gradually things got easier, and as wonderful as it is to be here with him now . . . with you . . . I know it's going to be hard to say good-bye again. I just don't know how many more good-byes I have in me, you know?"

Devon's hand found hers again, and he tugged her toward the

back door. "Let's not talk about good-byes just yet. We still have a couple of days."

Such a guy thing to say. Heaven forbid they actually have a real conversation about it.

"Stop it, Aussie!" Ryan screamed as he slammed the patio door shut behind him, trapping three of the balloons outside and popping one. A large dog barked and scratched at the glass, apparently not happy about being left on the deck.

Devon smiled. "Stella, meet Aussie, our golden retriever. The newest addition to our family and Ryan's best friend."

Aussie leaped toward the remaining balloons. "Leave my balloons alone!" Ryan shouted through the glass.

"They're Stella's balloons," Devon reminded him. "And that's no way to talk to your best friend."

Stella opened the door a crack and stroked the dog's head while coercing the stray balloons inside. "Nice to meet you, Aussie. I'm Stella." The dog licked her hand before she closed the door, leaving him outside.

Ryan frowned at the ground. "He made my red balloon pop. It was my favorite one."

Stella crouched down and lifted his chin with her finger. "Ryan, if you're through playing with the balloons, maybe we can let them go outside in the front yard and watch them fly up to heaven. Does that sound fun?"

Brown eyes brightened. "My mum's in heaven!"

"We can send them to her. I bet she'd love them," Stella said.

"Can we do it now?"

"Sure."

They walked out to the front yard. "Do you want to keep them tied together, like a bouquet, or would you rather separate them and send one at a time?" Stella asked.

"Together. I don't want any to get lost."

"Good point."

Devon rested his arm around Stella's shoulders, and a fleet of goose bumps coursed up and down her arms. She wanted to lean into him and soak up the affection, let it fill her up and give her something to hold onto.

"Whenever you're ready, Ryan," Devon said.

Arm raised high, Ryan's little fist opened, releasing the balloons. They bounced around in the breeze as they sailed high in the clear blue sky, picking up speed as they went. Before long, they disappeared behind the towering pines.

"Do you think my mum will get them?" Ryan asked.

"I'm sure she will," said Devon.

"Can we send her some more tomorrow?"

Devon shook his head. "Probably not tomorrow, but maybe we could send some to her on her birthday. Would you like that?"

"When's her birthday?" Ryan asked.

"December 12th," Stella answered. Was Lindsay watching her sweet boy right now? Did she see the balloons?

"December's not for a long time," Devon said to Ryan, "so you can't ask about it every day, okay? I promise I'll tell you when it's time."

"Okay."

"Why don't you go get your glasses so you can tell Stella the poem you learned in preschool yesterday."

Ryan dashed off toward the house and returned moments later, out of breath. Brown eyes sparkled through a pair of bright orange glasses made from pipe cleaners.

"I love them," Stella said. "You look very smart."

"Let's hear it," said Devon.

Ryan grinned. "I cannot find my shirt, I cannot find my shorts; I cannot find my socks and shoes, I cannot find my fork. I cannot find my toothbrush, and I don't know where the trash is. I'm going to have a rotten day until I find my glasses!"

Stella laughed and hugged him. There couldn't possibly be a more adorable child. "You are brilliant, Ryan. I can't believe you learned that entire poem in one day."

"He's a genius. Give me five." Devon held out his hand and Ryan slapped it. "And guess what else? Tomorrow Stella gets to come to your soccer game."

Ryan's eyes glowed. "You get to see me play soccer!"

"I can't wait," she said. "Let's go find a ball so you can show me all your moves."

They spent the afternoon playing soccer, throwing balls, and enjoying the beautiful fall weather. By the time dinnertime came around, they were all starving. Devon's parents had invited them over, so Stella climbed back into the rental car and followed them to the Pierce's house, where she would be sleeping. Devon didn't have a habitable guest room, so he'd arranged for Stella to stay with his parents—which was fine with her. Stella was thrilled to finally meet Lydia and Jack.

"I love spaghetti!" Ryan said when he saw what his grandma had made for dinner.

Lydia hugged Ryan. "I know, pumpkin. Why do you think I made it?"

"Again," Jack mumbled. "Ryan, aren't you getting sick of spaghetti?"

"No. It's my favorite."

Devon chuckled. "Dad, maybe if we didn't come around so much, you wouldn't be forced to eat it again."

Ruffling Ryan's hair, Jack said, "I love Ryan, so I put up with it. And who doesn't love homemade breadsticks?"

"I think everything smells wonderful," Stella said.

"You must be hungry," Jack said. "Everything smells good when you're starving."

"That's it." Lydia playfully swung a wooden spoon in her husband's face. "Now you have to eat two helpings if you want any dessert."

Jack took the spoon from his wife. "Let me guess. We're having homemade ice cream."

"It's Ryan's favorite."

"Of course it's his favorite. You rarely make him anything else."

"I do on Sundays."

"Only because the other kids come and you make their favorite foods. What about my favorite foods?"

Lydia shrugged. "You're a big boy. You can make it yourself."

Jack rolled his eyes and Stella laughed. "No worries, Mr. Pierce. I have some contraband in my suitcase. Ten packages of TimTams."

Jack looked interested. "No idea what those are, but if they taste different than homemade ice cream, you are heaven sent."

"I love TimTams!" Ryan said.

"TimTams?" Lydia said. "I've never heard of those, so they must be Australian. I wonder if I can get them anywhere here."

"They're at SuperTarget," Devon said. "But they're seasonal, so you can only get them between now and next spring."

"Really?" Stella said. "Why did I just bring ten packages through customs if you can get them here?"

Lydia frowned at her son. "And why have you never told me Ryan had another favorite treat?"

"I can't give you all my secrets, Mom. What am I going to use to bribe him with now?"

"Ryan doesn't need to be bribed," Jack said. "He's perfect."

"Yes, he is," Lydia added.

Stella smiled at the exchange. If it wasn't for the American accent, Ryan would look and sound like a Pierce. In fact, he was a Pierce, despite his last name. Ryan now had exactly what Lindsay had wanted him to have.

A real family.

chapter nineteen

"Go, Ryan!" Stella yelled as Ryan hustled after the soccer ball. The game was nearly over, and the score remained 0-0. The ball bounced near Ryan, and he charged as though nothing would keep him from scoring a goal.

"The other way, Ryan! Go the other way!" Devon called.

Ryan tried to turn the ball around, but two other children blocked his way, so he picked it up, ran a few feet in the opposite direction, then dropped and kicked it toward the right goal. One of the coaches blew a whistle and scooped up the ball, earning a glare from Ryan. Stella laughed. If only soccer didn't have any rules.

Devon nudged Stella's shoulder as they sat side by side on a blanket, watching from the grassy sidelines. "What would you think about hiking to a waterfall this afternoon?"

It sounded perfect. "I love hiking."

"I know." He winked. "But what I don't understand is why you'll voluntarily trudge through a forest filled with mud, bugs, germs, and who knows what else, but you still think my house is dodgy."

"I like your backyard," Stella offered. "And your front yard."

"Well, that's something, I guess."

Stella hopped to her knees and pointed at Ryan. "Look! He might actually score a goal. Go, Ryan!"

Ryan dribbled the ball and kicked hard, sending it three yards to the right of the goal. When the whistle blew, signaling the end of the game, Ryan frowned and stomped his foot. A teammate pulled out a box of treats and suddenly Ryan didn't seem to care anymore. Evidently treats made everything okay. Oh, to be four again.

They ate sandwiches at a nearby Subway before heading up the Columbia River Highway in Devon's red Jeep Wrangler. He'd taken the top off, so the drive was windy, bumpy, and breathtaking. Towering trees were splattered across the mountainside in a lovely spectrum of browns, oranges, reds, yellows, and greens. The wide breadth of the Columbia River made it look more like a lake than a river. What a perfect way to spend the afternoon. What perfect people to spend it with.

Devon pulled into a parking lot and shut off the engine. While he rummaged around in the back of his Jeep, Stella found the trailhead leading to a place called Triple Falls. 3.5 miles roundtrip. A long way to go for a four-year-old.

"Uh, Devon, I'm not sure Ryan's going to make it that far without any snacks or water."

Devon patted the pockets of his baggy cargo shorts. "Don't worry, I came prepared this time." The shorts looked no fuller than they had before.

"Doesn't look like it."

"You're just going to have to trust me."

Stella reached for Ryan's hand. "Okay then. Off we go." The dirt path was riddled with colorful leaves, and the crisp, humid air smelled of pine needles, timber, and vegetation. Nature.

About a mile into the hike, Ryan said, "I'm thirsty."

Devon fished inside one of his pockets and handed Ryan a small water bottle. "You want one too, Stella?"

"No thanks."

They continued on, and when Ryan said he was hungry, Devon pulled out a granola bar.

"You sure you don't want anything, Stella?" He pulled out another water bottle. "I brought enough for everyone."

"It's okay. Ryan might get thirsty again."

"I know." He handed her the bottle. "I have another for him."

Where? "How many did you bring, exactly?"

"Six."

"I don't believe you."

"Hold this, Ryan." Devon handed him another water bottle. Then another.

When he pulled out two more, Stella said, "Okay, wow. I never would've believed it. Those shorts are even better than my Mary Poppins bag."

"Ryan calls them my magic shorts," Devon said as he stuffed the bottles back in his pockets. "Don't you, buddy?"

With a nod, Ryan said, "They can carry lots and lots of stuff. But not my soccer ball."

"Nope, no soccer balls," Devon said. "Ryan made me try it once."

Stella laughed, then laughed some more. They were like a tonic. One afternoon with them, and life was all that it should be. Spontaneous, adventurous, happy. It wasn't that Stella didn't enjoy her life back in Australia, but when Devon and Ryan were around, everything was better. Brighter.

"Hey Ryan, can you hear that?" Devon said.

"I can hear it!" Little shoes started running. "Come on, Stella. It's the waterfall!"

"Whoa, slow down." The faint sound of crashing waves grew louder as Ryan pulled Stella along. A few turns later and three spectacular falls came into view, all generated from one river. It forked, then forked again, swelling around two vivid green islands before gushing over the hundred-foot drop.

"Wow," Stella said.

"You like?" Devon's fingers grazed her cheek as he brushed her windblown hair behind her ear.

"I like." Stella wasn't just talking about the waterfalls.

"It's not the Blue Mountains, but I thought you'd appreciate it."

"It's gorgeous. Really. I've never seen anything like it."

A little finger pointed to the river down below. "Can we go swimming?"

Devon chuckled. "Sorry, bud. Rivers aren't warm enough to swim in. You'd freeze. Besides, it's way too steep to hike down there."

"What can we do then?"

"Look at the waterfall."

"But that's boring."

"Toss a rock over the edge and see how long it takes to hit the bottom," Stella suggested.

Ryan found a rock and chucked it. A few seconds later the clatter echoed up the ravine. He grinned and searched for another.

"Wait. There aren't any hikers down there, right?" Stella should have asked that question before she'd told Ryan to throw rocks. Just to be sure, she leaned out over the railing, trying to get a better look.

Devon grabbed her by the waist and pulled her back. "Easy there, girl. What are you trying to do? Base jump without a chute?"

His touch felt good. Too good. "I wanted to make sure Ryan wasn't going to clobber someone in the head."

"Don't worry. That area's inaccessible to hikers."

"Good to know."

When Ryan tired of tossing rocks, Stella trailed behind the two boys as they headed back to the Jeep.

"Can we have pizza for dinner? And can we eat it at our house so Aussie can eat some too?" Ryan asked.

"Heaven forbid we leave Aussie out," Devon said. "What about you, Stella? In the mood for some pizza?"

"Sounds great."

By the time they got back to Devon's house, Stella was more than ready to eat the pizza, with its tempting aroma. Devon helped Ryan mix up a pitcher of lemonade while Stella foraged for the plates and cups. Then they all settled around the table on the back patio.

"Here, Aussie! Come here, boy!" Ryan picked off a pepperoni from his pizza and held it out for the dog. Aussie gulped it down and begged for more, so Ryan threw more pepperonis over the railing, then giggled when Aussie tracked them down. Before long, he discarded his pizza and dashed after Aussie, chasing him around the backyard.

Stella wished she could capture the moment and stay in it for a while—soak up the feeling of being part of a real, actual family. Stella wanted Devon to put his arm around her and pull her close. She wanted to rest her head against his shoulder and become a part of his life.

If only it were possible.

"Time to get ready for bed, Ryan," Devon called.

"I don't want to go to bed."

"There's a shocker," Devon muttered, making Stella laugh. "Come on, Ryan. If you get your teeth brushed before I count to thirty, you'll get an extra story. One . . . two . . ."

Ryan darted past them and into the house.

"Nice," said Stella. "I was worried you were going to have to lock him in the bathroom again."

"I've found that bribery works much better."

Stella smiled. "Mind if I read to him tonight?"

"Gladly. His new favorite story is *Five Little Monkeys*, and it has way too much repetition for me. I'm actually considering using it for kindling the next time we start a fire."

"You're terrible." Stella left Devon on the deck and found Ryan in his room. Four books were spread across his bed.

"I like all these books. Can we read them?"

"You bet." And she did read them, savoring every moment. Then she kissed Ryan on the forehead and turned out the light. When the ceiling lit up with over a hundred glow-in-the-dark stars, Stella couldn't resist the urge to snuggle with him a few minutes more.

"I like the stars," she said.

"That's called the Big Dipper, and that's the Little Dipper, and that's the Southern Cross."

Sure enough, there on Ryan's bedroom ceiling was the Southern Cross, a constellation typically seen only in the southern hemisphere. But here it was in Oregon, glowing bright for Ryan to see every night. A reminder of his homeland, his roots, his mom. *Thank you, Devon.*

Stella snuggled closer to Ryan, holding him tight.

Only one more day.

The thought pierced her heart, leaving it bruised and aching.

Stop! Stella wanted to shout at the passing time. *Stop! Stop! Stop!*

But the seconds ticked by, the earth rotated, and time continued forward unimpeded. Tomorrow there would be no days left. Only hours.

Stella stayed next to Ryan until both he and her arm had fallen asleep. It took all of her willpower to kiss his forehead and leave him alone in his beautiful starlit room. Rubbing the sleep needles from her arm, Stella found Devon lying on the couch, watching a sports game.

"I take it this is football?" Stella said.

His feet dropped to the floor as Devon moved to make room for her. "Yeah, and it's a lot different than rugby. These guys wear protective gear and play by normal rules."

"What's wrong with rugby's rules?" Stella said as she took a seat.

"If I could understand them, I might be able to tell you."

"You'll have to watch a game with me sometime so I can explain it to you."

"I'd like that."

The voice of the sports announcer filled the silence, but Stella wasn't ready to leave. She wanted to savor the time she had left with Devon, store it up for later days. But the longer she stayed, the harder it would be to go.

"I should head back," she said.

"Please stay." Devon turned off the TV. "Usually it's just me after Ryan goes to bed. It's nice to have another adult around, and besides, you haven't told me my random fact for the day."

Stella smiled. How could she say no to that? "Okay, fine. But only because I came prepared with a good one."

"All right. Let's hear it."

"Did you know it's impossible to lick your elbow?"

"Really? That's it? That's your 'good one'?"

"Did you?"

"No. But only because it's never crossed my mind." Like the good sport he was, Devon tried to raise his elbow to his mouth but couldn't quite reach. "Looks like you're right again."

"Did you also know that 75 percent of the people who hear that will actually try it?"

Devon chuckled. "And I was so hoping to stand out."

"Oh, no worries. You definitely stand out." Stella had meant for it to sound light and teasing, but when the words came out, they sounded anything but.

"I do?"

"Yeah."

"In a good way?" Devon moved closer and brushed her hair back, caressing her neck.

"Are you fishing?"

He inched closer. "You didn't answer the question."

"Yes," Stella breathed. "In a very good way."

Devon's thumb traced her cheekbone as he searched her face. Could he tell how crazy she was about him? How badly she wanted him to kiss her, to hold her tight and never let go?

Devon's lips brushed across hers in a feathery light kiss before coming back for more. Lost to a bliss-filled world of feelings, sensations, and Devon, Stella's fingers wound their way behind his neck and into his hair, clinging to him like he was the answer to everything. Her hopes and dreams. Her fantasies. A guy to love. A ready-made family. A place to belong. Devon offered it all.

Could offer it all.

Devon pulled back, his dark eyes raw and intense. A warm, hopeful feeling wound around Stella's heart, giving her reason to believe the unbelievable. He cared. Really cared. About her.

Devon's arm snaked around her back, drawing her to him. It felt so natural to rest her head against his chest, lulled there by the beating of his heart. It could work between them. It was possible.

But it was also Devon's choice.

Stella was tied to her job in Australia, but Devon was free. Free to span the oceans and bridge the gap between them.

The question was: did he want to?

Silence engulfed the room, and suddenly Stella had to know. She could no longer cling to the hope that a happy ending was possible without knowing he felt the same way. Slowly, she lifted her head. What if he didn't? What if his eyes were filled with regret? Please no.

They weren't. But they were filled with something almost as bad—sadness. Not hope, not joy, not anticipation. Sadness. As if Devon considered it a good-bye kiss.

So much for bridging the gap.

So much for happy endings.

Stella swallowed to dislodge the lump in her throat, knowing there was no way to dislodge the lump in her heart. She needed to get away. Now, before the tears came. Find a place to curl up and lick her wounds in private.

"Stella, I—"

"Don't say it," she whispered, blinking back the tears. "Please. Just let me go."

Stella felt his eyes follow her as she grabbed her keys and rushed out the front door.

At first, Stella allowed the tears to accompany her home, but as the distance lengthened between her and Devon's house, she swiped them away with an angry hand.

Why had he kissed her? If he'd already known it would be a good-bye kiss, why do it? Why put them both through that? Devon had ruined everything now. He'd crossed a line that shouldn't have been crossed, and now things would be different. They had to be.

Stella slapped her steering wheel repeatedly, hoping the pain in her hand would somehow lesson the pain in her heart. Yes, Devon cared about her, but not enough. Not enough to want to find a way to make it work.

By the time she pulled up to the Pierce's house, it was late, but Stella was too worked up to sleep. Not knowing what else to do, she perused the bookshelves in the family room, looking for a distraction. She pulled a book free and dropped down on the couch, flipping pages but not focusing on anything.

"What are you reading?" Lydia's voice startled Stella into dropping the book. "Oh, I'm sorry. I didn't mean to scare you."

"Oh no, it's okay. I scare easily." Stella picked up the book and turned the spine toward Lydia. "*To Kill a Mockingbird*. I hope you don't mind that I helped myself."

"Of course not. Have you read it before?"

Stella fingers slid across the cover in an almost reverent way. "My mum read it to me once when I was younger. It's such a sad story, really, but I loved Atticus. I thought he was so brave and kind. This book actually piqued my interest in law—in defending those who can't defend themselves. It was one of the reasons I chose to become a solicitor."

Lydia sat down on the sofa's armrest. "Isn't it funny how two people can read the same book and come away feeling completely different about it? Personally, it was too depressing for me, but it's always been a favorite of Jack's. While we were dating, he made me read it, and I told him I loved it because I wanted to impress him. Big mistake."

"Why?"

"After that, he considered it 'our book.' Some couples have a special song, but in his mind, we had a book. We had to read it every year around the time of our anniversary. And every year, I dreaded it. A few years later, when I was in labor with Devon, Jack brought that book to the hospital. We had decided on a natural childbirth, and I was in so much pain. The last thing I wanted to hear was that dreadful book. So I finally confessed I hated it."

"What did he say?"

A small smile played across her lips. "He said he needed to think. Then he excused himself and left the room. I thought I'd really hurt his feelings, but mostly I was mad that he'd left."

"He really walked out while you were in labor?"

Lydia nodded, her eyes twinkling. "About ten minutes later

he came back and told me he'd decided to forgive me. He even brought a peace offering."

"Flowers?"

"No. The anesthesiologist. Jack said that if I'd lied about *To Kill a Mockingbird*, I'd probably lied about wanting to have a natural childbirth. The funny thing is, he was right, bless his heart. I'd wanted that pain medication from the moment we arrived at the hospital. I was just too embarrassed to admit it—too worried he'd think he married a wimp."

Lydia gestured toward the book. "Admitting I hated that story was the best thing that ever happened to me and our marriage. From that day on, I stopped trying to be the perfect woman and learned to just be me. I was so much happier after that. Even though I didn't appreciate that book and I'll never read it again, it will always be one of my favorites," she said. "Maybe it really is 'our book.'"

Stella's quiet laughter filled the silence in the room. Lydia was wonderful. Jack too. How lucky Devon and Ryan were to have them in their lives.

That was it, wasn't it? The reason Devon wasn't willing to relocate. It wasn't about Devon not wanting to move to Australia. It was about Ryan. Lindsay had wanted Ryan to be an integral part of an extended family—to be raised with cousins, aunts, uncles, and grandparents.

And now Ryan had that. He even had a dog who loved him.

"I'm so glad you came for a visit," Lydia said. "It's been wonderful getting to know you, and I want to thank you for all that you've done for Ryan and my son. They wouldn't be here without you."

"It was Lindsay's doing, not mine. She loved your family, and I can see why she chose you."

"Chose Devon, you mean."

"He was part of it, I'm sure," Stella said. "But I like to think Lindsay saw the bigger picture. Somehow she knew that by choosing Devon, she was choosing your entire family. And I know I couldn't have found a better fit for Ryan in all of Australia. He belongs with Devon—and with you."

Unshed tears glistened in Lydia's eyes, and she placed her hand over Stella's. "Thank you, dear girl. For everything." With a gentle squeeze, Lydia left.

Stella fingered *To Kill a Mockingbird* once more with a sad smile. Somehow the book meant even more to her now.

chapter twenty

Sunday morning brought with it an overcast sky and an awkwardness that lasted much of the day, at least whenever Devon was near. As much as Stella had hated the thought of leaving, she now wished for an earlier flight. Normally, she was the type of person to confront problems head-on, but there was something about Devon that made her want to run—just like she'd done last night.

So run she would, just as soon as she could. In the meantime, Stella would stay busy in the kitchen until Devon's siblings arrived, then keep up a happy pretense through dinner. She could do it.

Devon walked into the kitchen. "Mom, why are you putting candles on the cake? Is it someone's birthday?"

"Ryan's," Lydia said.

"No, Ryan's birthday isn't for another month, which you already know," Devon said. "Are you going senile on me already?"

"She's doing it for me," Stella said. "I mentioned I'd be sad to miss Ryan's birthday, and the next thing I knew your mom had whipped up a cake. If I'd known she'd go to all that trouble, I would have kept quiet."

Lydia patted Stella's hand. "Never you mind, my dear. The idea was inspired. And Ryan will be thrilled to have a happy un-birthday party." Lydia pointed to a sack on the table. "Devon, there's some balloons and crepe paper in that bag, so feel free to make yourself useful."

"Yes, ma'am."

"Don't get smart with me."

"I wouldn't dare." Devon smiled. "What about the presents, Mom? Don't you need presents for birthday parties?"

"When the other grandkids get here, I'll have them each make Ryan a card. Presents from the heart are the best gifts of all, don't you think?"

"I do." Devon pulled a balloon from the bag and blew into it just as Ryan appeared. Letting it slip through his fingers, Devon smiled as Ryan chased it around the room.

"Do that again!" Ryan jumped up and down.

When Cora's family showed up an hour later, there were still no inflated balloons because Ryan had wanted to fly or pop all of them. Stella did manage to hang some crepe paper, though, so the room looked somewhat festive.

"You must be Stella," Cora said, hugging her. "I've heard so much about you. I feel as if I already know you."

"I could say the same about you," Stella said. "Ryan is always talking about his aunts and cousins."

"What about his uncles?" Jeff said. "What are we, chopped liver?"

Stella laughed. "'Chopped liver'? Really? Where do you Americans come up with such sayings?"

"From what I understand, you Aussies say some pretty nutty things too," Jeff said.

"Such as?"

"Spit the dummy, for one," Devon said.

Stella smiled at the memory. "All right, you win."

"Guess what? It's my un-birthday party!" Ryan shouted when he saw his cousins.

"No fair! I want an un-birthday party!" one of the cousins whined.

"Okay, it can be your un-birthday party too," Ryan said.

"What about me?" another asked.

"It's everyone's un-birthday party!" Ryan declared. "Let's go jump on the tramp!" The kids followed him out the back door.

"Hear that, Mom?" Devon said. "It's everyone's un-birthday party. Where's my cake and presents?"

"And mine?" Jeff added.

"Don't forget me," Cora said.

Lydia's gaze rested on Stella. "What about you? Any demands?"

Stella waved the question aside. "I'm just happy to be here."

"Suck-up," said Devon.

Emily soon arrived with her family, and the un-birthday party began. Devon's siblings drew Stella out, making her laugh and feel almost normal again. By the time dinner ended, she stopped wanting to leave and started hoping the flight would be delayed.

If only.

While Stella rinsed the dishes, the clock above the kitchen sink taunted her. Tick, tock, tick, tock. Enough! Stella had almost decided to toss it in the dishwasher when someone grasped her elbow and dragged her away from the sink.

"Devon, what are you doing? I'm not finished."

"Forget the dishes." Amused glances looked their way as Devon pulled her through the kitchen and out to the front porch. Rain drizzled down, and Stella folded her arms to stave off the September evening chill. She wanted to run back inside. Couldn't Devon see that she didn't want to talk?

"About last night—"

"I don't want to talk about it," Stella said.

"Well, I do. And I can't let you leave like this. Not until I've had a chance to apologize."

Apologize? He wanted to apologize? For what? "Are you sorry you kissed me?"

"To be honest . . . yes."

Was he serious? Stella turned away and glared at the dark shapes of the trees. "Honestly, Devon, what a way to say good-bye. I know you don't like to lie, but in the future, promise me that if a girl ever asks you that question, you will."

"You obviously took that the wrong way, which you wouldn't have if you'd have let me finish."

"Pardon?" She twisted back. "I don't remember interrupting you. You said yes and stopped talking. What was I supposed to think?"

"Nothing. That's my point. You jumped all over me before I could figure out how to explain."

"I'm not a mind reader, you know."

"I'll try to remember that."

Silence.

Fingers drummed against the railing as Stella waited. And waited. "Are you still thinking, or is the conversation over?" *Please say it's over.*

"If I had duct tape, I'd tape your mouth shut right now."

Fine. If he wanted her to wait, Stella would wait. Thirty more minutes and she'd have to leave anyway.

Devon took a step toward her. "Stella, I wanted to kiss you, which is why I did. I'll admit, it was selfish, but since the day I met you, I haven't been able to get you off my mind. I'd hoped if I let myself kiss you just once, I'd finally be able to move on and eventually think about another girl for a change. But it backfired. Now all I want to do is kiss you again and somehow keep you from getting on that lousy plane tonight."

No longer feeling the cold, Stella leaned against the porch railing, holding on for support. "Devon, I—"

"I'm not finished. Please, let me get this out." He paced to the end of the porch and back. "As much as I would love to follow you back to Sydney, I can't do that to Ryan again. For the past several months, he's finally had stability. He's happy—he has grandparents, cousins, Aussie . . ." Devon's fingers raked through his hair, leaving it adorably disheveled.

"Don't forget a father." Stella pushed away from the railing and rested her hands on his arms. "I know all of that already, Devon, and I don't expect you to follow me."

His fingers brushed her cheek. "This is killing me," he whispered. "But I don't know what else to do. I wouldn't be happy seeing you only a few times a year—it's not enough for me. But I don't feel good about taking Ryan back and forth with me either, nor am I okay with leaving him with my parents while I go."

Stella hated the finality in his words. Her stomach churned at the thought of never seeing him again. "What if I were to fly out here a couple times a year?"

"I've thought about that, and it might work for a while, but where would it lead? Your life and job are in Australia. It's not as though you can pick up and move here. You'd have to go through law school all over again, and I'm not going to let you do that. And Ryan should be here, with his family. Buying that house felt right to me, and we both know it's what Lindsay would have wanted. Ever since I sold my company and moved back, everything has fallen into place—everything except you."

Except me. Stella tried to blink away the tears, but a few escaped and wound a path down her cheek. Devon brushed them away with his thumb.

"I'm not sure I can do this," Stella said. "This isn't like saying good-bye to a close friend. It's like saying good-bye to part of me."

"I know."

Stella pulled away, wishing for inspiration—any solution that wouldn't involve her heart breaking. The blinking lights of an airplane pulsated slowly across the sky. Soon Stella would be on one, flying away from the people she loved the most.

"So what now?" she asked quietly.

Devon cleared his throat. "Lindsay wanted you to always be a part of Ryan's life, and so do I, so I'd like you to stay in touch with him. But maybe it would be better to have him call you once a week, instead of almost every day."

No, no, no! But she knew he was right. "Okay."

Devon took a tentative step toward her. When he took another step, Stella practically flung herself into his arms, soaking up his warmth and wishing it didn't have to be this way.

His lips found hers, and she kissed him hard, placing all of her good-byes into one last kiss.

By the time Emily and Cora had ushered their children into their respective minivans, Ryan had fallen asleep. Devon carried him to one of the bedrooms and laid him on the bed, kissing him softly on his forehead. Thankfully his parents had already gone to bed, leaving him alone with his misery.

Stella was gone. She'd kissed him one last time, hugged Ryan and his family good-bye, and then walked out the door. Devon had stood on the front porch as the car drove away, calling on every ounce of willpower not to run after her.

"You let her go. I can see it in your eyes." His mother found him in the family room and sank down next to him on the sofa.

"I didn't have much of a choice. She had to get back."

"Oh, I know. I wasn't referring to tonight. I was talking about permanently. You let her go."

"You already said that." As much as Devon loved his mother, he wished she'd leave him alone. He wasn't in the mood.

"Why?"

"Why did I let her go?" Devon asked. Was she serious? "What did you want me to do? Chase after her? Move to Australia and marry her? Do you really think that's a good idea?"

"If it would make you happy—yes," Lydia said. "Any idiot can see you're in love with her and that she's in love with you. I don't see a problem here."

"What about Ryan?"

Lydia's expression fell a little. "As sad as we'd be to see him go, your father and I would rather see you and Stella happy. If that happiness happens to be on the other side of the world, then so be it. We'll find a way to see you as often as we can."

If only Devon could believe that was the answer, the right thing to do. But he didn't. "I can't, Mom. I don't know how to explain it, but Ryan belongs here—with our family. With everyone. Living here feels right to me."

Lydia lifted his chin, forcing Devon to look her in the eye. "I'm only going to butt in this one time, so listen closely." Her words came out slow and strong. "A mother is far more important in a child's life than grandparents, aunts, uncles, or cousins could ever be. Don't you ever forget that."

chapter twenty-one

Stella stretched her arms as she walked to the window. Her office felt like a sauna, but she refused to keep her blinds closed during the day. There was something about natural sunlight that livened up the space and brought a certain hope and anticipation.

November had always been a beautiful month, but this particular one seemed warmer and more humid than usual—her damp and sticky skin attested to it. Thank goodness it was Friday and quitting time. Stella had worked late every night that week and planned to spend her entire Saturday holed up at the beach, relaxing, reading, and enjoying the cool ocean waves.

The perfect reward.

"Stella?" a deep voice asked.

"That's me." She finished closing the blinds and turned around. "Sorry, but I'm on my way—" Nausea filled her stomach. *No, no, no!*

"I can see by your expression that you recognize me."

Stella forced her voice to remain calm. "As much as I'd like to, I don't think I could ever forget your face."

Justin Wells offered her a slimy smile—one that she had come to loathe years ago. "I always knew you were jealous of Lindsay."

Hate filled Stella. Raw, bitter, hatred. "What do you want, Justin?"

He sauntered over to her window and looked out onto the street below. "The most interesting thing happened to me. A couple of weeks ago I ran into an old coworker of Lindsay's. She knew I'd gone out with Lindsay and mentioned how sad she'd been about her death. Imagine my surprise when she also mentioned Lindsay had left behind a four-year-old son."

Justin turned and faced Stella, probing her with his dark brown eyes. "Now, I know I've never been the best at math, but even I could figure out that the four-year-old son would have to be mine. Or is he five now?"

Stella tried unsuccessfully to swallow the bile in her throat. "Lindsay didn't know who the father was. And regardless, it's a moot point because the child now has a legal guardian."

"Didn't know who the father was?" Justin scoffed. "Like Lindsay could have found anyone else who would take her. No, you and I both know he's my son. And guardian or no, fathers have rights."

Stella's once stifling office now felt cold and clammy. "I'll ask you again. What do you want?"

"My son."

Stella folded her arms to hide her shaking hands. "Even if the child is yours, why would you want him?"

With a mock look of affront, Justin asked, "How could I not want my son? My own flesh and blood?"

"I'm no idiot, Justin." What did he want with Ryan anyway? He'd never liked or cared about children. In fact, he was the most selfish and lazy person she'd ever met. Had he changed? Not likely. It was in his eyes—the anger, the bitterness, the greed.

Suddenly, Stella knew. "You're after the dole payments, aren't you?"

Justin shrugged. "If Centrelink feels the need to pay me for taking care of my son, who am I to argue?"

"You're a pig, Justin. A lazy, good-for-nothing pig. And it's going to take more than a positive DNA test to get him back."

"Like what?"

"Like proof you'd make an adequate father and proof you're employed, for starters. You're only kidding yourself if you think any magistrate or psychologist won't see right through you. All you'll be doing is wasting your time and money."

Justin smiled. "But it's not my money to waste, is it? Not when I've found a sympathetic barrister willing to take on my case pro bono."

He was like a housecat—lounging around all day while expecting others to pamper and spoon-feed him. Stella wanted to slap him, but the solicitor in her held back.

"You're a mug if you think the court will grant you custody of Ryan," she said.

A moment of uncertainty was quickly masked by a seedy smile. "Maybe. Maybe not. I guess we'll find out." He nodded in her direction before striding out the door. "I'm sure my barrister will be in touch. Have a nice weekend."

Stella stood tall until the elevator doors closed; then she crumpled. If Justin followed through with his threat, Stella knew from experience that the battle for custody would be a difficult one. Not only was Justin a good actor but he was also Ryan's biological father.

She was 99 percent sure.

"Hey." Tess poked her head in Stella's door. "A couple of us are going out for dinner. Want to come?"

A thick fog seemed to surround Tess. What had she said?

"What's wrong?" Tess said.

Through the fog, Stella managed to tell her friend about Justin's visit. She needed someone with a clear head to tell her everything would be okay.

"Do you think he'll actually go through with it?" Tess asked.

"Yes." There was no doubt in Stella's mind.

"Well, we'll fight it then. You'll need someone to represent you in court, and I'm sure Gerald will serve as your barrister."

"It will take more than my word against Justin's to keep a magistrate from awarding him custody. You know that. Unless I can prove otherwise, we both know judges favor the family—especially if Justin can fool the psychologist into thinking he's a decent guy."

Stella dropped her head to her desk. "I feel ill. This can't be happening. What am I going to do?"

A hand covered hers. "No worries, love. We'll find a way. In fact, we'll make that nong wish he'd never fathered a child."

"Thanks, Tess." Stella tried to smile.

"Now enough wallowing. Come and get some grub with us. Everyone's waiting."

"Another night?" Stella was in no mood to socialize. She needed time to think.

A sympathetic wave and Tess was gone.

More than ever, Stella needed someone. She couldn't fight Justin alone. Sure Tess and Gerald would be on her side, working side by side, but Stella needed more than the law. She needed a crutch. Someone to lean on.

She needed Devon.

It had been over six weeks since Devon had watched Stella drive away. Six long weeks. Although she'd still talked to Ryan through the webcam once a week, it had been Lydia, not Devon, who'd sat beside Ryan. Devon had needed time to think. Time away from Stella to mull over things and figure out what he wanted to do.

And now, six weeks later, he'd finally decided. Tonight he would call Stella.

The opening notes of "Danger Zone" burst from his phone, and Devon laughed at the coincidence. Her timing couldn't be better.

"Stella?" he answered. "I'm so glad you called.

"You are?"

"I was actually planning on calling you tonight after Ryan went to bed."

"Oh. Well I need to talk to you too. It's important." Her voice sounded weak and shaky.

"Is everything okay?"

"No," Stella said. "No, it's not."

"What's wrong?"

"It's Ryan." Devon could barely hear her. "His father is going to try and take him away from you."

"His father?" Devon felt like he'd entered a surreal universe. "What are you talking about? I thought you didn't know who the father was. I have his birth certificate to prove it."

"Known or unknown, everyone has a father," Stella said.

"So you're telling me that some guy walked in off the street claiming to be Ryan's father and you believed him?"

"He is Ryan's father," she said. "I'm almost positive."

"Did you do a DNA test?"

"Not yet, but I don't need one to know."

Her meaning was clear. "Are you saying you lied to me? All this time you've known who Ryan's father was?"

"I'm telling you Lindsay withheld information."

"Yeah, but if you know this guy's the father, then you also know that she lied on the birth certificate, right?"

"I was Lindsay's friend, Devon, so no, she never flat-out told me Justin was the father—but only because I was her solicitor and she knew I'd be legally obligated to search for him. Yes, I had a good idea who he was, but I wasn't about to pry it out of her. Lindsay stuck to the story that the father was a one-night stand. That's why she wrote 'unknown' on the birth certificate."

A pit settled in Devon's stomach. "Are you sure it's him?"

"Ryan has his eyes. The resemblance is too close to doubt."

"Why didn't you tell me this before?"

"I probably should have," Stella said. "But it didn't matter at the time."

"It didn't matter?" he asked. "For crying out loud, Stella. Ever since I've met you it's been one secret after another. Haven't you ever heard of honesty and trust?"

"I never lied to you."

"You just didn't tell me the whole truth."

"You're right. I didn't," she said. "And I'm sorry."

Devon raked his fingers through his hair, fighting for a calm he didn't feel. "So what's going to happen now?"

"Justin will have to file for an appeal to have the parenting orders varied. Then the Family or Federal Court will review the situation and a magistrate will ultimately decide whether or not Ryan belongs with you . . . or with Justin."

"But I'm legally listed as Ryan's guardian."

"It can be overturned," Stella said. "If it was anyone but the father fighting this, the court would have no reason to remove him from your care. But a father changes everything—from the birth certificate to your guardianship."

"Okay, so if he files the appeal, what then?"

"In two to four months, you'll hear from an ICL—an independent children's lawyer who will be appointed to act on Ryan's behalf. You'll be required to bring Ryan back to Australia and the ICL will commission a child psychologist to interview both you and Justin and then report back."

"Report back on what?"

"Motivations to care for Ryan, parenting capacities, deficits in parenting skills, bonding, and attachment. They will also take into account the long- and short-term psychological impacts of Ryan being removed from your care at this stage of life."

That sounded promising. Better than anything else she'd said. "Well, that's good, right? The court wouldn't want to take Ryan away from someone who has been his guardian for nearly a year."

Silence. Not good.

"Right, Stella?"

"That's the hope. But it's been my experience that in situations such as these, unless the parent is proven incompetent, they usually get custody. In Australia, we place a great value on families, so the courts prefer to keep children in a home with their biological families."

"You're telling me they could take Ryan away from me just like that?"

"Yes," Stella said. "If the magistrate rules in Justin's favor, a common scenario would be for the psychologist to suggest a gradual increase in contact with the father—at least until familiarity and trust is built. Then a graduated move to the father."

"But we live in America."

"I know. Which is why the magistrate might give Justin full custody right away."

This conversation was going from bad to worse. She was making it sound as though there was no hope at all. "But you said Lindsay only dated drunks. Is this guy one of them?"

"Yeah. But Justin was never physically abusive like some of the guys Lindsay hung around. It was more emotional. He lost his temper and yelled at her all the time. He was also selfish and lazy, and expected Lindsay to support him."

"Why would a judge grant custody to someone like that?"

"The problem is that Justin knows how to charm and deceive most people into thinking he's better than what he really is. At least for a while. Yes, he was emotionally abusive to Lindsay, but I can't prove that—especially not now that she's gone. And unless Justin has done something that's been documented somewhere, our only argument is that he's lazy and looking for a way to live off the government."

"Live off the government? What are you talking about?"

"Justin knows that as a single parent, he can get money from Centrelink—a government-funded agency that assists those in need. They've tightened the reins over the years on single adults, but single parents are a different story. It's easier for them to receive help because they have a child or children to support."

"Are you telling me Justin is doing this for some welfare check?" Devon practically shouted. "You've got to be kidding me."

"Afraid not. When he and Lindsay were together, Justin faked an injury for the compo payments. He had no problem collecting government money back then, so why would it be any different now?"

If what she said was true, if Justin really placed a value on some government check, then there was hope. Maybe Devon could end it all before it began. "If that's true, why can't I offer Justin enough money to make him back off?"

"No, I don't want you to do that," Stella said. "That's not the answer."

"Why?"

"Because if you do, Justin will be able to puppeteer you any way he chooses. There will be nothing to stop him from threatening you again."

The sick feeling returned to Devon's gut. "Stella, there has to be some way we can fight this. I'm not about to stand around and let Ryan walk out of my life and into Justin's. Don't ask me to do that."

"I would never ask you to do that," she said. "And we will fight—in every way that we can. I promise."

"How? You just said we have no case."

"As soon as we hear that Justin has officially appealed, we'll hire a private investigator to dig into his life and hopefully find some witnesses to testify about his emotionally abusive personality. We'll also subpoena police and hospital records to see if he's ever been charged with anything, or if he's ever been admitted for mental health problems. Hopefully he's done something in the last five years that we can take to court."

"Tell me what I can do." Devon needed something, anything. The thought of sitting around and waiting held no appeal.

"There's nothing you can do—especially from America."

"Then I'll get us on the first flight out there."

"No," Stella said. "Justin may not even appeal the case, and even if he does, there's really nothing you could do from here either. As your legal advisors, Gerald and I will need to handle everything. Besides, I don't want you to uproot Ryan until you have to. It'll be best if you keep him in a regular routine for as long as you can."

"Stella, there has to be something I can do. I can't just sit around here waiting and worrying. Please. Give me something."

"You can pray," she said softly. "And be there for me when I need you."

"Always."

Stella dropped the phone to her desk and swallowed the dread in her throat, forcing her mind to think like a solicitor. Her fingers tap danced against the wood of her desk. Would Justin really go through with the appeal?

Yes.

The determination in his eyes alone would have convinced her. But then there was that barrister he'd already hired. Well, not "hired" exactly—not if they'd taken on the case pro bono. Stella's fingers stilled. Exactly who had Justin found to represent him? Or had that all been a lie? Stella could never tell with Justin.

chapter twenty-two

Justin greeted Janelle Renning with a flashing smile. "G'day. I'm Justin Wells. We spoke on the phone last week."

Janelle had drab brown hair, freckles, and eyes that looked too small for her face. When she peered over the rim of her reading glasses, a faint blush appeared on her cheeks.

"Yes, I remember. Have a seat, please." She gestured to a padded armchair. "What can I do for you?"

With his dark hair and eyes, Justin knew most women found him attractive. People often compared him to a younger Ben Affleck, and it was the reason he'd chosen a young, female barrister. Her homely appearance was an added bonus. Yeah. This meeting would go exactly as planned.

Justin had lied to Stella about the barrister agreeing to work pro bono. Janelle hadn't—at least not yet. But in the face of Stella's obvious hatred and accusation, Justin hadn't been able to resist. And it had been worth it. Even if Janelle didn't agree to represent him, the fear in Stella's eyes would make him smile the rest of the day.

Justin settled in the chair and replaced his smile with a look of concern. "It's my son." He let the words settle a bit before continuing. "You see, my ex-girlfriend was vindictive and emotionally unstable, at least toward the end of our relationship. When I told Lindsay she needed help, she lost it and basically threw me out. After that, she wouldn't answer my calls or speak to me, so I finally gave up and left for good."

Janelle watched with interested eyes. So far, so good.

He cleared his throat. "A few weeks ago I ran into an old friend of Lindsay's and found out some surprising things. Unbeknownst to me, she was pregnant when I left—with my son."

Janelle picked up a pencil and scribbled something on a paper. "We'll have to run a DNA test to be sure."

"I understand, but I know I'm right."

"How old is the boy now?"

"He has to be close to five."

"Where is Lindsay?"

"Dead."

Janelle's eyes flew to his. "Dead?"

Justin nodded and dropped his gaze, as if downcast. "Or so I've been told. According to her friend, she was diagnosed with a terminal illness and died shortly after. Lindsay left my son to some American without even telling me. I'm hoping you can help me discover where he is and help me get him back. It's not right what she did."

Janelle offered a sympathetic look. "No, it's not. And if this child really is yours, and what you told me is true, you could have a strong case."

"That's really good to hear." Justin forced a pained look to his face. "I have to be honest, though, and tell you that I can't afford you—at least not right now. I lost my job months ago and haven't been able to find work again." His eyes implored her. "Please help me. Five years have already been wasted, and I can't stand the thought of another year going by without me knowing my son. I want him back."

Janelle hesitated, but only briefly. "Well, you're in luck. I haven't taken on a pro bono case in a while and I suppose it's about time I did."

With a sigh of relief, Justin placed his hand over hers. "Thank you, Ms. Renning. I knew you were a special person just by looking at you."

Janelle smiled as she rifled through a desk drawer and pulled out some paperwork. "Well, let's get going. I only have thirty minutes until my next appointment."

"Of course." Justin accepted the papers. "I also need to warn you that the last few years have been difficult ones. After Lindsay broke up with me, I was heartbroken and became clinically depressed. Since then, I've been in and out of work, my credit cards are maxed out, and . . . I even considered taking my life at one point," he said, forcing his voice to shake.

"I'm so sorry to hear that, you poor thing."

Molding his features into a mask of shame, Justin said, "If you dig into my past, it's not going to be pretty. But finding out about my son has given me something to hope for—a reason to live again. Please don't let the courts keep him from me any longer. He's all I have left."

Janelle leaned across the desk and touched his arm. "You've come to the right place. I'm an excellent barrister, and I promise to do whatever I can to get you your son back."

It had been almost too easy. But Justin coerced a few tears to his eyes anyway. "How can I ever thank you? You're an answer to my prayers."

Janelle smiled, probably congratulating herself on her wondrous act of service.

An hour later, Justin walked out of the law office sporting a grin. Everything had worked out as planned. Janelle would officially file the appeal that week and all he needed to do was continue to act like a despondent father, find a decent temporary job, and clean up his apartment. Janelle would take care of the rest.

For free.

Justin passed by a pub and smiled. In a few more months he'd be able to spend his nights there once again. Days too, if he wanted.

He loved living off the government.

chapter twenty-three

Almost a year to the day of his last visit, Devon again rode the train through Sydney's busy streets, gripping Ryan's little hand in his own and hoping it wouldn't be his last trip. He wanted a reason to return, and if Ryan were no longer his . . .

Waiting and worrying. That had become his life during the past few months. And when Devon had finally heard from the Independent Children's Lawyer, he'd considered ignoring the summons and taking Ryan far away. Someplace no one would ever find him.

But that wasn't the answer, so there was no choice but to leave for Australia and let the worry fester. What would happen? How would it end? When would it all be over?

In two weeks, Ryan would meet his biological father. Two weeks and the psychologist would begin his rounds of interviews and observations. Devon's skin crawled at the idea of Ryan spending time with Justin, but there was nothing he could do.

Nothing he could do about any of it.

"Ow, you're hurting me," Ryan said, trying to pull his hand free.

Devon loosened his grip. "I'm sorry, champ. I'm just excited to see Stella again. Aren't you?"

"Yeah." There was that dimple. The one that charmed Devon every day.

The train reached Stella's stop, and they hopped off. When they reached her flat, Devon hesitated in front of the painted steel door. What would he find on the other side? Stella had sounded optimistic over the phone, but he knew better. No matter how hard she tried to hide it, there was always fear and worry. It unnerved him.

Devon sucked in a breath and knocked.

Seconds later, the door flew open, and there stood Stella, with her bright blue eyes, looking as gorgeous as ever in that baseball cap.

"I've missed you so much." Stella lifted Ryan off the floor and hugged him tight. "When did you get so big? I can barely pick you up anymore."

Ryan giggled. "I'm big and tall. Dad says so."

"You sure are, and you need to stop growing. If you get any bigger, I won't be able to pick you up."

"You need to lift weights," said Ryan. "That's how Dad stays strong."

Stella laughed, allowing the squirmy boy to slide to the floor. "There's sugar on the counter if you want to feed the birds."

"Yay, birds!" He needed no further convincing and ran off.

Stella peeked up at Devon from under the rim of her cap. He couldn't resist. Two steps and she was in his arms, holding him tight. If only he was there under better circumstances.

Taking a breath, Devon drew back and rested his hands on her shoulders, waiting. He needed Stella to tell him everything would be okay—that Ryan wasn't going anywhere.

"You're here," she said.

"I'm here."

Her lips stretched into a sad smile. "I wish you didn't have to be."

"Me too. But it's really good to see you."

"You too."

Devon's hands fell away, and he shoved them into his pockets. "Any new developments?"

"I talked to Gerald this morning, and it's looking good so far. We have Justin's overdrawn bank records, maxed-out credit card statements, and three witnesses willing to testify that Justin is lazy and emotionally abusive. Basically, we've done everything we can and now we're just waiting on the psychologist. Then it's off to court. By that point, we should have a better idea how the magistrate will rule since he'll rely heavily on the psychologist's recommendations."

Devon nodded. He didn't need to be reminded how important the next few weeks would be.

"I need to finish getting ready. Have you had breakfast yet?" Stella asked.

"Yeah."

"Well, if you're still hungry, there's some Vegemite in the cupboard."

"Gee, thanks."

"Just promise me you won't try to clean up."

Janelle Renning closed the file on her desk. "Justin, I have to be honest with you. Things aren't looking good." She had lost that sympathetic smile weeks ago. "Your financial situation is much worse than you led me to believe, and Gerald Larsen now has three witnesses willing to testify against you and your character. Do the names Bethany Marsh, Michael Woods, and Marti Lands sound familiar?"

Yeah, they sounded familiar. One good-for-nothing ex-girlfriend and two cocky bosses who thought they were better than everyone else. "I told you my past isn't pretty. Bethany is a deranged ex-girlfriend and the other two are old employers who think I'm unreliable. When I worked for them, I struggled with depression and couldn't handle going to work some days. They fired me because of that."

"Justin, I want to believe you, I do. You seem like a good guy, but since you never saw a doctor for your depression, there's no documentation, and I can't find a single decent character witness for you."

"But what about Jackson and Michael? They're willing to testify on my behalf."

"They're drunks, Justin. Putting them on the stand would only hurt your case."

Janelle was starting to sound snooty. Like she knew better than him. "Listen. I found a good job, just like you asked me to. I even moved to a two-bedroom flat."

"Yes, but a new flat and a few weeks of waiting tables won't convince any magistrate you're going to remain permanently employed. Not with your history. You need to show the court you really have changed—that you're ready to take on the responsibility of a child."

This woman knew nothing about him or his life. Janelle had probably never waited tables, stocked shelves, or cashiered for a paltry minimum wage. No, instead she sat on her swanky leather chair and looked down on everyone else from her office window. Everything came easy to people like her.

Unlike him. Justin could work his entire life and never get ahead, so why try? Why waste away his life trapped in a demoralizing, low-level job? He was better than that. He deserved better. Which was why he needed his son.

Justin looked down at his hands. "What more can I do? I can't live the rest of my life not knowing my son."

"Well, your case isn't completely hopeless. You do have a few things going for you. You're Ryan's biological father, which is huge. You're also Australian. In fact, this case would be easy if it wasn't for your unemployment history and an ex-girlfriend ready to testify that you're emotionally abusive."

Janelle twisted back and forth in her high-backed chair. "If only you were married or at least engaged to a nice girl. Then at least we could show that Ryan would have two parents."

Justin leaned forward, suddenly interested. "That would work? How long would I need to be engaged for?"

"I was only joking, Justin."

"I know a girl who . . . well, owes me a favor. If she agreed to become my fiancée, at least during the psychological interview and court proceedings, would that help my case?"

"Well, yes . . . but that's unethical. You can't do that." Janelle's voice was hesitant.

"Of course not," Justin amended. "The truth is, I really want to marry Nicole, and this might give me the courage to actually propose. If she accepts, would that be enough time to convince the psychologist?"

Janelle nodded slowly. "It could, but—"

"No buts, Janelle." Justin flashed one of his winning smiles. "Just leave it to me."

chapter twenty-four

The psychological interview was far more brutal than Devon had imagined. Over the course of two weeks, his life was peeled apart, bit by bit, exposing everything—including the glaring black marks against him: An American. Not the father. Single. Currently unemployed—although with that last one, his financial statements should show that wasn't an issue.

Worst of all had been the expression on the psychologist's face when he'd learned why Lindsay had chosen Devon. Words couldn't describe the disbelief, the "Lindsay must have been insane" look. Hopefully Justin was going through a similar, if not worse, experience.

Out of those two weeks, Ryan had spent four afternoons with Justin. It had nearly killed Devon to let the psychologist take him away, even though he knew Ryan would return. But if the day ever came that Ryan was forced to leave permanently . . . well, Devon didn't know how he'd react to that. He couldn't stand to even think about it.

Stella was the only reason Devon hadn't gone completely crazy. At the end of each grueling day, she was there with her planned outings, picnics on the beach, ferry rides, and movie nights. Anything to bring some normalcy back to their lives.

And it worked, for the most part. The only problem was that Devon's feelings for Stella grew stronger every day, and he couldn't do anything about that either. It was as though he was suspended, unable to move on with his life until the trial was over. And even then . . . who knew what would happen?

On the last day of interviews, Stella knocked on their hotel room door shortly after the psychologist had left. "Pack your bags," she announced. "We're getting out of town for a few days."

"Where?" Devon asked.

"Byron Bay. A beautiful slice of heaven—and my home."

Devon could have kissed her. A getaway would be perfect—exactly what they all needed. Click. TV off.

"Hey," Ryan protested.

"Didn't you hear Stella? We're going on a road trip."

Ryan leaped off the couch. "Yay! A trip!"

An hour later, they left Sydney behind and headed north. For the most part, the Pacific Highway followed the coastline, with views of the ocean as they drove through walls of tropical bushes and trees.

Devon loved the rural feel of it all. It wasn't anything like the Pacific coast in America. They didn't have to navigate through multiple dense, populated cities. Instead, the long, scenic highways led them through occasional rural towns. Every now and then they'd come across a larger city—but nothing like Sydney. The landscape was untouched and unsullied. Beautiful.

The sun set, taking the views with it. Ryan had fallen asleep in the backseat, so Devon readjusted the pillow and tucked a blanket around him.

"Are you doing okay?" Devon asked Stella. "I can drive if you're getting tired."

"I'm fine, but thanks."

He gently massaged the nape of her neck. Her skin felt soft and warm beneath his fingers. Even after hours in the car, she was still gorgeous.

"Tell me about Byron Bay," he said.

Stella smiled. "You're going to love it there. The city is on the easternmost peninsula, so it's literally surrounded by beaches. The weather is perfect, the water warm, and the views incomparable. It's the perfect seaside town."

"Why do you live in Sydney then?"

"After my parents died, I needed a change. Byron Bay has a lot of memories that were hard for me to deal with, so I didn't come back for a while. I graduated from law school and then took a job in Sydney before I started visiting again. Now Byron Bay is a lovely place I go to escape when I can. It may sound strange, but I feel closer to my parents when I'm there. I'm looking forward to showing it to you."

"And I'm looking forward to seeing it tomorrow when the sun comes up."

She tapped the clock on the radio. Twelve forty-five. "You mean later today."

"Wow. Time sure flies when I'm with you, doesn't it? What time do you think we'll get there?"

"Probably around two. I hope Ryan likes to sleep in."

"He doesn't."

A little over an hour later, Stella pulled into a driveway. The headlights highlighted a small rambler with a one-car garage. "Where are we? I figured we'd be staying in a hotel."

"This is the house where I grew up. My parents left it to me when they died."

"You kept it?"

"Of course. I could never sell this place."

Stella was full of surprises. "You never told me you were a home owner."

"You never asked."

"Fair enough," he said. "Who keeps it up?"

"My neighbor's son takes care of the yard, but the inside is another matter. Be prepared to find some dust."

"Good. Then I can tell you that your house is as dodgy as mine," he said.

"Hardly. My walls are painted, the floor isn't warped, and the cupboards all have doors."

"Ah, but mine isn't dusty." Wait. How long had they been in Australia? "Scratch that. It isn't *as* dusty."

Stella laughed.

Devon gently picked up Ryan and followed Stella into the musty house and down a short, narrow hallway. He tucked Ryan in bed and brushed the hair off his forehead. "Sweet dreams, kiddo."

Pulling the door closed, Devon sighed and leaned against it. "What am I going to do if they take him away?" he whispered.

"Shhh." Stella touched her finger to his lips. "They're not going to, so no more of that kind of talk. We came here to forget about the hearing, so we're going to have a fun few days and not worry about anything else, okay?"

"Sounds good to me."

Devon couldn't stop his fingers from touching the soft skin of her cheek. During the past few weeks it had been difficult to keep his distance, but he had. Now, though, he wasn't sure he could anymore. Whether it was the feel of her skin or the lateness of the hour, Devon caved to the temptation and brushed his mouth against hers. He meant to keep it light and brief, but a shockwave swept through him, and before he could think about the consequences, his arms were around her, pulling her close. He was like a starved person placed in front of a buffet of food. He couldn't get enough. She was too soft, too beautiful.

Stella finally broke free and took a step back, gulping in air as her wide eyes stared up at him. Devon fought the urge to pull her back; he wasn't ready to let her go. He didn't think he'd ever be ready to let her go again. But Stella was right. Not only was it late, they were both tired, and who knew where things would've led if she hadn't broken away.

What Devon needed was distance. The sooner the better.

"Which room is mine?"

Stella blinked, then pointed a limp finger at the door next to Ryan's.

It took all of Devon's willpower to step into the room and firmly close the door behind him.

chapter twenty-five

With Devon's kiss fresh on her lips, Stella somehow managed to find her room and crawl into bed. She snuggled under the covers and closed her eyes, but sleep never came. The kiss, however, came again and again, thumping around in her head like a ball in a pinball machine.

Why had Devon kissed her? Had something changed? Was he too tired to think straight? Would the morning bring a day of awkwardness where they pretended nothing had happened, or would he kiss her again?

And again.

And again.

Yeah, that would be nice.

When the sun finally peeked through the windows, Stella threw on some clothes and left the house. She needed groceries as well as some fresh air. At some point, she'd have to face Devon again, and she wanted an apron and a skillet to hide behind when he appeared. Especially if he intended to pretend like nothing had happened.

An hour later, Stella returned, laden with grocery sacks. She stumbled into the house and ran into a wet-haired Devon, looking refreshed and handsome as ever. Stella frowned. It wasn't fair that he looked so good—not when she had bags under her bloodshot eyes. She started past him, only to be halted by his hand on her arm.

"Let me help with those." Devon bent and kissed her cheek before taking the bags from her.

He'd kissed her again. In broad daylight with his senses intact. Or at least she hoped they were intact.

Devon set the groceries on the table, then reached for her hand and tugged her to him. "Ryan's in the shower, so we only have a few minutes."

"A few minutes for what?"

"For this." He kissed her again, this time on the lips. "I've decided to take your advice. For the next two days, I'm going to pretend like nothing is wrong and not worry about our future."

It was like Stella's head was stuffed with cotton. This had to be a dream. Either that or she'd gone mad and had fantasized an imaginary world. If so, forget therapy. She liked being delusional.

"Our future?" she repeated.

"Yeah. It's something we need to talk about, but not until we get back to Sydney. In the meantime, I plan to kiss you as much as I want—unless, of course, you have a problem with it."

"No." Stella shook her head. "No problem." Delusional or not, she'd enjoy it while it lasted.

"Dad!" Ryan's voice echoed down the hall. "The water is cold!"

Stella smiled. "I guess that means my shower will have to wait."

"Afraid so. I've learned to shower before Ryan. He won't come out until the water runs cold."

"You could have told me that last night, you know."

"Sorry. I guess I had other things on my mind." He winked.

After breakfast they packed a lunch, grabbed some beach towels, and walked the half mile to the beach. There they played, built sand castles, tossed a football, and picnicked on the sand. On a day like today, it was easy for Stella to forget about the trial and what life would be like after Byron Bay.

"I see Ryan made a new friend," Stella said when Devon plopped down beside her. Ryan dug in the sand several yards away next to a blond-haired boy. They looked to be about the same age.

"Yeah. He's here with his mom." Devon pointed to a woman who was reading on the other side of the boys. "They've decided to dig a tunnel, but I'll be shocked if they actually connect at some point."

"I'm glad Ryan found a playmate. It looks like they're having fun." Stella's toes played with the warm, happy sand. At least it looked happy. As did the ocean, the sky, and the landscape. Everything seemed happy to her that day.

Rolling to his side, Devon said, "I still can't believe this is where you grew up—a half a mile away from all this. I'm not sure I'll ever be able to leave here."

"I know what you mean." A light, happy breeze tickled her face.

"So is the surfboard in the garage yours?"

"Yeah. I'm no professional, but growing up here, how could I not learn to surf? My dad was a wonderful teacher."

"Why didn't we bring it with us?"

"Oh, I can surf anytime. Right now, I'd rather hang out with you and Ryan."

"There's always tomorrow."

"I'll feel the same way then too."

"Come on," Devon said. "I want to see you surf."

"Why?"

"Maybe I don't think you really can," he teased.

Stella smiled. "You think a dare is going to get me to surf? What are we, teenagers? You need to start spending more time with adults, and I'm not talking about your siblings—they don't count."

"Why not?"

"Because they're almost as bad as you are."

"I'm telling them you said that."

"See? There you go again," Stella said. "Honestly, how old are you?"

"You're asking to get dunked, you know." Devon moved toward her.

"You dunk me and it's Vegemite sandwiches for dinner."

"I'm a big boy. I can make my own dinner." He lunged, grabbed her arm, and swung her over his shoulder.

Her legs kicked and her fists beat against his back. "Let me go!"

"I don't think so."

"Ryan, save me!"

But Ryan only giggled.

Moments later, Devon dove into a wave, taking her with him. Salty water forced its way up her nose and into the back of her throat. She coughed and gasped until Devon grabbed her hand and pulled her to her feet.

"You are in so much trouble," she spluttered. Cupping her hands, she hurled a small wave of water in his face.

He splashed back before his arms caught her and pulled her close.

"I'll save you, Stella!" Ryan yelled as he ran toward them.

"Some knight in shining armor you are," Stella called back. "You're a little late."

Devon scooped up Ryan, and they played and splashed until salt stung Ryan's eyes and he wanted to go play in the sand again.

"Do you want to help make the tunnel?" Ryan tugged on Stella's and Devon's hands.

"Sure," said Devon. "But only if Stella helps."

"I'll help." They spent the remainder of the afternoon connecting tunnels and soaking up the warmth of the sun.

Later that night, Stella rummaged through the fridge and grocery bags, pulling out ingredients to make spaghetti Bolognese. While the pasta boiled, she browned the beef and sausage, humming quietly to herself. Hands snaked around her waist, and Stella smiled as she leaned back against Devon.

"Smells good," he breathed into her ear.

"It'll taste good too if you don't distract me."

"I wasn't talking about the food, although that smells good too."

Stella twisted around, and her hands traveled up his arms. "Ta. You clean up pretty good yourself."

Devon grinned and kissed her until she giggled and pulled free. "Stop. You're going to make me burn dinner."

"Okay, fine." He released her. "What can I do to help?"

Stella nodded toward a pan with boiling water. "The noodles should be done. Would you mind testing them?"

"Sure." He picked up a fork, fished a noodle out, and immediately flung it above her head. It ricocheted off the ceiling and landed on her forehead.

Devon's lips twitched. "Nope. Not done yet."

Stella glared as she picked the noodle off her face and threw it into the sink. "Once again, I'm questioning your age."

"Everyone knows that if a noodle sticks to the ceiling, it's done. If it doesn't, it's not."

"Of all the ridiculous things," Stella said. "Next time taste one or, at the very least, test it above your own head, will you?"

"But it looks so much better on you."

"Dad!" Ryan's voice carried down the hall. "It's cold!"

"Saved by the child," Stella muttered.

Devon brushed past her. "Yeah, I was really worried. What were you going to do? Tickle me?"

Stella scooped out a noodle and threw it at his retreating back. It stuck to his shirt. "Oh look, they must be done now."

Devon brushed it free as his laughter echoed through the house, warming every nook and cranny.

The meat forgotten, Stella admired his broad shoulders as he walked down the hall. Giggles and squeals floated through the house as Stella's eyes drifted shut. She felt the words as much as she heard them: *Please, God. Please let this be a taste of my future.*

The aroma of burned meat wafted into her nose, and her eyes flew open. She lunged for the skillet and quickly removed it from the heat.

Hopefully God wouldn't take "taste" literally.

chapter twenty-six

The night before the scheduled hearing, the hotel room was too small and stifling for Devon. Not even Stella, when she showed up at the hotel with Chinese take-out, could make it go away. Even Ryan seemed to sense something was wrong.

"I don't want to go to bed," he whined.

"You don't have to yet. Just get your pajamas on. Grandma and Grandpa will be here soon to read you a book." His parents' plane had landed an hour earlier.

"I don't want a story."

"You love stories. Especially *You Are Special*."

"No, I don't."

Stella only shrugged, looking as helpless and worried as he was.

"Let's go talk in your room for a minute." Devon lifted Ryan and carried him to the room, where he sat on the bed with Ryan on his lap. "What's wrong, buddy?"

Ryan frowned at the ground and folded his arms. "I don't want to live with Justin."

"Who said you're going to live with him?"

"He did."

"Justin told you that?"

Ryan nodded.

Devon wanted to rage out of the hotel, find Justin's house, and beat him senseless. What kind of person would say that to a child? Certainly not someone who cared about Ryan or his feelings.

Devon let out a breath and pulled Ryan against him. He wanted to tell Ryan not to worry—that he'd never have to live with Justin. But what if that wasn't true? What if Justin won? *Please, no.* "Listen to me. Justin shouldn't have said that to you. Stella and I will do everything we can to keep you with me, okay? Aussie and I would miss you too much otherwise."

"I wish Aussie was here."

"I know." Devon brushed his fingers through Ryan's curls. "But Grandma and Grandpa are coming, and I know they'll want to read you a bedtime story. Will you let them when they get here?"

"Okay."

A knock on the door reverberated through their hotel room.

"They're here!" Ryan said, running to greet them.

Lydia scooped up Ryan, and Devon hugged his father. Their presence elevated his spirits in a way nothing else could.

"Thanks for coming," Devon said.

"You couldn't have kept us away." His mother patted Devon's arm and breezed by him, carrying her grandson to the couch.

Lydia hugged Stella with her free arm and smiled. "It's wonderful to see you again, my dear."

"It's great to see you both," said Stella.

Burying Ryan in her arms, Lydia sat on the couch. "You've been gone for a long time, so you owe me lots of snuggles."

Ryan giggled and tried to wriggle free.

"Don't forget about *my* snuggles." Jack said, pulling a piece of candy from his pocket. "Look, I even brought a bribe."

"Yay!" Ryan jumped off Lydia's lap and ran to his grandpa.

"That was a low trick, Jack, even for you."

Jack heaved Ryan off the ground and hugged him tight. "If I have to play hardball to get some lovin' from my grandson, then I will."

Stella picked up her purse. "Well, it's getting late, so I should be going."

"I'll take you home," said Devon.

"No, your parents just arrived. I'll be fine."

"And we'll still be here when Devon gets back," Lydia said. "We'll see you in the morning, Stella."

Sighing, Stella nodded. "All right. Good night."

When the train dropped them off near Stella's flat, Devon threaded his fingers through hers. Their steps slowed, and he pulled her to a stop along the side of a dark and empty street. "I've been meaning to talk to you about something."

"What?"

"Us."

"Us?" she asked. "Right now?"

Picking up her other hand, Devon pulled her closer. "I wasn't going to tell you this yet, but now's as good a time as any, I guess. I've been doing a lot of thinking, and I'm considering moving to Sydney. Actually, I'm more than considering. I've already made up my mind."

"But—"

"If I'm granted custody of Ryan, which I hope and pray that I am, I'll bring him with me. And if I'm not," Devon said, not wanting to even think about it, "I'll come back on my own and hope the court will let me be a part of Ryan's life. Either way, I want to be where I can see you and Ryan every day. It's no longer an option for me to stay away from you."

When Stella didn't say anything right away, Devon added, "But if you feel differently—"

On her tiptoes, Stella pressed her mouth against his. Devon's arms encircled her, and he drew her close, loving everything about her. Her eyes, her hair, her charm, her kindness, her strength—everything.

Somehow, Stella had become a part of him, as though he was only a shell of himself without her. He needed her like he needed happiness and could no longer contemplate a life without her in it.

Not anymore.

Stella rested her head against the closed door inside her flat. Devon had said exactly what she'd wanted to hear and yet there were still too many what-ifs to really believe she could be that happy. What if Justin *was* granted custody? What if the judge didn't give Devon visitation rights? Could Devon still live in Australia, knowing Ryan was so close and yet still out of his reach?

On the other hand, if Devon was awarded custody, could Stella stand by and watch him take Ryan away from the Pierce family? Knowing Lindsay, Stella was sure she'd be fine with it. In fact, she was probably cheering them on from heaven's sidelines, yelling at her to stop being so stupid.

Sighing, Stella pushed away from the door. It was no use sifting through all the what-ifs—not when the list contained so many. One more day and she'd be able to narrow it down.

One more day.

chapter twenty-seven

No windows. Even with the rows of florescent lighting, the room was still dark and dreary. Or maybe it was just Devon.

"Why are they wearing those things on their heads?" Ryan pointed at the barristers.

Sure enough, the two barristers wore long, gray, tightly curled wigs. Like the powdered ones worn by men in the eighteenth century.

"They're wigs," Stella answered Ryan. "Barristers and magistrates always wear them in the courtroom."

"They look funny."

Devon ruffled Ryan's hair. "Just be grateful you don't have to wear one. I know I am." To Stella, he whispered, "Hey, is that why you became a solicitor rather than a barrister?"

"Are you saying I wouldn't look good in one of those?"

"You'd look better than those two."

Justin walked in wearing a tailored suit, holding the hand of a petite, blue-eyed brunette. His arm snaked around the girl as he stopped next to Gerald. "Stella, Devon, Ryan, I'd like you to meet Nicole Standing, my fiancée."

Fiancée? What fiancée?

"I didn't know you were dating anyone," Stella said, appearing unaffected by the news.

"For a while now. We made it official last week."

"How convenient."

While Stella remained outwardly calm, Devon seethed, wanting to throttle Justin and send the girl back to wherever she came from. Who was she anyway?

As Justin walked away, Stella laid a hand on Devon's arm. "Don't let him get to you."

"Too late."

"All rise for His Honour," a voice echoed through the courtroom.

"And it begins," Stella said.

If Devon thought the psychological analysis was bad, the hearing was even worse. It lasted three long, vicious days. One by one they were all called to the stand, with the exception of Ryan. Devon's turn came, and he calmly answered Gerald's questions, feeling more and more confident—at least until Janelle stood to cross-examine him.

"How well did you know Lindsay?" she asked.

"She lived with my family for nine months," Devon said.

"How long ago was that?"

"A little over ten years."

"Have you had any contact with her since then?"

"No."

"Why do you think Lindsay left you her son?"

"I don't know. I never got the chance to ask her."

"So you're telling me that you had no idea Lindsay had listed you as the guardian in her will?"

"That's right."

"I have to admit that I find it interesting Lindsay would leave her son to someone she hadn't spoken to in over ten years, don't you?"

"No," said Devon. "She did what—"

"It just doesn't seem like something a person in their right mind would do," Janelle said.

"Objection," Gerald called.

"Withdrawn," Janelle said. "Now are you currently employed, Devon?"

"No. But—"

"I only need a yes or no." Janelle's voice oozed sweetness. "You've had Ryan in your custody for over a year now. Has he had any trouble acclimating to American culture?"

Devon frowned. "Well, change is difficult for everyone, but—"

"Thank you."

Janelle continued in this vein for what seemed like hours. Sure, Gerald had allowed Devon to defend many of the same questions, but Janelle had a nasty way of turning everything around. By the end of his testimony, Devon wanted to strangle the woman. Did she have any idea what she was doing?

On the final day, the psychologist at last took the stand. Finally. Some answers. But would they be the answers Devon wanted to hear?

Magistrate Dover didn't waste any time. "Dr. Stephens, after conducting your interviews and evaluations, will you please share with us your recommendations?"

Silence coated the room and Devon leaned forward in his seat, clasping and unclasping his shaking hands.

Dr. Stephens scanned the courtroom, his gaze stopping briefly on Justin and then Devon. "It is my opinion that Ryan should be placed with his biological father, Justin Wells."

Nothing could have prepared Devon for the way those words impacted him—like he'd been struck in the gut with the world's fastest baseball. His hands flew to the armrests of the chair, and his fingernails dug into the wood. It was the only way he could keep himself from flying out of his seat and challenging the psychologist. How could Dr. Stephens possibly side with Justin? How?

Dr. Stephens went on, "This has been a difficult recommendation because I believe both men to be capable and able to make Ryan a good parent. Devon Pierce has proven to be a more than adequate guardian for Ryan. He's financially secure, and Ryan genuinely cares for him."

Then why are you recommending Justin? Why? Why? Why?

"However," the doctor continued, "Justin Wells is Ryan's

biological father. He's also Australian, which will allow Ryan to be raised in his own country. In addition, Justin has relocated to a flat with two bedrooms, has held down a steady job for the past two months, and has recently become engaged to be married. All of which show me that Justin is more than willing to make the necessary changes in his life to accommodate Ryan.

"As for the accusations against him, I have spent considerable time with Justin and saw no indication that he is emotionally abusive. Yes, he's awkward around Ryan, but they've had so little contact that it's understandable. I'm confident they'll become more comfortable together over time—especially if the court recommends counseling sessions. As for living arrangements, Justin's apartment is old and could use some renovations, but it will do for now. Justin is also deeply in debt, but he's working to free himself from those obligations. Regardless, I don't believe debt's a valid reason to keep a father from raising his biological son."

Dr. Stephens paused. "Ryan is now five years of age and has lived with Devon Pierce for over a year, so the change is going to be difficult for the child. That's why I'm also recommending a gradual move from Devon to Justin over the course of three or four months, assuming Devon will be able to stay in Australia for that long."

That's gradual? Devon wanted to shout. Ten years was gradual. Not three short months. That was nothing. Devon wanted to jump up and tell Dr. Stephens he was wrong—that he'd misjudged Justin. The doctor needed to understand the kind of life Ryan would be subjected to if he were placed with his father.

But an outburst like that would only make things worse, so Devon clamped his mouth shut. Not even Stella's gentle touch on his arm could ease the penetrating feeling of horror and helplessness that consumed him.

As soon as the official judgment date had been set, Devon leaped from his chair and practically ran for the nearest exit. He needed to get out of the courtroom and away from his parents, Stella, and Ryan. He needed to be alone—to battle his demons in private. Devon staggered out into the crisp June morning and circled around to the back of the building. A large tree trunk beckoned him, and he collapsed against it, slamming his fist into the flaky bark as he fought back tears.

How could he give Ryan up? And how could God have let this happen? Devon wanted to fight—to run back to the courtroom and tell the magistrate exactly why Ryan should belong to him. He wanted the judge to see the anguish on his face, to know exactly what would happen if Ryan were taken away from him.

A hand rested on his shoulder. "I'm so sorry," said Stella, a pained look on her face.

Devon was afraid to ask, but he had to know. "How often do magistrates rule against the psychologist's recommendations?"

"It happens, but it's rare."

An unseen weight pressed on Devon's chest as if trying to suffocate him. He couldn't do this anymore, couldn't handle the throbbing of his head or the sick feeling in his gut. Devon needed it to ease up. He needed relief.

Things happened for a reason, right? More than ever, Devon needed to believe that there was a wise, loving, and all-knowing God who was in charge—who knew what He was doing. Maybe the psychologist was right. Maybe Ryan should be placed with his father. His real father. Maybe Ryan would impact Justin the same way he'd impacted Devon. He didn't want to believe it, but it was the only way he could keep the pain from tearing him apart.

"Maybe Justin has changed. Maybe Ryan will be good for him and everything will work out for the best," Devon said.

Stella's eyes widened, and she shook her head. "He hasn't changed. I don't believe that for a second and neither do you."

"I have to believe that or I'm going to go crazy." Devon's fist pounded against the tree again. How could she remain so calm while he was dying inside? "Why didn't you just let me pay Justin to stay away in the beginning? This could have all been over months ago."

"If you'd have done that, Justin would use Ryan against you for years," Stella argued.

"That's better than losing Ryan permanently!"

Stella squeezed his shoulder. "There's still a chance, Devon. Please don't give up yet."

"But you just said—"

"Listen to me. It wasn't a good idea to offer Justin money before, but now the situation is different. At this point, if Justin backs out of this appeal, he won't be able to appeal it again later on. It will be over. Forever."

Some of the weight on Devon's chest eased up, and breathing came easier. Thinking came easier. Stella was right—there was still a chance. There was still hope. His hand covered Stella's, squeezing it. "Thank you."

Concern showed in her eyes. "What are you going to do?"

"You're my solicitor, Stella," Devon said. "So nothing."

Stella nodded.

"Would you mind telling my parents to take Ryan back to the hotel? Tell them I'll meet them there later. I need to get away for a while and think."

"Okay. I'll see you later." Stella left him with a kiss on his cheek.

As soon as they'd left, Devon pulled out his phone and called Stella's law firm. He waited while the receptionist put his call through.

"This is Tess."

"Hi, Tess, this is Devon Pierce, Stella's friend. Do you have a few minutes to talk?"

"Sure," she said. "What about?"

"I'm not too far away, would you mind if I stopped by in about ten minutes?"

"I'll be here."

Devon left Ryan with his parents and jumped on the train. Ten stops later, he exited and traveled the last few blocks on foot, stopping in front of an old, gray rundown apartment complex. No wild larakeets sang from the trees in this neighborhood. The entire street reeked of neglect and had a creepy, vacant feeling.

Devon was more determined than ever to do whatever it took to keep Ryan away from Justin.

He rapped loudly on the door.

Then waited.

And waited some more.

Was Justin gone? He rapped again.

Finally, the door swung open, revealing a dark interior and a groggy Justin. It was eleven o'clock in the morning, and the guy had obviously been asleep. Devon wanted to turn the hose on him.

"What are you doing here?"

"I'm sorry. Did I wake you?" Devon was anything but sorry.

"What I do or how I choose to spend my time is none of your business."

"Mind if I come in? We need to chat."

"Yeah, actually, I do mind. You've already had your chance to say whatever it is you wanted to say in court."

That's what you think. "Trust me. You're going to want to hear what I have to say." Another apartment door opened, and Devon added, "In private."

Justin glowered but grudgingly stepped aside.

Devon walked into a disaster. The odor alone made him want to walk out again. It reeked of soiled clothes, rotted food, and cigarette smoke. Several take-out boxes were scattered around, and discarded beer bottles dotted the floor.

"You've got to be kidding me," Devon said. "How did you ever make this place look good for the psychologist?"

"A maid service can do amazing things."

Devon's fingers clenched into fists in his pockets. Ironically, the only semi-clean place was the small card table in the kitchen. He brushed past Justin and pulled out a chair, gesturing for him to do the same.

Plopping down, Justin said, "What do you want?"

Devon shoved a piece of paper and a pen at him. "I want you to write a letter to the court saying you've come to realize that Ryan would be better off with me. You can make up whatever excuse you want, I just want you to be completely clear that your decision is final. You should also probably add an apology to the court saying how sorry you are for causing so much trouble."

Justin's arms folded, and he cracked a sneering smile. "You've already lost. It's just a matter of time."

"I'm aware of that."

"Then why would I write that letter?"

"Because I'm willing to pay you to write it—as well as stay out of Ryan's life for good."

Justin laughed out loud. "I wonder what the court will think when I tell them about your offer to bribe me."

Devon lifted his cell phone and snapped a picture of the apartment. "And I wonder what they'll think about the state of your apartment. And you for that matter." He redirected his phone at Justin and snapped another picture.

Justin lunged across the table, and Devon grabbed a hold of his dingy T-shirt. Through clenched teeth, he said, "I've had about all I can take of you. But as much as I'd like to use your body as a punching bag right now, I didn't come here to start a fight. I came here to make a deal with you."

Devon shoved a seething Justin back into his chair. "Now, we both know you have no intention of marrying Nicole, or vice versa, so let me explain something to you."

"You don't know anything," Justin spat.

"Fine. Let's talk about the future then. Assuming things don't work out between you and Nicole, and assuming you get that money from Centrelink you're after, in February Ryan will be old enough for school, leaving you time to work. That means Centrelink will reevaluate whatever amount they're paying you and start working with you to find a job. From what I understand, they're pretty good about checking up on people, but you already know that, don't you?"

Justin glared.

"In addition," Devon continued, "Ryan's not going to stay a child forever. At some point, any childcare payments you receive will stop altogether—which is only half your problem. The other is Ryan. A child isn't cheap. Clothes, food, school, and extracurricular events are just some of the expenses Ryan will cost you. And if you think for a minute that you can live like you've been living—" Devon gestured at the apartment "—and spend as little money as possible on Ryan, you're dreaming.

"If you win custody, I will move to Sydney, and between Stella and I, you'll always have someone looking over your shoulder, waiting for the day you mess up. You know Stella well enough to believe she will reopen this case at the first sign of neglect on your part. In other words, if you end up with Ryan, someone will always be watching."

Devon leaned back in his chair and folded his arms. "If, on the other hand, you decide to play the hero and write that letter we talked about, I'll wire one hundred thousand American dollars into your bank account one month after the case is closed. After twenty-eight days, an appeal is no longer an option, so you'll understand why I plan to wait until then."

"And how do I know you'll follow through on that?"

"You'll have to take my word for it."

"Forgive me if I don't," Justin scoffed.

"I'm here, aren't I? You know that Ryan is too important to me to risk your revenge. But as a show of good faith, I'll have five thousand dollars deposited within a day of the case being closed. The rest you'll get when I'm certain it's closed for good. And if I ever see your face again, I'll have records showing you accepted a bribe. It will look bad for both of us, but mostly for you, so I'd recommend staying as far away from me and Ryan as possible."

"You think I'd give up my son that easily?"

"Please." Devon pushed his chair back and tossed an old business card on the table. "Here's my cell number. You have my offer. If you decide to accept it, text me your account info. As for the letter, you can deliver it to your solicitor and she'll know what to do."

Without another word, Devon walked out, leaving Justin to his disgusting apartment.

chapter twenty-eight

Devon finished reading *You Are Special* to Ryan before tucking him under the covers. Tomorrow they would appear in court for the final judgment, and Devon still hadn't heard one word from Justin. The hope he'd felt weeks ago had dwindled and then died, and now Devon was having a difficult time masking his despair.

He had been so sure Justin would take the money—that this entire ordeal would have ended weeks ago. Maybe Devon hadn't offered enough. Maybe he should run over to Justin's apartment right then and double his offer. Would it make a difference? Would it sway him?

Large, trusting brown eyes stared up at him. "I want to see Aussie. He misses me."

Devon brushed Ryan's hair back. "I know."

"When can we go home?"

Devon hesitated. "You know we have to go to court again tomorrow morning, right?"

"I don't want to go. I want to go home and play with Aussie."

"Just one more day and then we'll be done, okay?"

"And then we can go home to see Aussie?"

Devon blinked and cleared his throat. He couldn't let Ryan

see him lose it. "I hope so, but it all depends on what the judge says. He might ask you to live with Justin for a while."

Ryan's lips trembled. "But I don't want to live with Justin. I want to live with you and Aussie." His face crumpled, and he started crying.

Devon felt tears wet his own eyes as he picked up Ryan and hugged him tight, rubbing his back and murmuring, "I know," over and over. Eventually Ryan quieted down and fell asleep, but the pain still throbbed in Devon's chest. Would he really have to stand by and watch Ryan get taken away?

His parents, solemn and quiet, were sitting on the couch in the front room. The feeling of gloom festered until Devon wanted to leave the hotel and hit the city streets—anything to distract him from the long night ahead.

Lydia patted the seat of the armchair, and Devon forced himself to sit down. Stella had left only an hour ago, explaining she had some things to get done before tomorrow, and Devon already missed her. He needed to see her, to feel her comforting arms around him and to hear her tell him everything would be okay.

As if reading his mind, his mother's quiet voice broke through his thoughts. "It's going to be okay. Whatever happens tomorrow, it's going to be okay." She said it like she was trying to convince herself as well.

Devon nodded but said nothing. He'd never believe that Ryan should belong with Justin. Never. Even Devon's faith gave him no relief from the darkness and misery that consumed him now. It made no sense that a loving God would prod Lindsay into choosing Devon, only to let something like this happen.

Leaning forward, Devon's thumb and finger covered his eyes as he wiped at the tears threatening to spill. He wanted to understand, wanted to believe there was a reason, but he couldn't summon the will to try.

His mother stroked his back, offering a comfort he didn't feel.

"Your mother's right, son," Jack said. "You've done all you can do. Now your only choice is to let the good Lord take over. He knows what He's doing, even if we don't."

Devon broke down. His shoulders shook uncontrollably as he

cried harder than he'd ever cried in his life. No words could describe the aching pit in his stomach, the sorrow that drowned his soul. He didn't have the faith to believe it was supposed to turn out like this.

And yet Devon knew it happened all the time. Children forced to stay with abusive parents. Children born into horrible circumstances. Children belittled, despised, and treated cruelly. It had happened to Lindsay. Sure, he could tell himself that there was a reason; that what didn't kill people made them stronger. But Devon couldn't wrap his mind around any of it—not now. Not when it was Ryan.

Ryan. His buddy, his champ. The boy who'd traipsed into Devon's life with his dimple, his charm, and his little Australian accent. The boy who giggled, loved Aussie, tracked dirt everywhere, colored on walls, memorized poems, and made castles for ninjas. The boy who sent balloons to heaven and couldn't understand why the Southern Cross didn't appear in the Portland night skies.

The boy who called him Dad.

"I can't do this," he said, his voice cutting though his sobs. "I'm not strong enough."

Jack laid a hand on Devon's back, speaking through tears of his own. "You're stronger than you think you are. We all are—even Ryan."

But Ryan shouldn't have to be strong enough.

"We're going to try and get some sleep," Jack said. "You should too. We'll see you in the morning."

His mom kissed the top of his head before they left, and as the door clicked closed, the thick silence of the room screamed in Devon's ears.

He had never felt more alone.

On the morning of the hearing, the weather reflected Stella's mood. The sky was filled with ominous, swirling charcoal clouds that promised a thunderstorm. Peeking through her bedroom window, she searched for one ray of sunlight. Just one. Stella needed a sign that Devon had a whisper of a chance, that there was still hope. But no sunlight appeared, and she felt suffocated by the darkness. After a few minutes, she gave up, wished the clouds to Hades, and yanked her drapes closed.

In the foyer outside the courtroom, Stella nodded at Devon, Ryan, and the Pierces. Everyone looked as miserable as she felt. Even Ryan seemed to sense the overall mood and stood there quietly, gripping Devon's hand and looking darling in a two-piece navy suit. Stella wanted to pick him up and take him far, far away where no one could find him.

The courtroom door opened, and Stella followed the others in slowly, glimpsing the room from the eyes of a client rather than a solicitor. Until that moment, she hadn't realized what a life-altering day this could be for people. Yes, she had sympathized with clients in the past, felt terrible when the ruling didn't go their way, but now Stella felt true empathy.

Finding her seat, she sat down. Devon's parents sat a few rows back, holding hands and fighting back tears. Janelle Renning sat quietly and erect, with a bland, unreadable expression. Was she gloating inside? Did Janelle have any idea what Justin was really like? Did she know what she had done?

Stella's fingers tightened around the pen in her fingers. She couldn't seem to look at anyone without becoming emotional in one way or another. Reaching for Ryan's hand, she held it tightly in her own, not daring to meet Devon's eyes.

It wasn't fair. It wasn't right. And for the first time in her career, Stella hated the law.

Where was Gerald? He should be here by now. Justin was nowhere to be seen either, which gave Stella some relief. She couldn't handle looking into his cold, dark, and triumphant eyes. Maybe he'd been hit by a car and wouldn't show up at all. If only.

Several minutes later, Gerald arrived out of breath, like he'd been running. "Sorry I'm late," he breathed.

"Everything okay?" Stella asked.

"Traffic."

A deep voice asked them to stand for Federal Magistrate Dover.

The magistrate entered briskly, took his seat, and scanned the courtroom. His gaze rested on the table where Janelle sat. "Where is your client, Ms. Renning?"

Janelle stood and lifted her chin. "Justin won't be coming today, Your Honour. I told him he needed to be here, but he insisted that the letter we delivered to you would be sufficient to excuse him today."

Stella's heart pounded as she stared at Janelle. What letter? What was she talking about? She waited anxiously for the magistrate to speak.

"He should have been here regardless of my decision."

"I know, Your Honour, but I couldn't force him to come," Janelle said.

"I could reschedule this hearing, you know."

"Yes, I know. But nothing I said would convince him to come."

What's going on? Would the judge really postpone the hearing? Please no!

The magistrate's eyes shifted to Ryan before resting on Janelle once again. "This case has dragged on long enough, so we will proceed with the decision. Your client, however, will be assessed a fine of one hundred dollars for thinking he knows better than the law. Mr. Wells filed the appeal, he should have been here."

"I understand, Your Honour. And thank you." Janelle said.

"Very well, then. Let's not waste any more time." The magistrate slid on a pair of reading glasses and looked down at the papers on his desk. "Yesterday, I received a letter from Justin Wells stating his intent to withdraw from the case. I don't understand why, nor did I appreciate the short notice." He glanced meaningfully at Janelle over the top of his glasses.

When she offered a solemn nod, he returned his attention to the papers. "That being said, I've since revised my orders. They are as follows: That the child, Ryan Caldwell, live with the respondent, Devon Pierce, permanently, and that the applicant, Justin Wells, have no parental responsibility for either day-to-day or long-term issues relating to the child . . ."

Relief and joy burst through Stella's body, drowning out the magistrate's voice. She couldn't believe it. Justin had actually withdrawn, even if he'd waited until the last day to do it. He'd probably delayed on purpose, hoping to get back at Stella and Devon. But none of that mattered now. It was over.

Finally.

Stella blinked away tears as she pulled Ryan into a hug. Over his head, she met Devon's eyes. A smile stretched across his face and she grinned in return, wanting to throw her arms around him as well.

When the judge finished speaking and dismissed them, Devon pulled Ryan to his lap. "Did you hear that, kiddo? You get to live with me forever. We get to go home."

Ryan's dimple was back. "Forever?"

"And ever," Devon said, holding him tight.

Lydia ran to them and wrapped her arms around Ryan and Devon. "I don't believe it. I mean, I know you offered Justin—"

"Mom, I have no idea what you're talking about," Devon interrupted with a smile. "And neither do you."

"She rarely does," Jack said, grinning.

"I'm sorry. It's just that I'm so happy." Tears streaked down Lydia's cheeks. She lifted Ryan from Devon's arms and hugged him tight. "I'm making you spaghetti and homemade ice cream with TimTams the minute we get back to Portland."

"Yay!" Ryan shouted. "Can Aussie have some too?"

"He can have mine," Jack said, for once not grumbling about spaghetti and ice cream.

Hand-in-hand, they walked out of the courthouse together and into bright sunlight. The clouds had actually parted, and Stella could literally see rays of sunshine forging through. It was as if they were telling her, "What just happened wasn't a dream. It's really over."

A moment later the clouds blocked the sun, thunder shook the skies, and rain came pouring down. Stella wanted to laugh and jump up and down, to dance and twirl in the rain. She didn't care about her dry-clean-only suit. Ryan would be where he belonged. With Devon.

And only one question remained: Where did Stella belong?

chapter twenty-nine

Jack and Lydia shooed Devon and Stella out the door. "Take her out to dinner," Lydia said. "You two deserve a relaxing evening, and we want Ryan all to ourselves tonight."

Stella was grateful for the chance to be alone with Devon. Now that the case had ended, she had questions. A lot of questions. She wanted to know what Devon had said to Justin and how much he'd offered him—how much more he'd had to sacrifice.

The elevator took forever to arrive, and when the doors finally opened, Stella pulled Devon inside.

As soon as the doors closed, she asked. "So how much did it take?"

"It doesn't matter."

"I want to know."

"Sorry, but you'll have to live with never knowing because I'll never tell you."

Stella squeezed his hand. The sacrifices Devon had made for Ryan seemed to rain down endlessly, like the weather from earlier that day. His job, his flat in Chicago, his former fiancée, his bachelor life of freedom.

And now his money.

"How can I ever thank you?" Stella focused on the glowing floor numbers. Five . . . Four . . . Three . . .

When the elevator chimed and stopped, Devon pressed the button to keep the doors closed. Two fingers lifted her chin, and his eyes met hers. "I love Ryan, and I would do anything for him. Understand?"

Stella nodded. Could there be a better man than him? A sensation she couldn't quite describe, a sort of intense rush, flowed through every part of her. She felt drawn to Devon like never before. He'd done so much. Enough. He shouldn't have to make anymore sacrifices—at least not for her.

Devon let go of the button, and they left the hotel behind. The busyness of Sydney's streets went unnoticed as a peace and calm overtook Stella, confirming the rightness of her decision.

As soon as they were seated in the charming and romantic seafood restaurant, Stella blurted, "I want to move to America." The decision had been easy—easier than deciding what meal to order.

Devon's eyes widened, and then he smiled. "No you don't."

"Yes, I do." She was absolutely, positively, undoubtedly sure.

"No. You don't."

"I can see Ryan has taught you how to debate," she said. "But I'll say it again. Yes, I do."

"Why? You can't use your law degree in America. You'd be giving up your career, and I won't let you do that."

Oh, he did not just say that. "You won't let me? I'm sorry, but you have no say in the matter. I can move to America if I want to."

"Why? I thought we'd already agreed that Ryan and I would move here."

"Because Portland is where you and Ryan belong. It's where Lindsay would want you to be, and it's as far away from Justin as you can possibly get."

Devon's hand reached for hers. "You didn't exactly answer my question."

"I did too."

"No," he said, his eyes twinkling. "You told me why Ryan and I should stay in America, not why you want to move there."

"Isn't it obvious?"

"Nope." Devon was teasing her. He knew exactly why she wanted to move, but the smile in his eyes challenged her to say the words out loud.

"Are you fishing for compliments?"

"One should do the trick."

Stella laughed. "Fine. I'm moving to America because I want to be where you and Ryan are. And unlike you, I'm sure I can think of something to do with my life. I could write for an international magazine, teach, or maybe even become a counselor. I did get an undergraduate degree in psychology, you know."

His lips twitched. "That explains a lot."

"Like what?"

"Your impressive ability to manipulate people, for one thing."

"Maybe. But that degree was also supposed to help me understand people, which I don't. Here I am, telling you I'm willing to move to your country so I can be with you and Ryan, and you're trying to convince me not to. Is this your way of telling me your feelings have changed?"

"My feelings for you will never change. I just don't want to see you give up something you love so much."

"Even if it's for something I love even more?"

For once, Devon was speechless. Brown eyes stared into hers before a gradual smile stretched across his face. "Would you be embarrassed if I kissed you right now?"

Chills ran up her arms. Delightful, happy chills. "No. I'd be embarrassed if you didn't. It's not every day I declare something like that in public."

Devon grinned as he brought his lips to hers in a kiss that made Stella forget they were in a restaurant.

Well, almost forget. A throat cleared next to their table. It was their waiter, holding two steaming plates.

Devon leaned back in his seat. "Sorry, man, but there's only so much temptation a guy can take."

Stella's cheeks infused with heat.

"No worries." The waiter grinned. "Will there be anything else?"

"No," Stella said. "And thanks. It smells delicious."

"Enjoy your dinner . . . and the entertainment." The waiter winked at Devon and left.

"You gotta love Australia," Devon said, then lowered his voice. "You know, we could always have the waiter wrap this up and take it back to your place so we can eat and 'entertain' ourselves in private."

"Oh, stop it." Really, though, Stella loved the teasing. It warmed her and brought a silly giddiness to her stomach.

"Then how about a race?" he suggested.

"A race?"

"First one finished gets to decide whether we live here or in Portland."

Stella dropped her fork. "Finished."

"Brilliant," he said. "Let's go."

"Devon." He couldn't be serious.

But he was already flagging down the waiter. When asked to box up their order, the look on the waiter's face made Stella cover her mouth to muffle her laughter.

The boxes remained on the table as Devon dragged Stella out of the restaurant, around a corner, and down a less populated, quieter street. Finding a dark corner, he pulled her into his arms and kissed her senseless.

Or at least tried to. Unfortunately, Stella's giggles interrupted them. She couldn't stop. Every time her eyes closed, the waiter's bemused face appeared, and she erupted all over again.

Devon finally gave up. "You're ruining the moment, you know."

"I know, and I'm sorry. But did you see how the waiter looked at us? Priceless."

"Obviously we need to get your mind off that waiter and back on me, where it belongs." Devon grabbed her hand and pulled her down the street. "Let's see if one of your random facts will do the trick."

It worked. The waiter forgotten, Stella groaned. "When are you going to stop making me do this?"

"When you tell me something I already know."

"Oh. Well in that case, did you know that chickens lay eggs?"

"No, I didn't. That's fascinating."

"Rubbish." She should've known he'd say that.

Devon continued to pull her along. The street had a dark, vacant feel, and Stella suddenly wanted to be back in his arms.

"Since you've finally run out of random facts, mind if I have a turn?" Devon asked.

"Do you really think you can come up with something I don't already know?"

"As a matter of fact, I do."

"By all means, then, have a go."

Devon's steps slowed, and he scanned the street, as if making sure they were alone. Brown eyes back on her, he said, "Did you know that when an American guy falls in love with a gorgeous Australian girl, it guarantees him good luck for the rest of his life?"

Stella's heart down-shifted from fifth to first gear, nearly stopping altogether. She could hardly breathe. "If that's true, you must not be in love with me. You've had horrible luck since we met."

"How do you know it's you I'm talking about?"

"A woman's intuition."

"Fair enough," Devon said. "And you're right. I have had horrible luck since I met you. On the other hand, I would still be a single workaholic living in downtown Chicago with no one to come home to, no one to call me Dad, and no one to kiss. Call me crazy, but I kind of like my new life."

"Really?"

Devon's arms circled her waist. "Really."

Stella felt like a teenager who'd been asked out by her first real crush. Only better. So, so, so much better. Actually, there was no comparison. "Well, that's all fine for you, but what about the Aussie girl? Does she get any guarantees?"

"Sorry, did I leave that part out?" He pulled her closer. "She is promised a ready-made family with a busy child, a dodgy house, a big dog, and all the fish she could ever want."

"That doesn't sound so bad." Actually, it sounded wonderful, like a slice of heaven.

"You have no idea how relieved I am to hear you say that."

Stella picked at a piece of lint from his shirt. "Correct me if I'm wrong, but did you just propose?" she teased.

"I don't know. Did you just say yes?"

Stella smiled. All her life she'd had the occasional girlhood fantasy of a guy kneeling down in front of her, speaking words of adoration, telling her how much he loved her, how he couldn't live without her—wait a minute.

"No, I did not just say yes."

"You didn't?"

"No."

"Why?"

"Why?" she repeated. "Because you forgot some very important words, Mister."

He paused. "Please?"

She could tell he was enjoying this. "Strike one."

"Abracadabra?"

"Strike two. One more and you're out."

"I didn't think Australians knew anything about baseball."

"Strike three, you're out."

"That wasn't my guess," he said.

"Fine. You get one more chance, so don't blow it."

Devon pulled her close and kissed her long and hard, leaving her breathless. "I love you, Stella Walker," he whispered in her ear. Then he reached into his pocket and pulled out a small gray box. Kneeling down on the sidewalk, he flipped open the lid and exposed a brilliant round diamond on a wide white-gold band.

"Will you marry me, Stella Walker?"

She gasped and entered a universe where time slowed and all noise disappeared except the sound of someone pounding furiously on a large bass drum. Or was that her heartbeat? The air thinned, the lights dimmed, and all that remained were her and him. Nothing else.

"I know this is a surprise, but I've had this ring for a couple of months now, waiting for that nightmare of a court battle to be over. I thought I'd jinxed everything when I first bought it, but then it became my hope for a future with you and Ryan. I carried it with me everywhere, not because I planned to propose right away, but because I needed the reminder. In fact, I wasn't even planning on proposing tonight, but after dinner . . . Well, I couldn't wait any longer.

"I don't know how things will pan out or where we'll end up, but so long as we're together, I really don't care." Devon's eyes searched hers, probing and wondering. "So what do you say, Stella? Will you marry me?"

Stella smiled through her tears. It had been perfect, even better than her girlhood dreams. "Yes. Yes, yes, yes!"

Then she was in his arms again—a place she never wanted to leave.

"Looks like my plan worked," Devon said. "I dare you to try to think about anyone else right now."

chapter thirty

Knock-ety, knock, knock.

Stella waited. Then waited some more.

When no one answered, she turned the doorknob and pushed it open. Quietly, she let herself inside and slipped off her shoes to walk across the beautiful knotty wood floor on her way to the kitchen. New maple doors hung on the cabinets, and the hideous mantle and fireplace were gone—replaced by two wooden bookcases that now flanked a gorgeous stone fireplace.

The once dodgy house now felt like a warm and cozy home.

A home that would soon be hers.

Ryan's voice floated through the open back door. Devon and Ryan were tossing a neon yellow football back and forth. Just like Lindsay had predicted. Once again, he touched Stella's heart. She wished she had a camera to capture the moment.

Ready to rush out the door and greet them, Stella paused. Devon's cell phone lay unattended on the patio steps. Stepping out of sight, she reached for her phone and called his number.

A few seconds later, the opening bars of "Danger Zone" from the *Top Gun* soundtrack rang through the air. Really? That's what he'd set as her ringtone? Or maybe it was just the regular ringtone for all his calls.

Through the crack in the door, Stella saw Devon jog over and pick up the phone without looking at the display. "Hey, beautiful," he said. "Seven days and counting."

The ringtone was hers, and hers alone. *What a toad!* Stella stepped out from behind the door and stared at his back. "Make that zero."

"What?"

"'Danger Zone'? Really? That's the ringtone you picked for your soon-to-be wife—the so-called love-of-your-life?"

Devon twisted around and a grin split his face. "If the shoe fits," he said, taking a step toward her.

Stella stepped back. "Well, it doesn't fit, whatever that's supposed to mean. You keep forgetting I'm an Aussie and not familiar with all of your ridiculous colloquialisms. And don't you dare take another step until you promise to change that song."

"To what? 'Ball and Chain'?" Another step closer.

A step back. "I'm not laughing. Try again."

"'Maneater'?" Another step forward.

Stella held up her hand. "If you keep that up, you might as well change it to 'Where Were You on Our Wedding Day?'"

"Why are we still talking on the phone?"

"You tell me."

Devon shoved his phone into his pocket. "There. Now if you come and kiss me in the next five seconds, I might change it to 'Hopelessly Devoted to You.'"

"That's a bit cheesy, isn't it? No, I want something brilliant, classic, not insulting, and definitely not cheesy. What about U2's 'All I Want Is You'?"

"Deal," he said. "And so true. Now come here."

Stella ran into his arms. He drew her close and kissed her long and hard, making up for the eight weeks they'd spent apart.

"Stella!" Ryan squealed, wrapping his little arms around her legs.

She knelt to give Ryan a hug and kiss. "I've missed you, love. But now we never have to say good-bye again. I'm here to stay."

Ryan grabbed her hand and pulled her to the backyard. "Come see Aussie's new trick. I taught him all by myself." He then demonstrated Aussie's newfound ability to run after a stick and bring it back.

"Do you want to try?" he asked.

"I'd love to." Stella heaved the slimy, slobbery stick across the yard. Aussie panted after it, and Ryan panted after Aussie.

Devon's arms wound around Stella's waist from behind. "We weren't expecting to see you until next week. Why didn't you tell me you were coming sooner? We would have picked out a balloon bouquet and met you at the airport. How did you get here anyway?"

"A cab. I wanted to surprise you."

"You did," he said. "And I'm glad. I was wondering how I'd survive another week without you."

Stella rested her head against his chest and laughed when Ryan tried to climb on top of Aussie. The dog bounded away, leaving Ryan in a heap on the ground.

Devon nuzzled Stella's neck. "Ryan wants me to make Aussie a saddle."

"Why don't you just upgrade to a pony? That way you can buy a saddle."

"No way. And if you ever bring that up around Ryan, I'm going to paint the fireplace white again."

Stella twisted and rose on her tiptoes to kiss him. "No worries. I love the fireplace too much. Besides, it's not as if I want a pony either."

"Good. At least we agree on that. No more pets."

"I'm hungry," Ryan called. "And thirsty."

"Me too," said Stella. "What should we make for dinner?"

Devon shrugged. "I had planned on ordering a pizza, but we could make hamburgers if you'd rather have that."

Stella clapped her hands and rubbed them together. "Or better yet, Aussie burgers."

"You'd better not be talking about our dog," Devon said.

"Very funny," she said. "Do you have pickled beets?"

Devon made a face. "No."

"Pineapple?"

"Maybe in a can."

"Bacon?"

"Of course."

"Eggs?"

"Uh, yeah . . . why? This is starting to sound like something we could feed *to* Aussie."

Stella reached for Ryan's hand. "We have so much to teach Daddy, don't we, Ryan?"

Ryan nodded happily.

"Just promise me the hamburgers don't have Vegemite on them," said Devon.

"Not on the burgers," Stella assured him. "But in case you're running low, I've brought several jars with me."

Devon groaned but followed them inside. Together they grilled the hamburger meat and loaded their burgers with pineapple, fried eggs, lettuce, tomatoes, and bacon. In the end, Devon admitted to liking them, and Aussie didn't complain either.

After they'd cleaned the kitchen, they snuggled together on the couch to watch Ryan's favorite movie. Or at least most of it. Ryan fell asleep near the end, so Devon carried him to his bed. Stella followed and knelt beside the bed, tucking him in. She loved watching Ryan sleep. He was so precious and adorable. Did she really get to be his mum? It seemed too good to be true.

Devon sat on the back patio steps, staring up at the sky. Sinking down beside him, Stella laid her head against his shoulder. His arm wound its way around her, and he pulled her close.

"I still can't believe you actually quit your job and moved to America," he said, weaving his fingers through her hair. "Or that we'll be married in just over a month. I feel like everything is too perfect, like a dam's about to burst or something."

His touch made Stella feel warm and cozy, like a cup of hot cocoa. "I think the fact that we're both currently unemployed, with a house payment and a five-year-old boy to raise, is enough of a problem to deal with for now."

"Actually, the house is paid for."

"Really?"

He shrugged. "My share of the company was worth a lot. And although there's no rush for either one of us to find a job, I've been thinking a lot about what I want to do. The renovations are pretty much finished, and Ryan starts kindergarten next month."

"What do you have in mind?"

"Well, I've been doing some consulting with my former company, and Brady has referred a few other companies my way. I never really pegged myself for the consulting type, but it's actually been fun. It would mean traveling, but I can be particular about the jobs I take and the time I'm willing to invest. If I start advertising, I'm sure I could build up a decent little business, and Brady's interested in joining me if that's what I decide to do. What do you think?"

"I think it sounds great."

Devon's fingers laced through hers. "What about you?"

"How would you feel about me going back to school? I've been looking into the certification required to become a school counselor, and I think I would really enjoy that. With any luck, I could work at the school where our kids might someday end up."

"Kids? As in, more than one?"

"Yeah. Don't you want any more?"

"Uh, how many are we talking?"

"I don't know. Two, four, six, eight—"

"Whoa! Slow down for a second. You're making a pony sound pretty good right about now."

Stella smiled. "Well at least a few more, anyway."

Devon appeared to consider the idea. "I guess Ryan could use a younger brother."

"Or a sister." An image of a toddler girl snuggled up on Devon's lap appeared in Stella's mind, and her smile widened. Yes, Ryan definitely needed a sister.

"But I don't know anything about girls."

"No worries. I'll teach you everything you need to know—not that you'll need much help. Whether you see it or not, you're a pretty amazing father. I think all you needed was a little nudge."

"It felt more like a shove, to be honest."

Stella's shoulder bumped against his. "It's good to know I'll be able to push you around. It means we'll have a happily-ever-after kind of marriage."

"Says who?"

"Me."

Devon chuckled. "So long as you're okay with me pushing back once in a while."

"I'm counting on it."

"Good. Now do you want to know what I think will make a happy marriage?"

"What?"

"This." He kissed her gently, then wrapped her into a warm and snug embrace. Crickets creaked, a breeze rustled the leaves, and Aussie snored from his place in the corner. Up above, the darkened sky glittered with dimly lit stars. Peaceful. Beautiful. Perfect. Had Lindsay foreseen this day? Had she known the far-reaching effect her decision would have? Did she approve?

Carried through the air by a meandering breeze, it was more of a feeling than an actual voice, hugging Stella as it whispered to her heart, *Yes.*

Thank you, Lindsay, thank you. For everything.

book club questions

1. Do you think Stella should have been completely upfront and honest with Devon from the get-go, or was she right to withhold information until Devon had really gotten to know and love Ryan?
2. Would you be willing to take on the young child of a virtual stranger?
3. What would you do if you knew a child was being mistreated and possibly abused, and how far would you be willing to go to save a child from certain abuse? Would you be justified?
4. After the psychologist gave his recommendation, do you think Devon was justified in his decision to payoff Justin? Does the end ever justify the means? What would you have done?
5. The decision the court would have made, before Devon's intervention, was actually very realistic—in both Australia and the United States. Is it fair that courts tend to side with the biological parent(s) in cases like these?
6. Today's courts often favor the mother. Do you feel that the mother is usually the best guardian, or should that bias be eliminated?
7. What do you think about Stella's decision to give up her life and move to Australia? Should she have done it, considering Devon was ready and willing to move to Australia?

8. If you could pick one place to travel to, where would it be? Would Australia make your top ten?
9. Would you ever try Vegemite?

about the author

When Rachael first saw *The Man from Snowy River* (and *Crocodile Dundee*, although she's cringes to admit it), she dreamed of going to Australia. Over ten years later, she finally got the chance and immediately fell in love with the people, the wild birds that eat sugar from your hand, the kangaroos, the beautiful city of Sydney, and the gorgeous place called Byron Bay.

Rachael is the author of two previously published books, *Divinely Designed* and *Luck of the Draw*. She lives with her husband and children in Springville, Utah.

Rachael would love to hear from you and can be found online at www.rachaelreneeanderson.com.